DAMASCUS BLUES

Nadel Harvey

Other Works by Nadel Harvey

Stilettos in the Sun
When a Body Meets a Body

This is a work of fiction. Names, characters, places, and incidents are a product of the author's imagination. Any resemblance to actual persons, living or dead, or to events or locales is completely coincidental.

Cover design by Solutions Website Design
Interior design by Cypress Editing

DAMASCUS BLUES
ISBN-13 (pbk.): 978-0-9911840-4-0
ISBN-13 (ebk.): 978-0-9911840-5-7

To Javier Atteya Harvey
A better friend would be hard to find

Blues is easy to play, but hard to feel.
—JIMI HENDRIX

Everything in excess is opposed to nature.
—HIPPOCRATES

The reward for work well done is the
opportunity to do more.
—JONAS SALK

1

Buraydah, Kingdom of Saudi Arabia

Zouhoor couldn't decide what to wear for her graduation ceremony, so she asked her husband, Khalil, for his opinion.

"Everyone will be wearing black, so why don't you wear something blue under your abaya."

He was right. In the Kingdom, women were obliged to wear black. There was really no point in doing anything to draw attention to yourself. Still, she liked asking for his opinion just to hear his voice. He was such a quiet man. Except when he sang, which he did only in the house or in the car—with the windows rolled up.

"You *do* like blue."

"Because it matches your eyes," he said.

Zouhoor was from Deir ez-Zour, a town east of Damascus, near the Euphrates. Blue eyes were not common there. But Zouhoor could not return to her village. It was besieged by Islamic insurgents. It was no longer safe for her. She was far away from that life, because she now lived in the Kingdom. But Deir ez-Zour was history. That was not so in the Kingdom, where they had been living for three years. Life in the Kingdom was marginally better. The town of Buraydah was vast with some 500,000 inhabitants. Camels and date palms were found in equal and overwhelming quantities. Still, Buraydah was as slow a city as the vast numbers of camels there. They too were a constant reminder that no matter the number of new buildings, they would remain centuries behind.

"I'll be so glad to get out of this dump!" she was inclined to say to Khalil.

"More glad than leaving your little village?" Khalil said.

"Yes!" She said. "They are out of step with this century, and don't have the money to do better."

"But here the government is doing all it can to modernize life. Look at the shopping malls. Also, we live comfortably. And we are in a safe environment."

Just as Khalil spoke, a car drove by, leaving in its wake a series of explosives.

"Oh, how I wish the delinquents would crash!" Responded Zouhoor.

"You should be used to it by now. This is their only outlet, well, this and shisha. Oh, and drifting. I almost forgot," added Khalil.

"Just be glad we won't be here forever. Hopefully, you'll land that job in Quebec. You won't hear that there I bet. The Canadian police wouldn't allow it."

"The price of gas won't allow it!"

Khalil pulled his wife toward himself. The heat of her body made him feel good. She nibbled his neck and grasped his hand.

"First, graduation," she said.

*

Khalil met his future wife on occasion in Damascus while studying in medical school. He was one of the only African Americans there. As he did not study sharia like the other African Americans, he had little to talk about with them. If he saw them at all, it was at the Jumah prayer. After the prayer, everyone went his own way. Khalil completed his studies in urology. He had been awarded a fellowship and remained in Syria until he found a post in Saudi Arabia. He met Zouhoor in the relaxed atmosphere of Damascus. There, men and women met over coffee in the open parks and museums. Khalil had made a few friends in medical school and among them was Latif, who liked him to the extent he wanted him to meet one of his sisters. He had six sisters, so there was some concern in the family about who would be the first to marry. Their ages ranged from twelve to twenty. The family pushed for education, and the young women also saw the benefits of higher education as part of their continued striving for improving themselves. Zouhoor was the oldest. She was not the most attractive one, but possessed a quiet beauty. She was very thin and her face had freckles. She did not like dairy product, which contributed to her being gangly. She had very long hair and her eyes were a match for any standard of beauty in Syria. She was the object of glances from both men and women. Khalil was in hopes of finding employment first. He had had no serious female companion during his studies, and by then, had abandoned the notion of finding a permanent companion there. He felt it was because he stood out in a crowd, being so black in a sea of whiteness. "Oh, nonsense," Jamal, an Algerian student, would say. "In my family, we are every color, even black! Don't forget, it is against Islam to discriminate." Khalil believed that may have been true for the Prophet during his time. Khalil would never know how it was then. He (among them) gave lip service to the Hadiths Muslims shared. But that did not change the fact that Khalil was a black pearl in that Mediterranean world. He was sure that things would have been different had he won a fellowship to Sudan or Morocco, but they offered him nothing in his search for a new home. (The schools in Sudan never bothered to reply to his queries.) His studies were really his only fixed companion. When he wasn't studying, he would pick up his baritone sax or bass clarinet. He would walk around his room, and sometimes stand in front of a sketch of three pomegranates in red pastel and charcoal taped on the wall, which he had drawn. The fruits looked open and translucent. The blood red seeds, some promiscuously running along the tablecloth, some still contained within their skin, all available to be devoured. He had done well without any distractions. Why change now? He was nearing the completion of his stay there anyway, so he had agreed to meet Latif's sister. It was not without trepidation. It would take a while to get to know Zouhoor and her family, so he had little reason to think that meeting this woman would mean anything more than a gesture from Latif to show his brotherhood, which he was fond of saying about Muslims in general. And why meet his sister, and presumably, family now? "We are all brothers anyway, right?" If that were the case, why all the killing in the region? "Oh, they're not true brothers." No, Khalil would be the first to agree, but they considered themselves such, so the notion of brotherhood remained undefined. *Didn't Cain kill Able?* And Hadiths about the Prophet, while leaving a legacy of superlatives, gave no help to the warring factions of these political foes, if they bothered to read them at all. There were Sunnis, Shias, Alawites, followers of Sulayman al-Murshid, Ismailis, Druzes, various others, and Christians. They couldn't blame Israel, when their brothers in Syria were *bumping each other off* every day! There was always someone to point a finger at, but like the American Khalil met in Buraydah said, "When you point your finger, three more are pointing back at you."

No, he would meet this woman, and continue looking for a job. Marriage was most likely the reason for the meeting. Otherwise, why would have Latif offered to introduce him now? He had known him for two years, and never once mentioned his family. Khalil was familiar with the mores of the Arabs: never ask a question about women in someone's family. Women were never even mentioned in conversations. *It was just as well,* thought Khalil—He did not want to mention any female of his own family in the conversation. He had his dark secrets, which he kept hidden. Khalil was sure that his character had something to do with this meeting. No, he had no time for shisha, a pastime that consumed the Middle Eastern men. He found more solace in listening to Monk, Khalil's own playing of the baritone sax and bass clarinet, or catching one of the street musicians doing his version of jazz on saxophone. The regimen of meeting the family members would remain, whether Zouhoor were interested or not. He remembered a sermon back in Philadelphia at the Albanian mosque where the imam said it was the woman's choice. But he knew cases where the woman did not make the choice. He laughed at the thought. In Afghanistan, that was the case. If there is any truth in the newspapers and Khaled Hosseini's novel *A Thousand Splendid Suns,* women have no choices. But he read far too much for that part of the world, with few people to talk to about his musings. (Khalil considered the issue of consent, but where was consent when a girl the age of nine says yes to a man well over thirty?) Music was so much more rewarding than street conversations.

*

Deir ez-Zour, Syria

"So, you and Latif are friends! Good!"

"We have known each other for some time."

"So why am I just meeting you?"

"Only he can answer that question."

Latif, his father, and Khalil sat in the tearoom. An Indian brought in a tray of biscuits, samosas, and tea. He placed them on the table in front of the three men.

"So how long have you been a Muslim?"

"A lifetime."

"So, you were never a Christian?"

"It comes as a surprise to you, doesn't it?"

"No, I understand that there are many Muslims in the United States."

"And Canada, and Jamaica, and South America."

"*Al hamdulillah!*" chimed both Latif and his father.

"So do you plan to stay in Syria after you graduate?"

"No. I want to return to the US."

"I have never been there. What is it like?"

"For the professionals, it can be great."

"You can raise a family there," said Latif's father, stirring sugar into his tea.

"Yes. There are good schools," Khalil said.

"I hope you are hungry. My wife and daughters have prepared a meal I trust you will like."

"Do you have other sons, too?"

"No, just Latif."

"You must be proud of him."

"Yes, as your parents must be of you. Is your father a doctor?"

"No."

"What does he do?"

"Time. My father is in prison."

To this response, Latif's father bristled. He seemed at a loss for words, but he was innately inquisitive. He was a man who needed to know everything. Behind his glasses, he darted quick glances at Khalil, that at his son.

Khalil interjected, "Oh, it's okay. I have grown accustomed to all the questions about my family, and when I became Muslim, and if was I born in the US. A foreigner like me gets used to that and more."

"It must be hard on the rest of your family, your father being away. How long has it been?"

"Five years."

"May Allah protect him! And the rest of your family?"

"You are looking at it."

"Excuse me?"

"I am an only child. I have no brothers and sisters."

There was a knock on the door. Dinner was ready. The men moved to the adjoining room, and sat on the floor. The women were not around.

"May I wash my hands?" asked Khalil.

Latif showed him to the washroom. As he was returning, one of Latif's sisters stole a glance at him through a cracked door. As Khalil walked back to the dining room, it was as though he were walking through a house with hidden passageways that he would never have permission to enter.

"And the rest of your family?"

Was the old man deaf? Should he tell him that his mother was an alcoholic who committed suicide? Hardly an icebreaker.

"My mother died a while ago."

"May Allah grant her Paradise," he said.

Does Allah grant Paradise to those who commit suicide?

The men ate their fill. Khalil was not in the habit of eating much. He had eaten more than he would ordinarily, sampling the Syrian delicacies.

"I'll be getting back. I have a lot of reading to do."

"But it is so early," said Latif.

"And were you not interested in meeting my daughter?"

"Is she even here?"

"She is," the father replied.

"Perhaps the next time I am invited."

The father looked offended. He had gone to some trouble, having spent money on a floral display in the patio, extra Indian hands to spruce up the place, and on those who prepared an exquisite meal.

"Are you engaged to someone?"

"I am only engaged to my studies."

Khalil looked at his watch. "Before I leave, I would like to meet this woman, if it's not too much trouble."

The old man spoke to his son, and Latif left the room.

"Let us go into the tearoom."

There sat Latif's sister and mother.

Both women were wearing pastel colors. The father introduced everyone with greetings in Arabic. They smiled as Latif introduced them to Khalil. Everyone sat on cushions, with silence consuming the air, until the father spoke.

"Khalil, this is my eldest daughter, Zouhoor. She hopes to finish her studies abroad, perhaps in Italy."

"I have never been to Italy. It is a place of some interest to me, though. I have seen some movies by Roberto Rossellini," said Khalil.

"I do not know him," said Zouhoor, not yet looking up. "I am interested in journalism, and read as many periodicals as I can."

"What about literature? That is an interest of mine," said Khalil.

"And mine, too. Who do you like?"

"Do you know Phillis Wheatley?"

"No, I do not. What has she written?"

> 'Twas mercy brought me from my Pagan land,
> Taught my benighted soul to understand
> That there's a God, that there's a Saviour too:
> Once I redemption neither sought nor knew.
> Some view our sable race with scornful eye,

"Their colour is a diabolic die."
Remember, Christians, Negros, black as Cain,
May be refin'd and join th' angelic train.

"That was so beautiful! Would you write it down, so I can study it?"

"Of course, I would. I agree it is quite beautiful. She is a poet few people know, but she is very lyrical. I wish I had memorized more of her poems."

Khalil felt his cheeks warming up. He was much too dark to blush, but he imagined himself doing just that in their presence.

"And do you know Italian?" asked Khalil.

"Yes, I speak it," she said, holding her mother's hand.

"Maybe you and your family will go one day," Khalil said.

"I have never traveled beyond the borders of Syria," she said.

"And Syria is the only foreign country I have visited. I did come through Lebanon to get here though. That was so brief. I can't say I saw much. I need to go to Mecca before I return to the States. Maybe I will see Italy too."

"How did you meet my brother?"

"In chemistry class. We would review notes sometimes."

"Khalil is so good in chemistry. I thought he would make an excellent pharmacist," said Latif.

"Your brother is very generous. In all fairness, Latif was far better in science than I was."

"You both finished chemistry, so who is to say who is better?" interjected the father. He had been listening, in addition to watching his daughter's reactions.

"Sir, you and your family have been very kind, but I must be returning."

"Must you leave so soon?" offered Latif, looking over at his sister, who cast her eyes down again.

"Oh, perhaps you and your sister could come to Damascus one day."

"Yes, that is certainly possible," said the father.

2

Khalil took no time in getting back on the highway. It was a polite encounter, as those staid visits would most often be. Everyone seemed on pins and needles, except Khalil. He had no expectations. He had nothing to lose.

In his journal, he entered,

> *Zouhoor, the first Syrian woman I have met socially, and I am nonplused. I would have had more to say, but the family, like a guided missile in pursuit, caused me to redirect my flight, until I thwarted my mission, and cast myself back into the sand.*

"He's a little arrogant! Imagine the nerve of him! We invite him over to meet our daughter, and he wants to leave without even meeting her!"

"Perhaps, we should have had him over before. I have known him for more than three years. He might have thought that Zouhoor had another love interest that didn't work out," said Latif.

"How could he have thought that, unless you told him so," said the mother.

"You saw his reaction. I had never even mentioned our family to him!" said Latif.

"We will just have to invite him again." The mother had finally spoken.

"I still say he is arrogant. He showed no real interest, only in Italian films," said the father.

"And a safe topic. If you had let me speak on my own, I could have gotten him to talk," said Zouhoor.

3

Buraydah, KSA

"You didn't say anything about the letter," said Zouhoor.

"Letter?"

"The one that came today. Everything okay?"

"Oh, sure. We better get going or we'll be late."

"In this country, nothing starts on time," he said, dodging the query, his unwillingness to discuss news from America. Were it just the news of the Obamas, he might have been willing: what they had had for Thanksgiving dinner, or if Khalil's home team, The Philadelphia Eagles, was going anywhere in its conference. Those weren't questions of any concern to Zouhoor. *She had yet to see America, and better to shade her eyes from what she would know in time*, thought Khalil.

This was a subject he hated to broach: his father and how much longer he would be in prison. Passing bad checks came easy for someone skilled at counterfeiting. But $300,000 was where his skill ended. Ten years was what Joe Baptiste (later Ali Bilal Baptiste) received for his skill set. He should have stuck to printing certificates for the Boy Scouts, and wedding invitations. No, he wanted to become a forger of signatures. "Just because one is good at something doesn't mean he should pursue it," he later told a judge on his review board. Khalil wondered just how many African Americans are named George Washington, Lincoln, Hamilton, Jefferson, or even Andrew Jackson. Being named after a President didn't get anyone any closer to the Treasury, so why should forging signatures of the dead ones?

"Mr. Baptiste can you say that your time here has been used for your betterment?" asked the parole advisor.

"Oh, I have more than learned my lesson." said Ali Bilal.

Joe Baptiste was going nowhere, and neither was Ali Bilal, at least for the next six months. The parole board was taking its time deliberately to review the case. In the interim, Ali Bilal would be perfecting his calligraphy. He had taught himself to write just like Thomas Jefferson. It was a skill he would never use. It was a pastime, and he had plenty of time to pass. He read the classics of Robert Louis Stevenson and Dostoyevsky, the novels of Chester Himes, the plays of Albert Camus, and the poems of Gabriela Mistral. Reading gave Ali Bilal a chance to take flights from his cell. While reading about Miguel de Cervantes, he discovered that like him, Cervantes also spent five years in prison. Miguel and his brother Rodrigo were captured by Turkish ships in 1850.

*

Ali Bilal's son found more meaningful use of his mind and hands.

At least he found Islam, thought Khalil. With nothing but time, he learned Arabic, which he continued to read with fervor. Ali's writing had always been a joy for his son to read, but being in jail was nothing he ever discussed. He never liked to discuss, even share the details of his family with his wife.

He wished he could erase them. But she found out eventually, thanks to the Internet. And Khalil's mother? Zouhoor had yet to hear how she met her end. The Schuylkill River is no place to be in which to be, anytime of year. When a river patrol fished her out of the river with weights around her waist, her arm was entangled in a tree limb. She might have changed her mind after jumping, but with a broken neck, it was indeed too late.

Zouhoor was receiving her Bachelors of Arts in Journalism, a degree that took her six years to earn. When she had a miscarriage, she lost the time and her enthusiasm.

"We'll have plenty of little ones running around," said Khalil. He held Zouhoor, but she seemed unmoved by his words. She felt her soul had been ripped from her, stolen from her body. The premature fetus had forced its way out of her two months too soon: a son without a name they would never forget.

*

Before that event, she read assiduously, telling stories to their yet-to-be-born child. She envisioned herself working for *Al Jazirah,* or maybe her favorite journal *Corriere de la Sera.* She had taught herself Italian, and made friends with some young women from Milano in Damascus.

"Next summer we should go to America. Do you want to?"

There she goes with that again!

"Oh, sure."

"Why do you hate America? I just want to see where you grew up."

*

Philadelphia, Pennsylvania, 2003

"Is Joe Baptiste, here?" Asked a tall, well-built white man with gray eyes, showing his badge. A black man of equally strong features stood by his side. Both were expressionless in their blue serge suits.

"Dad, it's for you."

Khalil stood transfixed, holding his physical chemistry book. The men did not move. Nor did Khalil.

The blond detective displayed his badge to Joe, while reciting the Miranda rights. The black officer proceeded to put hand cuffs on him.

They took Joe away in full view of the news-reporting neighbors. They stood at their brick-faced public housing project, gawking like hungry ravens.

The emptiness of watching his father depart was shared with no one. He was an only child, and his mother had walked out on him and his father four years prior, in search of something better. She wasn't a mermaid, but they had found her near the banks of the Schuylkill River: a suicide victim, with a lead chain around her waist. Houdini she was not. Her stomach held granite schist, chicken, kidney beans, and rice. She loved her creole cuisine. Jambalaya was something he would have to go to the Atchafalaya Basin to find. No one in Philadelphia had come forward with a comparable recipe. She could cook okra like Khalil would never forget. The green slippery plant that his forkful of rice would sop up would remain a permanent memory on his tongue and its smell, in his nostrils. His vision vanished, as his cravings dissolved. He had no choice but to come back to reality.

Who was it that sang, *Each of us is born alone, so welcome to the twilight zone. You can leave with only what you bring...?* Khalil really had to focus and finish his assignments. There was no future for him in the city where his father had set such a precedent.

So, it was no surprise that Khalil never told Zouhoor about his family: there was nothing he cared to tell. That, however, did not quench Zouhoor's curiosity, nor her desire to see America.

Back to his mother, Khalil was the only one available to identify the body; a duty he accepted with the detachment of a coroner. He never thought he would see her again anyway. He kept his memories of her in the closet of his room: not a locket of her black hair. No. A faded black silk blouse she had left behind, a bottle of Dewar's Scotch, all but empty, its inch-level content inside. It reminded him of how vacuous her life must have been. *Why hang around for death to extinguish the flickering light?* How she came to that end was a mystery he wanted the answer to, but more important to him was his own life, and where it would take him. He held nothing dear, save his education and his future in medicine. Anything else was a lattice-work of intangibles. He was alone in the world that had neglected him. Were it not the case, his mother would not have walked out, leaving him with a father, preoccupied with a scheme that led him straight to serving time in the penitentiary. Was there really anything else? If so, he hadn't found it.

*

Khalil had waited twelve long weeks for his letter from the University of Damascus Medical School. He had been accepted, but more importantly, on full fellowship. His colleagues at Cheyney University who had applied to American schools were going to face exorbitant debts, once they completed school.

*

"What about the war over there? You could get shot!"

"And I couldn't get shot here?"

This was the talk of people who had never left their own stoops. They would still be sitting at McDonalds, bumming cigarettes four years from then, when he returned, if cancer hadn't claimed them. He might not return at all. He did not know what Damascus held for him. It was the chance to begin anew, and that was good enough, given how his life was devoid of any history in his hometown. He had found no brotherly love there. He was more than willing to take his chances abroad. If he had not been so eager to pursue his medical career in Africa or the Middle East, he would have gone to Latin America. He had friends from Colombia and Chile who encouraged him to go there. "You'll love it!" some said. "I am afraid I won't finish!" Khalil replied. "Those sisters are a real distraction." He recalled fondly the Chilean coed he had danced with at the International House. They held other around the waist, and there was no place in the world he would have rather been, no other cloud he would have rather floated upon, and no other indigo sky he would have rather been under. No, in the end he would follow his plan.

*

It was a *bon voyage*, as he chose to go by vessel across the Atlantic. It was eight days at sea. He occupied himself in reading novels and listening to music. He filled his head with what was new. As he had few friends back in the States to write to, so what memories did he care to conjure? And who would be interested in his parents' lives? An embarrassment and a disappointment. Take your pick, which was which.

The third day at sea came with turbulence, so people at the dinner table were talkative.

"So, where are you headed?"

"Damascus."

"Business?"

"You could say that."

Khalil had little to offer the inquisitive middle-aged traveler. He was dressed well in a suit, though Khalil saw no need for the formal attire.

"I love the sea. And you?"

"Yes," said Khalil.

"I will have the chicken marsala," said Khalil, pointing to the menu as the waiter wrote down his choice.

"Lamb," said the middle-aged man. "I have noticed you are always reading."

What interest was it to him?

"It's an interest I have developed."

"And a fine one too" said the man. "I like to read, but don't have the time."

"To each his own."

The man seemed dissatisfied at the abrupt closure of the conversation, so he proceeded with more questions.

"Are you traveling alone?"

"Yes."

"You know, there are dances every night, upstairs in the hall. Many of the young people go there. I have not seen you though."

"Then you should find plenty of company," added Khalil.

"Oh, I was just mentioning it. It's something to do if you like to go."

"Well, it's not something that interests me at the moment. You should take advantage of it, as you may have already."

"Oh, I just like to be around young people."

Young people or young men?

I am enjoying the voyage at any rate," he said, sipping his white wine.

"How is your chicken?"

"Delicious. And your lamb?"

"Excellent."

The remainder of the meal was only broken by the dropping of a knife and the sound of glasses clicking here and there.

"Would you like to come by my room for a drink?"

"No thanks," answered Khalil. "I have too much to do. Good evening."

Khalil was not looking for friends, and certainly, was not looking to see the inside of that guy's room.

"Oh, hi. See you have company for dinner," said a short, pudgy, olive-skinned man with a beard.

"You can join us," said the first middle-aged man. "What is your name?" The first one asked Khalil.

"Call me K."

"I am Barish. This is Hasan. We are partners."

"So are you traveling alone?" asked Barish, holding in his stomach as he maneuvered into his chair at the table.

"Yes."

"American!" Said Barish.

"I can't be the only one on this ship." "No, I guess not."

"I think I'll be running along now," said Khalil. "Good evening."

Khalil did not wait for the inevitable request for him to stay.

As he walked away, Barish said. "Mmm, fine young man. He'll make someone happy."

"Yes, if he isn't already," added Hasan, whetting his lips.

"You're so predatory!"

"Yes, so unlike you! And you scared him away."

"He's not interested. You would have known that if you had met him earlier."

"Well, I'll never know for sure, will I?"

"Sooner than not, you would have found out. I am just avoiding the disappointment."

"So, do you want to go back to my room for a night-cap? I have a bottle of scotch."

The men left, already full of anticipation.

*

The ship rolled, rocked, and chopped through the waves. Khalil took some Dramamine. A minute later, he was bailing into the bathroom sink the wine he had drunk earlier. While the vessel continued to sway, Khalil no longer felt anything other than relief. He had cleared his stomach, then his throat with Listerine, and into the shower he went.

4

At breakfast the next morning, Khalil found the two men sitting together, but avoided contact with them. There was a woman sitting alone at a large round table. He greeted her, but she said nothing, so he spoke again.

"Good morning," Khalil felt he was intruding, so he found himself another table. A young woman sitting there greeted him.

"Good morning," she said. "I noticed you yesterday, but you were with friends, so I didn't say anything."

"Oh, I am traveling alone."

"I am with my mother. Is this your first voyage?" she asked.

"Yes. I hope my stomach endures it."

"It is my first one, too." she said, cutting her lettuce and tomatoes.

"My name is Shamsa."

"Mine is Khalil. Nice to meet you."

"You, too."

"Where are you from, Shamsa?"

"Tunisia. And you?"

"United States. It's my first time out of the US."

"Where are you going?"

"I am headed to Damascus."

"For business?"

"To study medicine."

"I am returning to my country because I completed my studies in banking."

"Congratulations."

"Thank you."

The two of them sat eating their food. They did not utter another word until they finished eating, at which time Khalil asked Shamsa if she wanted to go for a swim later.

"I haven't seen the pool yet," she said.

"We can see it together."

*

The water was cold and refreshing, as Khalil eased himself into it. Shamsa slid in the pool from the side. The water was indeed cold. Shamsa's arms went red with goosebumps. That did not stop her from taking to the water and doing some laps. Her body glided effortlessly, as though she were on a team. Khalil was at once aroused and taken in by her grace in the water. She swam without a cap; something for which Khalil was grateful, for when she swam to where he was standing, black hair shone full of iridescence. *Her radiant smile would brighten any dawn*, thought Khalil. She was just the levity he needed, without even having uttered a word. Khalil watched her with rapt attention. She laughed and her breasts rose and fell with every guffaw. Her black one-piece bodysuit was what women in her country often wore, she told Khalil when he asked about it.

"You find it strange?" she said, looking down at her body.

"I like it!" he said.

The black bathing suit would cast no shadow on the morning, he thought. "You may start a craze somewhere, if not America. There they love the immodest."

"Enough talking. Let's swim!" she said, taking off like a young porpoise. Khalil was no great swimmer. He could only catch up with her when she stopped, which she did, so they could enjoy the same space and hear each other.

*

They later climbed out of the pool and sat on the lounge chairs.

"You're quite good!" offered Khalil. "I couldn't keep up with you."

"It wasn't a race."

"You would have won, if it had been."

Shamsa dried her long hair.

"That swim was just what I needed," said Khalil. "You're lucky your studies are over."

"Now to find a job."

"Your country has been in the news a lot, with the change in government."

"Yes, like starting from scratch, as you say."

"You will have a chance to make history. Maybe the first female head of a bank."

"That is a little too fast. I haven't even gotten there yet. Those who were there during all the fighting have a distinct advantage."

"Still, you are coming with a fresh perspective. I read a book by Muhammad Yunnis. He was able to help women improve the banking system in his country, Bangladesh.".

"I don't know him. Maybe I can do the same." She said.

"That is what I am thinking. Since he won the Nobel, people might listen to his ideas. Let's discuss it over dinner, if I am not being too forward." He suggested.

*

"I was going to ask you about him. It is a good place to start."

"How about six thirty?" he said.

"I'll meet you in the dining room then."

They left the pool. The waiter, who was serving drinks to the people at the poolside, watched them leave.

Khalil had a bounce in his step. When he arrived at his room, he kicked off his sandals and plopped on his bunk. He felt a new exhilaration. He had had his first exchange with a new female in years. There was the blind girl he had met waiting for the bus at Broad and Lehigh. With her he had exchanged banter, and once, she had touched his hand, which he kissed. She pulled it away, and color rose to her pale cheeks. It was winter, and the rose perfumed lotion remained in his nostrils long after the day was through. He hoped to run into her on the way home, but it was several months before he saw her again. By then he had graduated from college. Whatever excitement he felt earlier, had long since faded into the ethos of the two seasons that had passed. The next time he saw her, she had the color of summer in her cheeks, and her hair had grown longer. Apart from her name, Nilda, and the rose scent, her memory had faded. He wondered what she would be doing. He did not plan on seeing her until he returned, if he ever would. She would be a secretary by then.

*

And Shamsa? That had been fun, and he hoped for her as well. She was great company, and he wished she thought so too. He was a loner, with few connections to the world outside of his trunk of books. *Don't make any plans involving anybody. You'll only be disappointed.*

*

Khalil had dozed off. After waking up, he shaved and showered. He put on a grey suit and a sunset-colored tie. He removed his black shoes from a plastic bag, still polished. He squirted on some 4711 cologne and left.

He took back what he said about there being no need for a suit and a tie.

He arrived at the dining hall before Shamsa. In fact, he was the only one there.

He asked the waiter if there was something wrong.

"You are early, Sir. Would you like something to drink?"

"Some of that coffee, please."

"Oh, good evening, Khalil."

It was Barish, looking as if he was enjoying the voyage. "You have been scarce."

"Oh, I haven't jumped ship."

"I saw you at the pool. What a lovely young woman!"

"She was, wasn't she?"

*

Khalil left Barish and returned to his cabin to check his appearance. He wanted to look his best when he met Shamsa for dinner. He thought of changing his tie to a blue one. But on second thought, he stuck to his first choice. He was full of anticipation of what the night had in store. Maybe some dancing in the moonlight. Who knew?

*

When Khalil arrived at the dining room, he passed by Barish, yet again! *Barish's broad smile is so sinister*, thought Khalil. A nod of acknowledgement was all Khalil showed. Then he spotted Shamsa, but she was sitting with a woman.

"Hello," said Khalil. He stood for a second before taking the only available seat, next to the heavyset woman.

"This is Mrs. Rakman, my mother."

"Pleased to meet you," said Khalil. Her voice sounded more like *surprised to meet you*.

"Shamsa says you are an excellent swimmer."

"I could take some lessons from her, with your permission."

"Oh, of course."

Mrs. Rakman was decked out in emeralds and gold, looking like royalty. She wore an overpowering perfume. Khalil did not have a sensitive stomach, but he had no intention of sitting for a meal next to that woman.

"Please excuse me," he said. "Perhaps, I will see you after dinner."

Khalil did not want to offend Shamsa's mother, but he had to move.

There was another table at some distance from Shamsa and the others. When Khalil sat down, with his back to the table he had just left, he cleared his head from the noxious aroma of that perfume, though a hint of it remained in his jacket. There were two couples sitting at the long table; one couple to his left, the other opposite him.

"Hello," he said in a general tone.

The men returned his hello, and went back to their conversations. Khalil occupied himself with the menu. A salad was all he was interested in. The presence of Shamsa's mother had taken away his appetite. Khalil added sugar to the tea the waiter had served. The tea helped clear his head and regain his mood. He contented himself as he listened to the instrumental music in the air.

*

Khalil had finished his salad, when he heard Shamsa's voice behind him.

"Khalil. Are you all right?"

"Yes."

"You left so abruptly."

"Sorry. I am allergic to your mother's perfume. I saw no way to tell her."

"Oh, I apologize. I didn't know. I told her about you, so she wanted to meet you."

"Perhaps, tomorrow."

"We are traveling together, so we spend our time doing the same things."

"Except swimming," Khalil interjected.

"She doesn't swim."

As Shamsa finished her words, Mrs. Rakman arrived. Khalil stood.

"I am going to turn in early, ladies. Good night."

Khalil did not wait for a reply because the fumes smelled just as toxic as before. He was not aware that he was allergic to anything prior to this experience. Maybe it wasn't an allergy, just what might have been a cheap perfume.

*

An hour later, there was a knock on his door. Khalil was reading. He walked to his door.

"Sir, a lady gave me this."

Khalil accepted it and closed the door.

> *Khalil, my mother is offended by your behavior. She wants an apology. I told her that her perfume irritated you. That is right, isn't it? In any case, maybe you can meet us in the morning for breakfast. She won't wear that fragrance.*
>
> *Shamsa*

Offended by what? Khalil didn't know the woman. Maybe she wanted to get to know him—had missed an opportunity. Khalil was not looking to make a commitment with Shamsa. He saw her as company, and nothing more. He was on his way to Syria. His goals were already large, and they did not include a wife, nor the baggage of a mother-in-law. No, he would cut out any further meetings unless they were in passing. He had met Shamsa because they were traveling in the same direction. Her mother had created a fork in the road. He was moving on.

*

The next morning Khalil purposely sat in a faraway location from the seating he had chosen the night before. The table was full, save for one seat which meant two guests could not possibly sit there. His back was faced to anyone entering the dining hall, to avoid contact. There was only one day remaining before they arrived at Carthage. He would never see either of them again. His sunglasses and dark suit allowed him to remain as inconspicuous as he could be.

*

"Good morning, Khalil."

There were the two of them, standing behind him. "We thought you might join us," said Shamsa.

"Oh, but I am finished. I got an early start, sorry. What about tomorrow?"

Shamsa looked at her mother, and offered, "Maybe." They turned and walked away.

Without anything fixed, there was no chance that they would meet again.

*

Back in his room, Khalil pulled out his anatomy book and read through the section of the respiratory system.

There was a faint knock on his door. Khalil opened it.

"Hello."

"Hello."

"May I come in?" asked Shamsa.

Khalil motioned she could. It was an awkward visit. Khalil didn't plan on seeing her again.

"You see, we are leaving tomorrow, and I wanted to say goodbye."

"Thank you."

"You didn't plan to do the same, did you?"

"No. I don't like goodbyes."

"I thought we would have a little more time together."

"It was inevitable that we would part. No sense building a ship of dreams."

Khalil had spoken without hesitation, though the words sounded cold.

"I liked the short time we spent together, and wanted more. Do I sound forward?"

"Yes. It's okay, though. We don't have much time. Can I offer you something to drink?"

"Do you have any wine?"

"They furnish the bar with bottles of it. How about a Bordeaux?"

Khalil opened the bottle, and poured two glasses.

"It's fitting that we toast to your return to Tunisia, embarking on your future."

"And what about *your* future?"

"That, too! I don't know what to expect, besides political unrest."

"That's in my country, too."

They clicked their glasses. The wine pinched his palate, and Khalil grimaced. But Shamsa seemed to like its taste.

"You know, you might end up in Tunisia one day."

"Four years from now. I might deliver one of your children."

"I don't plan on having children."

"It's a long way off. Who could have said we would be sitting here drinking wine?"

"Two Muslims at that!"

"Two moderns."

"Like Rumi said, 'If Allah didn't want us to drink wine, why did he make grapes?'"

"And what about corn? My grandfather loved sour mash," added Khalil.

"Sour mash?"

"Whiskey."

"Listen to us. Discussing the benefits of alcohol."

"Right out of the Quran."

"Haven't times changed?"

"But people haven't. We repeat the same mistakes over and over."

Khalil spoke with a lucidity that wine can give.

"Let's make a plan to meet in four years, if neither of us is married," suggested Shamsa.

"Good."

Khalil committed himself, believing they would never see each other again.

By the third glass, Shamsa was in Khalil's arms. They embraced like newlyweds, short of undressing.

Khalil had not held a woman in a long time. It was a strange feeling. The pleasant scent of jasmine fluttered in his nostrils.

"And your mother?"

"Let's not talk about her."

"You're right. Let this be our moment."

Khalil held her hands to his lips. He caressed her fingers, then she, his. They lost themselves in the fleeting moments, as if making up in advance for the times they would not be together.

Shamsa broke away, not wishing for what she could not have to keep. How could she explain him to her mother? He was not one of her people, Muslim or not.

5

They arrived at Carthage. Khalil could not take anything in because of the dense cloud cover. It looked like
rain was on its way the cloud-cover was as thick as
sheep's wool, and everyone who had a raincoat donned
one. Khalil and Shamsa had already said their goodbyes,
so they avoided the last-minute handshake, as that was
all they would be afforded, given the presence of
Shamsa's mother. Khalil watched the passengers disem-
bark in silence, but for that rolling of grey waves against
the port and the ship. The passengers disappeared into
the early morning darkness. The old port had seen ships
since the time of the Phoenicians. A freighter coasted
by. The ship was loaded down, and seemed barely able
to reach the port. A sailor tossed a rope to two men
waiting to bind it to the wharf. They knew their work.

Men worked together. Where had he seen that before? Certainly not in his personal life. His father
worked alone in the basement and in collaboration with
people unknown. Maybe they were in prison too. Khalil
never interested himself in finding out who was involved. Who could he have asked? Any telephone conversations would be channeled to the police, which
shortly thereafter would ricochet back at him. Hot

lamps and questions he could not answer. Maybe that was why he hadn't been questioned, because they knew who they were after, or at least the only person they wanted behind bars. Counterfeiting was serious enough. Where was a man in a housing project going with fake twenties? How could he explain those nice clothes on a janitor's wage? He couldn't bank anything. It was only an artistic endeavor. It would have been better to paint signage. That was honest work; not a get-rich-quick scheme. Didn't he know that ever since slavery, the black man has been under the microscope? How else could the government have found Obama? The government has never been too busy not to watch black people. No man escaped its purview: not James Brown, not John Coltrane, not Richard Wright, not Franz Fanon, not Andre Watts. There is no *Invisible Man* of Ralph Ellison, notwithstanding. Every black man, indeed every man with a social security number, is significant. If for no other reason, his number matters to the war machine. That is reason enough to track his movements.

*

Still, watching men engaged in work with a common purpose intrigued Khalil. Marcus Garvey might have observed men coming together with a productive purpose before realizing his shipping enterprise, Black Star Line in June 1919. And what about his successful winery with grapes harvested from Ethiopia?

Why had Khalil never seen such a scene in his own community? Was it the threat of black men working?

Men played blackjack and poker. Men rolled dice, and played numbers, but that was the extent of it. Black and brown men played dominoes, and sold shots of coquito in plain view of police cars. (How did they get away with it?) Black men found solace in the underworld or bars. But in the time of war, there was high employment for black men. Adolph Hitler made sure of that. Black and brown men defended their country abroad. The irony of the statement gave Khalil a moment to pause. The great wars provided employment for blacks in Europe and elsewhere, when none was available for them in their birthplace. Jim Crow made sure of that. Khalil did not plan to engage in any warfare, or save the war against diseases. But he had a dog in that fight—even though the enemies were microscopic. His hero was Louis Pasteur. But in the States, the post-Civil War black population was the cancer that guarded itself against eradication, or at least that is what he felt. How was a country, so rich in resources and so ready to come to the aid of foreign lands, blind to the needs of its own? How long would it take for ex-slaves to be thought of as more than three-fifth of a human being? These were the questions Khalil pondered. He was not a philosopher, so the answer to that would have to hit him like a car he did not see coming.

He watched the dock workers move in synchronicity: heads wrapped for protection from the sun, and to keep from having to mop their faces. They seemed small to be doing such arduous work, but that did not stop them. They knew what they were doing.

*

"Excuse me," said a man passing Khalil. He was leaving the ship. The man was dressed in clothing typical of Tunisians: a red fez, yards of off-white fabric, and some sort of sandals. He seemed at ease, and, his garment, bellowing as he walked. Khalil had not noticed anyone boarding the vessel, though he did see men taking stock from the ship, loading it on the dock that continued to mount up on pallets, to be hoisted away at some later time.

On the street, a boy, perhaps twelve, rode a bicycle, while carrying bread on his head. It seemed to be laid out on a board, stiff enough to hold the load, light enough not to weaken his neck. He was quite deft as he negotiated the street traffic with the poise of an acrobat. Khalil reflected in that instant on what boys that age were engaged in back in Philadelphia: slinging plastic bags of slow-but-sure death. When the future looked dim, why not extinguish the light altogether? Crack, the craze of the latter years of the 20th century, ate away at everything, but a vivid and distorted imagination to get your hands on a bag of power. Crack is concentrated in central cities, particularly those with large Black and Hispanic populations. The cities experiencing the highest average levels of crack are Newark, San Francisco, Philadelphia, Atlanta, and New York. Tell a story that sounds believable the first time you hear it, but wouldn't fly any time after that. It was like the little girl he remembered seeing, presumably selling candy for her school, but really to support her parents' habit. By the time she was fifteen, she was selling her own brand of candy, now to support her own habit. Khalil had been propositioned more than once, and he was still running from the ugliness of his neighborhood. But what he at once realized was that he could not run from his memories. The bad ones were never on life-support. They thrived under the harshest conditions. He noticed that they required no resuscitation. Unlike anatomy, they required no memorization. He wondered why that was so. They often crowded his head when he needed that space for important matters. He was, however, grateful for the physical space between his family and himself. A family of one he remained, and he would only be visited by his father in his dreams, were he to appear at all. And his mother? Did he ever really know her? She was a beautiful woman, he remembered. She had a slight build with almond eyes, which narrowed when she smiled. She was so quiet that she was easy to miss, were it not for her long black hair, something that got her stares of admiration in her twenties, given the photographs in the albums he would look at from time to time. He, curiously enough, had no pictures of his mother with him. His father might have taken them with him to prison. Then again, he did not really care. It was too painful to feel—he did his best to bury those thoughts: a father in prison and a mother dredged from the river. Still, he could not forget either. One could forget one's ancestors. They were the people he never knew. But one's parents were another story—a story he played a part in. He had lines that he still remembered, beatings he still felt, embarrassments he never hoped to share.

6

Khalil found himself in the pool. There were others there, but he spoke to no one. He took some laps, which felt good. After some twenty laps, he had had enough. He left the pool, wondering why the ship was still docked.

"One of the motors needs repairing," was what a manager told him.

Khalil went back to his room. It was dinner time. Feeling glum, he put on a suit to cheer himself up.

In the dining room were several couples. When was the last time he sat with a woman? No, he could not count Shamsa. He had no relationship with her. That was happenstance. He did not have to think hard.

*

"Do you want some more spinach?"

"No, but I'd like some of that cabbage, please."

Khalil had struck up a clandestine relationship with a college biology professor. Mrs. Avo-Muuri was not divorced, but even if she had been, seeing each other openly would not have been tolerated—the Puritan mores of the school would force the continued secretive nature of their relationship. Integration was all right in the calculus class where Leibniz was revered, but Martin Luther King's books and papers on integration were another story. Mrs. Avo-Muuri was in the habit of cooking him dinner on Sundays. Khalil had no family, and Mrs. Avo-Muuri was alone after a year of being separated from her husband, who also taught biology in Finland.

Khalil carried some flowers across the quad and Khalil's friend, Paul, saw him and greeted him, "Hey, nice touch! They for your queen?"

"You know me," said Khalil.

"I sure do!" chuckled Paul.

How much did he know? Khalil could not be sure. But why had Paul chuckled? If he had followed him, there would be no doubt. Khalil walked into the biology department building. Mrs. Paivi Avo-Muuri was in her office with a female student. Khalil sat in the hallway until the student left.

"Happy birthday."

"They're beautiful! How did you know I like chrysanthemums?"

"The picture in your apartment: that was my clue."

The flowers were as white as Paivi's complexion. Her eyes were light grey. She wore her blond and silver hair in a chignon, or a braid that ran half the length of her body. She was about five foot nine, with the figure of an Olympian.

"I will have to thank you for these, at the appropriate time."

"In the appropriate way," added Khalil.

Paivi knew what foods Khalil liked, and she always served him dessert afterward.

"Sometimes, I wonder," she said. "How long will it take to forget me? When you are in medical school, I mean."

"I will never forget you. I am going to marry you one day."

"Seriously. I want to know."

"I'll send you a ticket, and right after graduation, we'll find an imam, any imam and—"

Paivi covered his mouth, stifling his words. She did not want to hear what might very well in time prove to have been an untruth. Her future plans had already been derailed by a marriage that had not worked out. "Who wants a wife who cannot bear children?" were her husband's stinging words. *She is so much more than a barren wife*, thought Khalil. She was accomplished, beautiful, but was not what her husband wanted, anymore. There was no denying that, so why should she pretend, only to be hurt again?

"You know my situation, and I have heard you say you want a family someday."

"There is always adoption," he offered. "There are so many children mothers give away, or drown in rivers, some still harnessed in car seats."

"How can they do that?"

"Because they see children as a burden, and they are heartless," replied Khalil.

"You are different," she said, holding his hand to her lips. "You make me wish I were younger, if only ten years."

"Don't I make you feel younger?"

"I feel almost giddy with you. Would you like some wine?" she said.

"It's the wine that's making you giddy."

Paivi took another sip and surrendered to Khalil's embrace and the breeze that came through the kitchen window. It would be another unfinished dinner. His napkin fell onto the floor. Her hair pins led a trail to the bedroom. They would find themselves looking out the bedroom window again, as the pine trees danced that final summer semester together.

7

Apart from Paivi, Khalil had had no other intimate relationship. He avoided fraternity parties, because he could not go with her. They did go to concerts and jazz events. They once went to see McCoy Tyner perform in Philadelphia, and spent a week in Manhattan where they had caught Ahmad Jamal. While there, they heard The New York Philharmonic play a Beethoven piano concerto. Paivi and Khalil were free of the gawking they sometimes engendered in Philadelphia. In New York, they were anonymous and loved talking while they walked across the Brooklyn Bridge.

But in Damascus, he was nowhere near any of those experiences. There were ruins and bombed out remains. The pillars of Palmyra lay parallel and perpendicular to the ground, Still, the evenings were busy with pedestrians. He loved the activity, but he was not a part of any of it. He was truly alone. He knew enough conversational Arabic to get directions. He would, no doubt, learn a lot in the next few years. Paivi had given him a set of Arabic language recordings, which Khalil completed listening before leaving the States. They would be his companions for his stay, he felt. There was going to be no dating in Syria—he was sure of that.

*

He sat in the dining room, toying with the string beans on his plate. The little green logs rolled against the lamb chops, then back to the potatoes.

"Did you like the last piece," Paivi asked.

"Of course!" he answered, while applauding.

"Who is the drummer?"

"Vernel Fourier."

"He is wonderful. He looks like you."

"If I had his talent..."

"You might not do medicine."

"I would be a magician."

"You are already that."

"I don't understand you sometimes."

*

Those were the times Khalil savored. More than string beans, artichokes, and lamb chops, those simple, ever-refreshing moments with Paivi. The biology teacher danced in his head. Paivi, with eyes of quicksilver, Paivi, with the twenty-four-inch waist, and all that hair. *Nice to keep a memory alive.*

*

"Sir?" The waiter's voice interrupted Khalil's reverie.

"Yes," answered Khalil. He was finished eating, so the waiter removed his plate.

Another waiter came by with tea. *How efficient they are!*

Khalil dropped a sprig of peppermint into his glass, along with a cube of sugar.

As he was stirring the tea, he decided to watch a movie that evening. There was no reason to hurry to bed.

Persona. Ingmar Bergman was his choice. Then *To Kill a Mockingbird* was showing. He had not watched a black and white since *La Strada.* Paivi was always exposing him to foreign films. She liked Ingmar Bergman. Also, she liked that Gordon Parks, maybe poetry, and his story about the Brazilian boy, *Flavio.*

Paivi had a compelling interest in cultural contributions made by blacks. Instead of picking Khalil's brain, she seemed more interested in filling it. She talked at length about George Washington Carver's study of the sweet potato. As she sat on a pillow in her apartment, with a glass of Chablis, she stocked Khalil's head like a vessel with researches or speeches Carver had made. Paivi loved botany, so she made Carver's work enjoyable to listen to. Khalil would have to go far to find someone like her, and where he was going, there was no guarantee he would. He was hoping to return and make good on his promise. There was no one in the world he cared for as much, and the circumstances by which he had met her seemed quite unlikely.

*

It was raining. Khalil was waiting for a bus to take him back to campus. He had been to a theater in Germantown, and was now at the 69th Street Station. A woman had taken the same long bus ride from

Germantown, and was also waiting at the station. They were alone in the terminal. It was a Sunday afternoon. Khalil had seen the woman on campus, but never met her. She was a faculty member after all, and they did not always mix with students.

"Excuse me, but I saw you at the theater. My name is Khalil Baptiste."

"Paivi Avo."

She had a firm handshake, one that equaled Khalil, and they were nearly the same height.

Khalil looked at the lightest eyes he had ever seen. They were a piercing grey, but her rose lips were full, and cheekbones high. Her hair was in a chignon. Her appearance was not one that invited him at first glance, but once she said her name, she followed with a few questions that surprised him.

"Are you in Dr. Young's Physical Chemistry class?"

"Yes."

"That's where I saw you. You were talking to him after class. I was outside the classroom waiting for him. You left by the door on the opposite side."

"How do you even remember me?" he asked.

"The red parka you are wearing."

"How observant!"

"I remember colors."

"What did you think of the film today?" he asked.

"I liked it. And you?"

"It was a little crazy, the way they fought. Years later, they were tearing each other's clothes off."

"They needed that distance to awaken their old passion."

"Are you Swedish like Liv Ullmann?"

"I'm Finnish."

"The only person from Finland I know of is Jean Sibelius."

"What do you think of him?"

"His music seems great for films, but I haven't heard that much of it."

"Have you heard the Violin Concerto in d minor? It's his famous one."

"I don't know it. I'll have to check it out in the public library."

Khalil felt nervous talking so casually to a teacher. His stomach churned with anticipation. *How had the two of them ended up in the same physical space? Where were all the people who normally bustled in the station?* Khalil got up from the bench to look for some answers to his question. A sign posted on the wall announced *During Construction Shuttle Bus Will Be Available Here*, and that the bus came every two hours. They had another hour to wait. He shared the news with Paivi.

"I wondered too where the bus was," she said, straightening her beige raincoat.

8

The old bus lumbered through Delaware County until it reached the campus. The driver was careful on the narrow roads that led to the small series of school buildings. The rain had not let up. Khalil and Paivi descended the bus and stood for a moment under his umbrella.

"Next week starts a new group of films. Do you know María Félix?" asked Paivi.

"I have never heard of her."

"Maybe we can go together for her film," she asked.

"I'd like that," said Khalil, enthusiastically.

Khalil walked Paivi back to the resident housing where some of the professors lived. Paivi lived in a house surrounded by tall firs.

They exchanged telephone numbers and goodbyes.

The rain had ceased and Khalil had made a new acquaintance.

*

Back in the dormitory, Khalil turned on the radio to classical music. A symphony orchestra played Strauss, and Khalil danced a waltz. He was happy beyond his recent memory. Even if it goes nowhere, he had something to do next week besides study. A trip to the movies with Paivi gave him a new interest. He would enjoy discovering all the Sibelius compositions he could. This woman was full of culture. Apart from the Olympics in Helsinki that Mr. Flaerty, one of his chemistry teachers talked about whenever he could, Khalil had never given Finland a thought. He was eager to explore that country through The Britannica. He conjured images of a snowbound land, where because of that, people stayed indoors most of the year. In Paivi, he found someone who could bridge whatever he read with a person willing to share time with him.

In the following weeks, Khalil met Paivi every day for lunch in one of the male dormitories. Those meetings alone might have been enough, but Khalil found himself falling further in love with the mere mention of her name. Her name came out of nowhere when a coed on the bus-ride back to Philadelphia said to a friend of hers, "I got a B from Mrs. Avo. With that I maintained my average."

*

Khalil's heart sped and he had the urge to get up and run. Run off the bus and find her! It was almost too much for his immaturity to bear. *Why did being in love make him so out of control?* He would have to get a grip on himself.

"You know Mrs. Avo, right?"

Khalil realized the coed was talking to him, when she tapped on his seat in front of her.

"Uh, yes."

"I have seen you two together. Oh, it's all right. I like her too," she said.

Khalil wondered if she had noticed how he sat up when she first said what she did. It had to have been obvious to anyone who watched him. Of course, it was! He felt so guilty being in love. What added to that guilt was he did not know how she felt. He knew he would have to find out before he lost his mind. No, he had already done that! He just wanted to complete his education, but not without losing Paivi. Losing Paivi? He didn't even have her! He didn't have anyone! He was completely alone in the world. What did he have to lose? No mother. A father in prison. Paivi might not even be in reach. What wouldn't he do to hold her now? But why worry? He had his new life ahead of him.

*

He stood in line at the check-out counter at the campus bookstore.

"Excuse me," asked a coed behind him. "That woman wants to talk to you."

Khalil looked behind the coed to see Paivi. His fingers were no longer sure what to do, as they found the bills to pay for the books he was about to buy.

Khalil wanted to talk to her as well, not that he knew what to say. As his father had once said, "If a woman is interested, she will find a way." Khalil was in a sea of uncertainties. Now, he was looking into those grey eyes, wondering how he could see his way out of them. Could she see clearly through him with them?

"You were looking at me a short while ago, so I thought we might have a chat."

Khalil did not want to chat as much as he wanted to hold her.

"I have been listening to Sibelius. He speaks to me, daily! Through the violin, I mean. Does that make any sense?"

"Of course, it does."

Khalil was suddenly trembling like the last leaf of autumn.

"I am on my way into town. Can you come?"

"It's Friday and my classes are over. I am going in town, too."

Khalil marveled at his spontaneity. *A jazzman must think like that*, he mused.

*

"Did you get anything good?" she asked him.

"*Arrowsmith*, Sinclair Lewis."

"I have never read that," she said, sounding as if she had actually, but not wanting to appear so knowledgeable. "But is it true he turned down a Pulitzer?"

"I have no idea. How could he turn down such a prestigious award?"

"Maybe he didn't need the money," she offered.

"I wouldn't have. He could have given it to charity, if nothing else."

It was at that moment that Paivi slipped her slender hand into Khalil's. It was the surprise of it all. It felt wrong, yet he wanted that feeling. What he did not want were the stares his holding a white woman's hand engendered. The City of Brotherly Love is only a slogan maybe originally on parchment. Still vivid was his memory of waiting with a Puerto Rican woman, Olga Melendez, for a bus on the 5ᵗʰ and Walnut. A car was driving by, when its passenger called out, "What you doin' with that nigger?" In a knee-jerk response, Khalil had yelled back, "Your mother!" It was a tit-for-tat city, where no offense went without an equally offensive re-action. All that reading of the Quran had not hushed Khalil's instincts that simmered inside, which had slipped out of his tongue. On that cold winter night, Olga had leaned in close to him and said, "No one will say that in Puerto Rico." Paivi might have said the same thing to him. There was no reason to read too much into her holding his hand, and he could think of no-where else he would rather be.

*

They sat side by side in the restaurant. When the waiter came by, Paivi held Khalil's hand to her lips.

"What will you be having?"

"Seafood salad."

"The salads are big," said the waiter.

"Then just give us one," said Khalil. "And a bottle of sparkling water."

When the waiter returned, Paivi was studying the mole on Khalil's left palm with the interest of a mas-seuse. She showed little interest in the octopus, so Khalil, with his right hand free, ate it and the oysters too.

*

They found their way to Sansom Street, where there were always foreign films playing, and no one staring at a very dark man and his Nordic date. While the Swedish dialogue was lost on Khalil, he was able to understand heated scenes, as was Paivi. Her mouth even devoured the scent of the seafood between Khalil's fingers. He loved this woman's attention to detail.

"Let's find a hotel," suggested Khalil.

Paivi squeezed his hand in confirmation. Her full lips caught the glow of the street lamps. Khalil could not remember a time in his life when he had been so close to fulfillment. Maybe he would go to Finland and get away from the legacy of the embarrassing, memories of his family brought him. He held her hand and they walked in and out of the shadows on the sidewalk.

"Khalil. Is that you?"

From across the street, it was Bilal Ishak. They had grown up together but did not go to the same college. Bilal Ishak crossed the street, if only to get a closer look at whose hand Khalil was holding.

"What's up, Khalil?"

"Everything's fine."

"I can see!"

"This is Paivi. Paivi, Bilal."

"Pleased to meet you, Paivi."

Bilal shook hands with her and smiled a nervous glance. He liked her too. "You aren't from here, are you?"

"No. Finland."

"When did you have time to go to Finland?" he asked Khalil.

"I go every chance I get."

"Oh! Well maybe I should go with you next time."

"All you need is a ticket," answered Khalil.

"Call me," said Bilal.

"Okay," said Khalil, and they walked in opposite directions.

"Who was he?" asked Paivi.

"Just another hound. A smart hound though."

"We were friends in high school, but I don't see him anymore."

"That might change, it seems," said Paivi.

"I think so, too. But neither one of us has the time we once had."

*

By the time Khalil and Paivi had gotten to 13th Street, they had found a bed and breakfast. They dropped off their belongings and went out for some necessities.

*

It was 11pm when they got back to their room. Khalil and Paivi were where they wanted to be. They had not known each very long. The walls were enough to contain the secrets they would share, starting with the birthmark on Paivi's back and the one on Khalil's rib cage; hers the shape and color of a peach, his, the color and shape of an eggplant. Those two objects slid against each other in unexpected ways, revolving like planets in orbital bliss. Was Andromeda ever more in love with itself? If so, Khalil and Paivi would never care. Paivi coated rose lotion on Khalil's dry skin, while he massaged her toes between giggles. He was in need of some levity. He couldn't remember when he had been so playful. And laughter—was there still a possibility that he could find the childlike joys he never knew? And the ever serious Paivi Avo? A failed marriage had no place in that space of playful souls and tears of joy. Was she shuddering in that muslin cocoon? The rebirth of a *Calinaga buddha* that had found its way to America, aboard an ocean vessel, and was now in a hotel in Philadelphia, about to find itself a new chrysalis. And she was more than ready. Her body throbbed with ecstasy and Khalil's too. She repeated his name, as if saying it empowered her. Then she hers, now alternating it with his.

*

When dawn broke through the window, the bedroom lights were still on. That was the least of their concerns. Slivers of warm rays, razor-thin, passed through the curtains, each one silent, coruscant, and joyous.

Leave the lights on, was what Paivi had said. She did not want to miss any portion of Khalil's anatomy. What did tangled limbs care about lamplight or sunlight? A sheer curtain shielded them from the bold amber of the sun. Still, it painted Paivi, as if she were a canvas, and Khalil took her in to him with a freedom he could not on campus. There were just too many eyes, eyes most interested in saying "nay" to what these two had been drawn to do.

9

Beirut, Lebanon

The steamer pulled into harbor. Billows of smoke were in the air. The air smelled of olive oil, but also of animals being cooked. Was there a feast taking place? There was plenty of excitement. To Khalil, this was a great event, and he had arrived just in time. He was certainly eager to begin his studies. While descending the ramp, he was jostled by other passengers, who were in a hurry to get in the lines ahead. He smiled. *A rowdy bunch*, he thought. Men carried makeshift boxes of belongings. Some women helped their elderly parents, while others carried their children and more boxes. Khalil had a suitcase, a baritone sax, a bass clarinet, and a steamer to claim. That was all.

He stood there, looking through his black book for the address of his contact, Dr. Ishak Munir.

"Khalil, do you need a ride? If so, I have a friend who is coming to get me." It was Barish, standing next to a young man.

"Thanks just the same. I'm ok. Nice to have met you," Khalil replied, hoping to put a closure to their contact.

"Oh, I'm sure we'll meet again," said Barish.

Khalil looked up just long enough to see the hopeful expression on Barish's face dim, and then, he went back to his book.

*

Boom! Rat-tat-tat! An explosion and a machine gun fire. It was impossible to gauge the distance or direction from which the shooting came. People that could, dropped to the ground. Some could not get back up. A big woman splayed herself on the ground. She covered her face. A little girl huddled herself next to the woman. There was a volley of bullets, then another. A sign that had just prior read "Suleiman Muhandis" in Arabic, now, riddled with holes, only read "handi." *What a welcome! They will need doctors—or coroners!* Khalil still had his steamer to forward to his final destination, but that was no longer a priority. As he stood up He got to his feet after having crouched down to save himself from the bullets. His legs locked. He wanted to run but how when he was frozen with fear. But just as quickly, his adrenalin overtook him.

He saw several men running with automatic rifles, all in uniforms. It was not the most reassuring sight. It did give a police presence to Beirut. *Were they under a state of emergency?* This was not the same notion the Bible gave him back in his comparative religion class. Isaiah 35:2 It will blossom profusely And rejoicing and shout of joy. The glory of Lebanon will be given to it, The majesty of Carmel and Sharon. They will see the glory of the Lord, the majesty of our God.

It was going to be four years of dodging bullets, perhaps. *Did they sell Kevlar vests in the open market? They sold scimitars, so why not?* These thoughts made Khalil feel uncertain about being able to survive his studies. But what were his options? One could get shot anywhere. So settle in and absorb the beauty of this ancient city! He dusted himself off. The choice to wear a suit did not appear to be the best option, although its sand color served him well, as it His suit now held the scent and color soot from the diesel truck engines.

From Beirut, Khalil would have to find some transport to reach Damascus, and have his steamer put on a truck, separately. The chaos of the present environment made him feel he might be seeing his belongings for the last time, even though he and his few things were already separated. *Just get there in one piece!* It was not going to be easy to find Dr. Munir, given the turmoil. *Was it like this in Damascus?* Dr. Munir at least knew what Khalil looked like. But how would Khalil recognize his contact? Given the dearth of dark faces, Khalil would not be hard to find. The chaos heightened his sense of bewilderment. People running around, scrambling for cover, or trying to gather their belongings was Khalil's welcome to Beirut.

*

Khalil boarded an old bus that would take him to Damascus. By the time the bus pulled out of the station, it, with its thirty-plus passengers, smelled of goats, and athletes who had played their best, though there were no goats or soccer players on the bus. A woman was sitting by herself in the front. Khalil amused himself by watching the shepherds moving through the street with their herds. There were shepherds in the road. Barefoot boys were playing soccer, perhaps hoping to play in a World Cup for some country, far away from the gloom that surrounded them. Looking at them he wondered, *how could anyone question that education is not the only sane way out of this?* Not the rote memorization of facts with the inability to apply solutions for a better world. These roads needed someone to ride on them and turn the clock forward to catch up with centuries of time. *Where were the great minds that gave the world algebra and astronomy? Were they heading the world into a valley of internecine wars?* Khalil let the bumps muddle his thoughts, and like the other passengers, found himself counting sheep.

*

When Khalil opened his eyes, it was to lights and honking horns. *This has to be Damascus*, he thought. It was just too big, and had too many people to be another sleepy village. The bus ground to a halt into the station. A guard boarded it. He checked passports or whatever identification the passengers had. He only stopped when he came to Khalil, but knowing little English said nothing after a cursory examination. It was after 7pm, so Khalil thought he might still be able to catch up with Dr. Munir. No. He could find a hotel on his own. Dr. Munir would be the next day's task.

He did not know where he would find his contact anyway. *Boom!* Was it another explosion? The last one had been in Beirut. Who was setting off these bombs? What did they hope to accomplish? A diversionary tactic? If confusion was their aim, they had already succeeded. Khalil helped an old man to his feet. The man had urinated on himself. A father consoled his daughter. A woman screamed uncontrollably and Khalil was back on the ground again at the sound of another burst of gun fire. When Khalil opened his eyes, he saw blood on his hands. He felt dizzy, but no pain. Had he been shot? He quickly examined himself. He was intact as far as he could tell. But blood was streaming from another man's leg. He had fallen and was lying next to Khalil. The old man winced, holding on as best he could. "I'll get you help," said Khalil. *But from where?* he wondered. He needed help himself, but at least he had not been hit by the fusillade. The heat of the sidewalk and Khalil's face felt one and the same. Another man got up and ran right into a vehicle. He didn't get back up. Khalil heard an ambulance. *Or was it a fire engine?* He could not be sure. He hoped he would not be riding in the back of one of those trucks, bouncing around on a gurney. And where was Dr. Munir? Would there be no one to receive him? No. *This* was his reception. Nothing could be more confusing. Welcome to Damascus! You may kiss the ground. But he was already doing that! The salt-taste was both his sweat and the earth, now filthy. *Get used to it,* he told himself. *Be patient, or you may find yourself like the one who tried to make a dash for it. He* would never run again! He checked his disheveled garments. He was glad his attaché was still strapped around his arm. His hands were scraped a bit. He still had his mobile. *Good!* He walked down a street, disoriented but intent on locating Dr. Munir. People were still running, but they perhaps knew where they were going. He did not. He stopped in an alley, and now stood between two walls. The smell of garbage from a bin near him commanded his olfactics. No windows were blown out to cut him into shreds. He tapped in the country code and number. The message in Arabic was clear: he could not complete his call. He would make the call from one of the shops, if they would allow him. *Why wouldn't they?* Or was it like America, where they were quick enough to say no to a stranger's request? At least he had dollars. Who would turn *them* down? *Rat-tat-tat! Rat-tat-tat!* In another minute, the money he had might mean as little as it did to the man lying contorted in the street. The plumes of smoke gave him little hope, except that he was sure Dr. Munir could help him understand what was going on. But he had to find him, and soon. Behind him, he heard a commotion. He turned and saw uniformed men with machine guns running his way. He froze. They slowed down, and went past him. He was not who they were after.

A flash of life in Philadelphia overcame him: he was walking home from the Free Library on Logan Square on a Sunday afternoon in spring. Police pulled over next to him and asked him where he was coming from. The library. What did he have in his bag? Books. They wanted to see. Sure enough. He had books: microbiology, differential equations, *Tieta* by Jorge Amado. He did not expect an apology. None was ever forthcoming—to him anyway. He knew better than to give them any pretext to pull out their night sticks. They moved on to interdict some crime, he supposed. North Philly was full of it. Chestnut Hill, no creature stirred. He told himself that there might be some honest cops riding around. There might have been a couple, but he had his doubts.

*

Damascus

Khalil broke from his reverie and walked into a small shop. He found a vendor unloading tomatoes onto a display. He greeted him with a brotherly *As-Salaam-Alaikum*, and then asked if he could use the telephone. Without hesitation, the vendor obliged. Khalil made his call.

The phone rang.

"Hello, this is Khalil Baptiste. I would like to speak to Dr. Ishak Munir."

"Hello Khalil. I am Ishak Munir. Are you in Damascus?"

"Yes. A shopkeeper was kind enough to let me use his phone. Where should I meet you? It's kind of dangerous where I am. Explosions and gunfire."

"Catch a taxi to the Damascus University Medical School. I will meet you at the gate. It will take perhaps a half-hour."

Khalil thanked the shopkeeper, and went outside to find a taxi. He saw people walking around as if nothing had happened. *Were they so used to seeing people lying on the street and hearing the bursts of Kalashnikovs?*

The first taxi motored past him, as if on its way to a hospital. Minutes later, a rickety Fiat came to a halt, as if out of gas.

"Damascus Medical School, please."

The cab driver turned to look at Khalil with his to-bacco-stained grin. As he started the engine, the Fiat coughed its way through several alleys first, and then braved the highway. Everyone was in a hurry. Damas-cus struck Khalil as a city of impatient ones, young and old.

Khalil asked the driver in Arabic, "So what were all the explosions? Did you hear them?"

The driver did not respond immediately. Khalil thought he had misspoken. But surely, even if the driver had not heard the commotion, it would at least be the most current news. After Khalil had resigned himself to his silent ride, save for the missing engine, the driver spoke.

"It's the opposition. They want the president gone." Glancing through the rearview mirror, he asked, "*Sudani?*"

"*La.*"

"*Somali?*"

"*Ameriki.*"

"*Ameriki!*" the driver responded in the quizzical way Khalil would have to get used to. This was the third world, but Khalil felt it should be the first world. It certainly had a recorded history that would make a clear contender, but that is not how placements were assigned.

Now it was Khalil's turn to turn a deaf ear. He had had enough to fill his journal with a near-death touch-down at the port. He would save any conversation for the coming days.

Khalil exited the cab, but not before snagging his pants on the spring protruding from the seat. Khalil had no local currency and tendered the driver five dollars. The driver took off before Khalil could have asked if what he gave him was enough. The taxi sped away.

*

Among all the myriad faces, there was none that looked Khalil's way. Or no, they all looked at him in the same way: with curiosity. *Curiosity is good*, thought Khalil. Nothing like disinterest. He was only too familiar with *that* look. It was the look he hoped he had left behind, once he stepped aboard the transatlantic vessel. *Is this the right entrance?* He asked himself. It must be. Dr. Munir had given no indication of another. He stood where he was to be easily identified. But how could there be any doubt? No one else looked like him!

"Hello! Are you Khalil Baptiste?"

"Ishak Munir. This is Tarik Ali. He will assist you."

"Pleased to meet you both."

The men shook hands.

"I trust your voyage was pleasant," said Dr. Munir.

"Yes. I am glad I came by ship."

"That way your luggage stays with you. Where is your luggage?"

"Because of the confusion at the port, I have decided to claim it later."

"We have to apologize for that. Most unfortunate times we live in. We will secure it today."

Dr. Munir spoke with an assuredness that made Khalil feel that he was someone who understood the current happenings of Damascus. As he talked, his eyes moved about as if someone might be watching them.

This made Khalil uneasy, but he walked just as quickly as they did.

"Where are you from in the US?" asked Tarik Ali.

"Philadelphia. Ever hear of it?"

"Yes. In geography class."

His answer made Khalil chuckle, though he did not elaborate in his answer.

"You will want to pick your bags after we get you to your room. It is in the dormitory. It will do for now. You will want to find a new location after you have gotten to know the city a bit," said Dr. Munir.

As they walked past the old buildings, Khalil had the feeling he was going back in time. He remembered a conversation he had with his friend Bilal.

"You know, you may see some of our ancestors in Syria. Let me know if you do."

Khalil had yet to spot any ancestors. He did, however, see some women he would like to know. But that would have to wait. More importantly, he hoped he could stay alive long enough to finish his studies. He had yet to start, and the afternoon had been anything but calm. The sky was now cloudy, and he yearned to hear no more explosions.

They arrived at the dormitory. It was another old building with wooden floors that creaked. Dr. Munir and Tarik Ali escorted Khalil to his room. When they arrived, an Indian with keys scurried behind them. He greeted the men, and tendered Dr. Munir the keys. Another Indian followed Khalil, Dr. Munir and Tarik Ali into the room, holding a tray with fruit and bottled water.

It was hot in the room. A second Indian opened the window. With the door still open, a breeze blew into the room.

"You have four days before anyone can register you in school. The administrators are all away. Don't worry. It will be fine."

Why wouldn't they be fine? Khalil had copies of all the documents he had forwarded to the school.

"Let us go down to the desk, so that I can call the customs office," said Dr. Munir.

"We will have a lorry meet us there."

*

"When Khalil, Dr. Munir, and Tarik Ali arrived at the customs office, the parking lot was empty and the door was locked. A lorry driver arrived shortly after Khalil. Ten minutes later, the customs officer arrived, apologizing. He was a corpulent one, with his stomach hanging over his belt. He had gone to make *asra*, the afternoon prayer. Khalil thought of the ironic blend of the call to prayer and staccato of the sirens. Damascus was a busier, more dangerous place than Philadelphia. Khalil did not necessarily want a city of brotherly love, just one of brotherly survival. He was not sure if, when he asked the old man he had helped to his feet, was the same one the customs agent was referring to, until the agent said he wore a long black shirt and held red prayer beads in his hands, until he said, "May Allah accept him."

That made two deaths he had witnessed in two hours!

Khalil signed the receipt for his steamer and suitcase, and the truck driver loaded them onto the truck.

"This evening Tarik Ali will take you out for dinner. We will drop you off so that you can rest. We eat late here. Can you be ready by 20:30?"

"Of course."

*

After returning to the dormitory, Khalil took a shower. The scrapes on his hands burned when the water hit them. The bed was stiff. *A new mattress*, he noticed. He set his alarm clock, and drifted off to sleep with the patter of rain that splattered off the windowsill onto the floor.

10

Khalil was ready when Tarik Ali showed up at 21:12.

"I didn't think you were coming."

"I was not going to disappoint you," Tarik smiled. "Are you hungry?"

"I am."

"There is a place not far. It is home cooking, I think you call it."

"I just hope they give me enough!"

"Oh, they are not stingy. You will see."

*

The two men walked on the skinny sidewalks and rubbed shoulders as they got out of the way of cars driving by them. It had stopped raining, but the streets streamed with warm water, which evaporated into the evening light that shone from the shops. The alleyways were just as crowded as the big streets. Khalil took in the crumbling facades. Civil war had left its scars of honeycombed buildings, grey and chalk-white, which no one talked about, but must have been on the minds of anyone raised in Damascus. Paint-chipped and lattice windows served as reminders of what was once, now only history. Khalil saw a mule cart go by and the mule relieved itself of its lunch: dark-brown mounds, dinner for the flies, already there.

"How do you like Damascus?"

"A city of history and surprises!"

"How does it compare to Philadelphia?"

"Oh, mine can't compare to this place!"

"No, I mean by modernity."

"I have no way of telling. It's too soon," replied Khalil.

It is noisy, to be sure, thought Khalil. Car radios blared the vocal hits of the time and drivers honked impatiently at pedestrians and fellow drivers alike. The traffic crawled nonetheless, so what was the point?

"It's a city for fun!" said Khalil. "What year are you in?"

"Oh, I graduated last year."

"In medicine?"

"No, business. Dr. Munir is my uncle. He thought I could get you oriented. I think you will be fine here."

"I am eager to start my studies."

"Studying isn't easy here because of the government upheaval. You must have followed it while in America."

"I have, particularly since I was coming here."

"It will probably get worse. There is a strong opposition to the government. But he is stronger."

Khalil was not interested in politics, as he knew that it was a volatile topic. And also, the Damascus University stamp appeared on letters granting him a fellowship. If President Al-Assad were ousted, his fellowship would be in jeopardy. No, he would walk the tightrope and balance his way through school.

*

When Khalil and Tarik Ali walked in the restaurant, they were greeted warmly. The male host recognized Tarik.

"Welcome Tarik. And friend."

"Hi, this is Khalil Baptiste from America."

"Welcome to Syria."

Tarik smiled as he watched the smoke rise from the kitchen. He was familiar with the smell of lamb that wafted through the air. Khalil picked out cumin, nutmeg, onions, and coriander. The waiter walked them upstairs. The tables for two were snugly situated, so Khalil asked that they have more room. The waiter removed one of the tables and a set of chairs.

*

Music swirled in the air. A female vocalist sang of a lover who *did not deserve the love he had betrayed. Why was it always the same?* Khalil could not help but notice that there were only men in the restaurant.

"Where are all the women?" he asked Tarik.

"Women are so boring. They are probably making the shopping lists for tomorrow." Tarik answered.

What a banal answer, thought Khalil. Is that the extent to which he thought women engaged themselves? Khalil could see he would not be spending much time with Tarik.

"But if you want to see women, I know a place."

"Now we are getting somewhere!" said Tarik Ali.

Khalil was aroused by this new awakening Tarik had come to. Khalil was possibly mistaken by Tarik's sexist words. Still, Khalil said what the present atmosphere substantiated: some of his misgiving about Tarik. Men sat around and smoked, content in their own world. It looked like a scene from Saudi Arabia Bilal Ali had described. Khalil's friend Bilal had made Hajj and he talked of the days of heat and the constant company of men, of their preoccupation with women, to have several wives, and while they encouraged him to do the same, had a very complex system of finding one wife, let alone more than one. *Brotherhood was good, but nothing could compare with the company of a sister.* When Bilal said those words, Khalil added Paivi to that list. She was not Muslim, but he loved her company all the same.

"You seem far away," said Tarik.

"It's a lot to take in. Even with knowing the language, I have so much more to learn."

"And you will learn, too! You will like it."

How was Tarik so sure? Khalil wondered. *Had he seen others experience a transition to his culture before? He had to have!*

*

Khalil was practicing his horn. The Buffet series 400 baritone sax was his most dear friend. Oh, he had his clarinet too. His baritone was older than he was. He named her Meryam, Surah 19—so he always addressed her with reverence. Oh, she coughed a lot when they first met. The humid air made it difficult to breathe. But with time (with proper nurturing), Khalil coaxed the charm she held captive, or as he was inclined to believe, and the years of practice were paying off. He loved to see the sunlight transform the tarnished loops of brass into splendid arms he brought to life when he raised her to his lips. She was all lyricism in his arms. He took the chords from Sam Rivers' *Beatrice* and fashioned a charming melody. He played it at the window and some passers-by clapped. This acknowledgement was the encouragement he needed. Before this, he alone knew that he liked music so foreign to this land. Finally now, he owned the song that had no name, only a feeling. Call it *Damascus Blues* for the haunting echo that followed the sigh of all he had left in his hometown—the home he had left forever. No, he had to return to Paivi: the svelte silhouette who had him playing Sibelius passages in his own composition, as if he, Khalil, had composed them himself. Paivi's gait was what he measured to bend the notes that gave his tone all the warmth he now knew. When Paivi called him a genius, and after hearing what he had done to Romance opus no. 9, Khalil would never be the same again. And on baritone saxophone? Had Coltrane and Sibelius ever been more kindred spirits in Khalil's hands? *Those days in Paivi's place.* The walls white like snow or *lumi*, as Paivi said. There was no denying that she would always be with him. But she would not be there. Not the way she was. He was already a different person. *Just keep playing.* It was starting to sound better. He ran a Phrygian mode in D-flat, starting on F. He liked the sound. He had one foot in Damascus and another on Fifth and Somerset in Philadelphia. That intersection was part of *El Bloque de Oro*, shops where you could find great pastries like flan and some of the best Puerto Rican meals, or both, in *El Restaurante Bohio* in the homes of neighbors if you were lucky enough to know someone who lived on Somerset Street. This gave the tune a Spanish feel. He borrowed a lick from Dave Valentin. He wished Dave were there to hear it. The musical ideas that rushed to him launched him forward. He was not going to question his muse. He just hoped she would stay. The sound swelled. The walls would never be the same. He would have to send for Paivi. The more he thought about her, the more he wished he had invited her to come with him, as crazy as it might have been. *Man was not meant to live alone!* True she would be gawked at to no end! The walls seemed like paper. The neighbors' conversations filtered through the walls. No one had complained about his playing yet. Then there was a knock on the door.Khalil was still full of trepidation. Was his playing disturbing someone? Was he not allowed his only therapy in this land of shifting horizons and early crepuscules?

"Hello, brother. We are here to meet you."

"Meet me about what?" Khalil's jaws collapsed after he spoke.

"Well, we see you are new around here, so we wanted to introduce ourselves. I am Hamid ad Din and this is Yusuf as Sahara, and we are from the New Students Committee."

"Khalil Baptiste. Thanks, but I am quite busy. Pleased to meet you."

"No, you don't seem to understand. We want to greet you! To welcome you to our country. Your Arabic is quite good!"

"Thank you very much. Well, maybe some other time."

*

At that point, Khalil closed the door. Even to him, it seemed like a rude gesture, but he was not in need of any reception committee. He was in the country for the sole purpose of a medical school education—and maybe, some music during his down-time. But, perhaps he was taking on the wrong attitude. *Arabic good? Of course, it was!* He passed with native fluency at the university. Why should he pretend that it wasn't? This was an opportunity to make friends—or to meet spies! Yes, he was sure that's what they were. Spies! What was his real reason for being in Damascus that was in the midst of - civil strife?

His curiosity took over. He opened the door again. There was now a third man standing there. This last one was older than the others. *A professor,* thought Khalil.

"How can I help you?"

"Now, that's more like it! We just want you to have a tea with us. What's the harm? Cultural exchange is all we're after. America is a place we know so little about. You are American, right? I should not assume that you are. And we can practice our English. I feel ashamed that my English is not equal to your Arabic. But Arabic is your first language, correct?"

"You are full of compliments. I guess a cup of tea can do no harm," said Khalil realizing he might have appeared caustic in his reception.

Khalil wiped his instrument down the way he normally did. The chamois was full of moisture. He laid his instrument inside its case.

He caught up with the students downstairs.

"Actually, we want to help you," said one of the three men standing in the lobby.

Khalil sat with the men in the outside seating of the café. He relaxed, exchanging light conversation with the talkative one of the three.

*

"I just wonder why a man would come so far, from America nonetheless, to study medicine."

"If someone is fortunate enough to have school pay for his education, he would take advantage of that, wouldn't he? He would have a chance to read from ancient, revered texts, left by the brilliant scholars."

"Of course, of course! Medical school must be expensive there."

"Extremely. In America, I read about the Transition Period, a time in Islam when scholarship was highly valued in Iraq and Syria. I was drawn to study medicine here because of the contributions of that period. That was during the Umayyad Caliphate, I believe. You see my point?"

"And has your stay been—?"

"Fine," replying to the student before he had completed his question.

Khalil did not care to embellish his answer. He did not know these men.

"So how did my name come up? Did I win a lottery?"

"Lottery?"

"I mean, out of all the foreigners here, how did you choose me?"

"Oh, we asked at the school about you. We were curious where you came from."

"So I am being followed?"

"No, no. We are a curious people. You would have to admit that you stand out. In a good way, that is."

Khalil now noticed that people were interested in why he was in Damascus. He would use these chance meetings to gather information too.

The steam swirled from the tea. Khalil added a spoonful of sugar. He was warming up to their attention. He was not used to meeting people at all. He was not even looking for associations. He *did* want to know he was in a cordial environment. He would have to appear like the friendly American. What notion did they have of one anyway? Sidney Poitier? Morgan Freeman? Clint Eastwood? Marlon Brando? Had they ever heard of them? Well, they would not get a stereotype with him either. They would have to form an opinion based on these tea sessions, presuming that there would be more.

"So, where are you from?"

"Philadelphia. It was the first capital, back in 1776."

"Damascus is very old. Before the Romans came—it has a long history. We are proud of our past."

"I have so much to learn," said Khalil.

Another student arrived. This was a woman dressed in magenta blue-green hijab.

"Hello, sister," said Hamid. "This is Meryam. She is a medical student, too."

"Pleased to meet all of you,' said Khalil.

"You meet many students, and we hope to get to know all about you," said Hamid.

"All about me? I don't think my autobiography is too interesting. Well, and I about you."

Khalil began to feel nervous. These Syrians were indeed in need of information and he decided then and there to give away as little as possible.

"Are all of you med students?" he asked.

"Just Murad and Meryam," said Hamid.

Neither Murad nor Meryam had spoken beyond introducing themselves.

"So, I may see you two at school."

"You may," said Meryam.

"I feel I should mention that I named my saxophone Meryam. Please don't be offended."

"Why should I be? It is your saxophone."

The reply was followed by tension-breaking laughter. A few smokers' coughs from the older student in the group trailed behind.

*

"You have been quite nice to invite me out,"

Meryam smiled, hiding her crooked teeth with a raised hand. She was wearing a gold ring with a blue stone. Her hair was covered in a magenta-blue smock. She was a tall woman dressed in jeans. Her presence created a distraction. Khalil was quick to pick up her purpose for being there: draw all the information she could out of Khalil.

"I have always wanted to go to America," she stated. "Have you ever been to Hollywood?"

"No. I have never been to the west coast. I have only been to New York."

"America is so vast," Meryam offered. The men just remained silent. Their eyes darted back and forth, moving with the alacrity of scriveners. How did Meryam know so much? Was she just filling the air to sound smart for the American? That was what the silence seemed to tell.

*

There was a knock on the door. Had Khalil overslept, again? He had done a lot of that in his new home. Would he ever get the feel of this place?

*

Xandra in Damascus

Khalil received a package at his apartment building. He could not have been more surprised. It was from Philadelphia. What was more surprising was who sent it: Julian Exposé. Julian was his uncle, married to his mother's sister. He had never heard from him before. These people did not write, unless there was a death to report, or an emergency where money might change the outcome: someone in the family had gotten locked up. The Baptiste family had the distinction of walking the tightrope of life without a safety net. So, what good news was in this envelope? Being so far away from home, Khalil was happy to hear even bad news. Coming from his family, it could only be bad news. Those DHL packages were so hard to open! Was his father dead, too? Why did it have to be bad news? Because that was the only kind his family was capable of bearing. What a negative legacy! Didn't the delivery guy even resemble a vulture, circling, to patiently to pick apart his carcass? He was still standing there—after Khalil had paid him, including a tip! He smiled at Khalil as if he knew the contents.

"You can go!" Khalil said, unable to hide his irritation. Was the guy waiting for him to open it in front of him?

Now Khalil did not want to open the package. He went back to his bedroom and dropped the package on his bed. He looked at it. Hadn't he run away from home? Did he need any reminders of the pain that still pulsated in his body? But no, this might be good news. Another dead relative? He was running out of guesses! How many did he have left? No, stop this insanity! It was only a package. How could it harm him?

It was a letter and a composition book.

Dear Khalil,

I'm somebody you never expected to hear from, I bet. I never did no writing in school, so here I am, sending you this little note. Your Aunt Eve Marie was holding on to something I felt belonged to you. It is your mother's journal, I think you'd call it. Yes, that's it. I didn't know she wrote. Eve held onto it, because it was all she had left of your mother's things, except for the bottle of Dewar's scotch she still hasn't opened. Funny how you hold onto something long after

*they're gone, waiting for them to come back,
when you know they done gone to the other
side! Your mother sure did love her scotch.
The good stuff she called it! I'd agree, but
can't drink like I used to. Oh, remember
Sonny Boy? No, you probably don't. He
wasn't in your crowd. He died last week.
Cirrhosis. Came as no shock. Sonny Boy went
like his father. Wasn't nothing but drunks,
that bunch! But I'm off the subject. This is a
fine book your mother left! I wish I could
write, but I don't have the patience. Your
mother, Xandra, did though. She didn't talk
much. She just lay it down on paper. She
didn't care who it was. You'll see how her
words can cut. I know it is going to be in the
right hands. A man of letters like you!*

So good news *was* in the envelope!

He could hardly believe it. But it was in his mother's
hand! This was a secret she had managed to keep from
him. And to imagine that he never would have seen it if
his uncle hadn't sent it! The pages, some stained with
liquor. The coffee, still lilting through the desert air
brought her back to life. She was alive. Like a memory.
Does anything ever really die?

Page after page brought back the life his mother had
lived.

*Bilal is not a bad man. Not all bad, any-
way. I love him, even though he has hit me.
But when he hit me, he was striking himself.*

The pain is in his bloodshot eyes. He has big dreams, but those are not things I see him reaching. They are mushroom clouds full of mush. He shouldn't reach so high. This world will not let him realize those dreams. Better to reach for something attainable! Steady work like a dishwasher! You can't spend integrity, but when you clean out a grease trap, you bring home a dollar.

How could his mother put a cap on his father's future, without putting one on her own? She was a realist. She looked at things and saw them for what they were: in black and white. Xandra was not a fascinating person, but she paid the bills on time. As Khalil turned the pages, he felt the impressions of blue and black ink, which brought to life a world unknown to Khalil. He did not know his mother at all. And if he did not know her, he did not know himself. The journey into her life made his more meaningful. His father, Bilal, was a gambler. That's how he found himself in prison. Khalil stuck to the attainable dreams. He had good teachers, even if they did not see themselves as that.

Khalil put down the notebook. It was a lot to take in, but he knew he would devour it. Oh, had to pick it up! He was so far away from everyone he knew; his mother could shed some light on why he hated his homeland. He read with the enthusiasm of the boy who reads *The Three Musketeers* and *Platero and I*. Xandra may not have talked about herself, but she had plenty to say about others.

That Tina Roberts thinks nobody knows what she's doing. She's sleeping with my man. Well, I can't really say he's mine. He's hers! Anytime she wants him. But one of these days his stomach is going to explode in his shorts. That will be a pretty mess to clean up. Her bed linen won't ever be the same. Those chocolate brownies that he loves, but laced with Ex-Lax. It was a shameful thing to do, but no one will be ashamed as he must have been. And if she ate some too? I would have loved to see them both!

So Dad was getting down with Miss Tina! I wonder if they still see each other, Khalil thought. Miss Tina was a head-turner. She must have made it easy for him. Maybe she helped him pass the bills. If so, it didn't come up at the trial.

Khalil was glad he knew nothing about what was going on with his father. He was equally happy that he had no knowledge of the relationship of his parents. But now he had a window into their lives; their sorted lives.

*

"So what do you think of Khalil?" asked the older student.

"What's there to think? He's an American guy?" answered Meryam.

"I mean, why come here to study? There are so many schools in his own country."

"True. Maybe he has an ulterior motive," said Meryam.

"I don't think so. That seems a bit of a stretch. Based on what?"

"We don't know what his motives are. He seems so serious."

"He could still be a spy."

"If he is, he will have to do something to convince me," said Meryam.

"That's what I want you to find out. Find out as much as you can. Get close to him. Find out if he is here for a reason other than to study medicine."

Meryam did not like the idea of spying, but she would do what she could. If these young people were going to build a new country, she had to play her part, which might mean doing something unpleasant, like spying. The fact that Khalil was there on funds that the government provided. Was it true? Khalil would give her that information. What was the government going to earn by giving an American anything? America, where the streets were paved with gold! Even if she didn't believe that, what if they were? Yes, this Khalil was full of information for her to mine.

*

"You know, we should study together," Meryam said.

"That's fine with me, but I usually study alone."

"I mean, we could help each other."

Khalil was fine with that. He worked alone. He was more than happy to see her when she came by. She broke up his day. She was a distraction, not a nuisance. When he wasn't studying, he was practicing his saxophone. He filled his room with notes, and had a musical conversation with himself. It was call and response time every day. The notes were the friends he wasn't going to see. The guys he missed in Philly, or his conversations with Paivi. He missed her. There was no denying that. But now Meryam had wedged her way into his life.

"Yes. Company is good." She said. "I am amazed at your Arabic. You don't even hesitate!"

"Well, I have been speaking it a while. And we can speak in English if you like."

"Whenever you like, but I enjoy speaking Arabic with you."

"So, what does your family do?"

"My mother is deceased. My father is a printer."

"I am so sorry. Do you have brothers?"

"No, and you?"

"I have three brothers and two sisters."

"The families here are much bigger than in the US."

"We live together. We are close."

"Some families are close in the US, too. My family is not, though."

"Why is that?"

"I have no idea."

Khalil did not like where the conversation was headed. He hated talking about his family.

A family that gave him no pride. He swept every thought of them under the rug. The rug had a mound under it. So the questions about them started answering themselves. Khalil found himself talking about them just to relieve the pressure cooker in his chest.

"My family is all here, but yours is not," Meryam offered.

"True. We aren't the writing type. I do call from time to time."

"And do they ask about Damascus?"

"No. I wish they did. There is so much to talk about here."

Khalil found himself wishing he had a better relationship with his father. *Better?* He had none with him at all! That was all his fault because of the stain his father put on the family. But why look at it that way? Every family had things they would rather not discuss. Just talk about the good times they once shared, but they were so few.

"You know, there is something I used to do with my Father. I would take a trolley with him through the city. I never knew where he was going, but along the way, we would sometimes stop for a banana split. Do you know what that is?"

"No."

Khalil drew a picture of a banana split and Meryam beamed with delight.

"We don't have anything like that."

"You've got plenty enough."

"Still it looks delicious!"

Khalil smiled and asked, "Are you hungry?"

"No. A little envious though."

"When you go to the States, you'll have plenty of things to try."

The likelihood of that happening was very remote. Meryam was planning on building a new nation. Going abroad was not in her future. She was to get whatever information she could, and pass it on. She would keep probing until Khalil told her something useful.

"So, whatever made you leave the US, and why Syria?"

"All the history is here. And as I had shared before, I was lured by the free education."

"Who in the government is giving away free education?"

Khalil was disturbed by Meryam's tone of voice. "I don't know exactly. I think you should take that up with your government. Just look at it as a way governments work to establish working relationships with each other."

Meryam backed away momentarily. She would try an alternative line of questioning to see how much Khalil knew about Syria.

11

Three years in Damascus

"Hello Paivi"

"Khalil? Is it really you?"

"It is. How are you?"

"Fine. I should have asked you first."

"I was crazy to leave you there. I miss you so much."

"No more than I miss you. And the trip there?"

"Long and eventful."

"You've got to tell me all about it!"

"I'd rather send you a letter. I don't trust discussing it over the phone."

"That bad, eh?"

"Action packed, just like a movie."

"You've piqued my interest."

"Nobody would believe it."

"I would. If it comes from you, I would believe every word."

"Well, the voyage was nothing compared to the bus ride from Beirut and the arrival in Damascus."

"In Beirut, there was an attack and several people were injured."

"I wish I kept you here. But you were so adamant."

"Nothing could have stopped me—short of death."

"Which sounds like you barely escaped."

"I got pretty dusty, rolling around on the ground."

"There you go, making light of a pernicious situation."

"They keep you on your toes."

"I don't like it."

"It's not all bad."

"Tell me something good?"

"I'm alive."

"And I am here."

"And who's got your back?"

"You do!"

"How many oceans away?"

"You're just an air ticket away."

"My first break, and I am coming there."

"No, not here. Let's meet in a neutral country."

"Why not there. I am dying to see Damascus."

"Don't say dying. Say eager, or anxious. No, not anxious!"

"Every time Damascus is in the news, it's never anything good. Crumbling buildings, cars on fire, bodies in the street, that's what you can count on."

"Oh, that's how they keep you wanting more."

"Seriously though. How can you study in that chaotic environment? You should have gone to Finland. It's safe there."

"Maybe post doctorate."

"You have to survive this first."

"I will."

"And what was that sound?"

"A truck backfired. It's quite common."

"I'm sure it's too common."

"So, let's meet in Madrid. It's romantic, I hear," said Khalil.

"Or Paris."

"Or both!" said Khalil."

"I miss you. I love you. I don't think I can wait till the end of your semester."

"Really, you can come whenever you like, but I would rather we meet elsewhere."

"Are you ashamed of me?"

"Are you used to being stared at?"

"I can get used to it."

"There's another thing. We aren't married. Here, they really get into your business. Your business becomes their business, and they can't get enough. They are the most inquisitive lot."

"I think I understand."

"And someone as blond as you, they may even ask for your autograph!"

"So, they may take me for star?"

"Don't be surprised."

"Let's meet in Madrid."

"Now you're talking!"

"You say when, and I'll make hotel arrangements."

"I love you."

"I'll send you all the details by tomorrow. I love you, too."

The conversation ended as quickly as it had begun. The streets were as quiet as they had never been. Suddenly, Khalil was filled with anticipation. *Was he really a few weeks away from seeing Paivi?*

He walked out to the café. He ordered his tea with a sprig of mint. It arrived with the customary two cubes of sugar. As Khalil dropped the cubes into his glass, he asked himself: *Why do I love Paivi?* Why had he never had a girlfriend before? He had been interested in some. Barbara Brown, the chocolate beauty with the scent of bergamot in her hair, Nana Rodrigues, an African-American-Portuguese flower from Rhode Island, who wrote poetry in her chemistry lab book: *would you give me the time of day if my eyes weren't green and my wrists not small, would you sing my name in the Rodin Museum, and my hair not like Rapunzel?* Both from Cheyney University. Yes, he had shown interest in them, but they had not reciprocated. It was easy to dismiss them. His heartfelt sentiments had died like uncultivated plants.

Paivi showed him love. He had found nothing like that at his home. It was a barren land. He had to go outside to find life to nurture him. Paivi provided a selfless love. How could he question that?

He had gone to Damascus, hoping to complete his studies, which he had all but done. But it was a country in turmoil, caught in the vise of societal unrest where distrust was pervasive. If you went to the mosque, it was with trepidation. You could pretend that all was well. Khalil took the words of the imam to heart whenever he said, "Pray as if it were your last." He anticipated a hand grenade rolling on the carpet in front of him. People ignored him. He was invisible in a different way than he was in America. In Damascus, he was a novelty, but people did not care where he came from. That would not be the case if Paivi were there with him. All the men would want to be his friend. What was his association with the tow-headed beauty? Was she his wife? Did she have sisters? He had gotten to know their motives, while wearing their cloak of religious camouflage and inquisitive analysis: But where are you really from? And have you ever been to prison? The latter were cultural surprises to him, but he accepted them with clinical detachment. The edginess of life in Damascus had become a part of himself he was eager to shed by the way of meeting Paivi in a city neither of them had ever seen.

*

Khalil arrived in Madrid on a sun-filled morning. He felt most relieved to be in a city that was not under siege. There was a military presence, but he discerned no anxiety on the faces of the pedestrians. And people singing on the streets was something he had not seen since as a boy he heard teenagers sing songs by the Temptations in City Hall. This was not Damascus, or any place in his recent memory. Who was he kidding? In any memory! And what was that going on over there in the airport? A woman dressed in what looked like a gaucho outfit, serving complimentary glasses of wine. People singing and drinking wine in broad daylight? Khalil was in another world. He would be waiting for Paivi right there for five hours. He had joined the cadre of students who attended classes sporadically. With the spate of car-bombings clashes of insurgents, students ventured out as little as possible. They burned the midnight oil in their apartments. More and more, they enrolled in online courses.

Khalil joined the revelers, hunching his shoulders to the rhythm of the guitarists strumming. Yes, Madrid was the paradise where Khalil would free himself of the crazy world that Syria had become. Khalil felt himself relaxing into his breakaway sanctuary. It was almost immediate. He was only at the airport, and he could already taste freedom in the air. As he walked through the mall, he took in the advertising. Huge colorful signage displayed watches and perfumes. Fashionably dressed women lured the shoppers. Khalil wanted to buy Paivi something. He would wait until she arrived. He checked the arrival of flights from Munich, where the second leg of her flight began. Lufthansa flight 1292 was due at 18:47. Khalil walked into a shop that sold CDs. He browsed through the music. He had heard of few of the artists. He spotted one by a cellist, Sol Gabetta. It contained the music of Vivaldi. He decided to buy it for Paivi. He did not want to meet her empty-handed. Getting her a gift helped relieve his anxiety, the feeling that stirred in his gut. Why did he feel he was doing something wrong by leaving Damascus? He was going back after this little break. Was he like anyone else who had left that war-torn city, so glad to find a haven? Khalil looked around at the travelers, sitting alone, or embracing and laughing. A group of men held some packages. They perhaps had gifts for their children. Khalil had only Paivi. At least he had her.

Khalil had to remark that he was in a place where people expressed their feelings. Where was the last time he had seen people singing and playing guitar? He couldn't remember. Compared to Madrid, Damascus was a morgue. It was not because of the war. It was just the cultural differences. Joy was not a bad thing. It's just that people in Damascus kept their happiness corked.

And now with the war, everyone walked around as if carrying a keg of dynamite. One never knew when the next keg would go off. For Khalil, Madrid was a heaven where the angels sang.

Khalil left the airport to see for himself what Madrid was like in the open air. Congestion was nothing new to him. People loading into cars and children wanting to have candy, all universal. Khalil was eager to see Paivi's reaction. He would just be happy to see her! Khalil sat on a bench, his suitcase and bass clarinet by his side. He listened to a man singing in his car. He thought that he would become like him in a short while. Paivi and Khalil would conjure melodies that they knew in common; that no one would tell them to be quiet, at least he hoped no one would. Now, there silence again. Khalil sat alone. The noise would pick up again and the next flight would generate the usual activity.

*

The silence prompted Khalil to take out his instrument. He played slowly. The long tones reminded him of molasses cascading over mounds of ice cream. The sound was sweet, like the way he used to play for Paivi. He noticed the woman who was giving out samples of wine earlier pass by him. She liked what he was playing and nodded in approval. She paused, taking in the notes. She did not leave until he had completed his phrase. He felt an unusual freedom. He was as free as the drizzle that fell. He was under the canopy though, so he continued. He had drawn a small group of listeners.

He lilted into *Contemplation* by McCoy Tyner. He wondered if any words existed for it. He thought it would make a beautiful song if the right singer sang it. Someone like Nancy Wilson, he thought.

> *Memories of us in the rain,*
> *My hand contained all I wished for*
> *Whispers and dreams still make my heart swell*
> *All that has changed is the season.*

He had never even heard anyone play it on a bass clarinet. He was glad he knew it. Maybe he would find a singer to accompany him. He was getting ahead of himself. He was enjoying himself, away from the rigor of study, amid the pedestrians.

"*Otra!*" said a man in the group. Khalil's playing had drawn a few people. *Naima* came to mind. He conjured Paivi's face. Her piercing steel-colored eyes made him close his own as he played. He realized why he liked playing bass clarinet more that the baritone sax. It was the warmth of wood that worked for him, which the saxophone did not have. There was something celestial about that tune. He knew what it was in an instant: He was away from everything he knew that held him back: his neighborhood, his country, and even his Damascus. He played with the freedom of the expatriate he had become. He ended to a nice applause. The little group dispersed.

"No. I don't play in a group. I play for therapy."

What he said may have been lost on the man who asked if he played in a band. The man did not ask for any explanation. There was the universal exchange of smiles. That was enough for Khalil. He was ready to return to the terminal to meet Paivi.

Inside, Khalil sat down and was overcome by the sadness of thoughts of the summer job he had back in Philadelphia when he worked for the public housing department. He couldn't get over why he was even thinking of that experience. The present place was the furthest ever away from that dismal environment.

It was a veritable retirement community of clock-watchers, ex-offenders, and chronic drug users. Most of the men had grown up in the 60's, so the conversations about the Drifters, Hank Aaron, and Mario Lanza filled the break room like the wall clock that would not know the twenty-first century.

While those men had acquired their knowledge by the seat of their pants, through repetition and memorization, they didn't trust the knowledge contained in books. Nor did they trust anyone who read them.

"Whatcha readin'?"

"Oh this?" said Khalil, with a *what do you care?* in his voice. Then, again, maybe it was someone of his ilk.

"*Gabriela.*"

"Sounds like a girly book."

Khalil closed the book and turned the book with the semi-nude cover facedown.

"You'd have to read it to judge. Or, you could just watch the movie."

"You tryin' to say I can't read?"

"No. I see you reading the Daily News."

"That's right, so don't get smart, brainy."

There was no envy in the coworker's voice. This *homo erectus* (and he looked just like something out of an anthropology journal) found books intimidating. Khalil's summer job couldn't end soon enough, but not before he had earned every penny he needed.

These guys were the kind you could not open your wallet around. They never had any money, so you never wanted to appear that you had any. Khalil would jokingly ask for ten dollars to borrow on certain occasions just to keep them at bay. These guys lived in abandoned cars, or with girlfriends, because either their wives, or the families had put them out. Because how many times had they gone home wasted on pay day, after spending their paycheck on crack? They cursed their women for making them appear in family court to pay what they owed for child support. One of them *borrowed* his transpass, only to never return it. Khalil found these men to be no different from the men in his own neighborhood; though they had jobs, they were suffering from the same lack of a place to stay, or a place to go. They occupied the bottom rung of society where the ceiling was glass and low.

"You don't have no kids, huh? No. I didn't think so." It sounded like an indictment. "Maybe he ain't into women," another one snickered. "Leave him alone. Can't you see him readin' that girly stuff? No offense." "None taken." "See how he is? So civilized!" "Oh, he was raised by white folks." "Is that true?" "No." "What kind of name is Khalil anyway?" "It means close friend in Arabic. I really have to go now."

*

Khalil was so glad to be away from that xenophobic-homophobic bunch! He looked around the airport for what would be the refreshing sign of Paivi. But more than anything, he enjoyed his invisibility among the sea of unfamiliar faces.

Was that Paivi? No. He wasn't sure what she looked like now. He played a game with himself but he really could not say how she would look. He did see a woman who resembled Altagracia Llores. She was standing with him one night after coming from a movie. *The Elephant Man.* Altagracia wept on his shoulder in the theater. As they waited for the bus, Khalil caressed her gloved hand. He felt so much joy as she leaned in to him on that cold November night. A car roared by and the passenger shouted, "Nigger!" And continued on. Altagracia looked up into Khalil's eyes. She knew the words were directed at him.

"Why do they hate so?"

"That's their nature. They must learn it from their mothers when in the womb."

"All of them?"

"No, just most of them." Khalil had no way of being entirely certain, but he had seen enough of that behavior to leave him thinking that most white people felt that way. Altagracia kissed his hand, and then, his lips. That was the warmest gesture he had ever felt. He needed that to renew his faith in humanity.

Now, there she was! Khalil could not believe his eyes. But he had to believe. They embraced and had nothing but joy to share. They stood silently, smiling at each other. Khalil could not remember being happier.

He was still wondering what he would do, now that they were together in Madrid.

They caught a taxi to Plaza del Angel where Khalil had found a modest hotel. What did they care about the modesty? Would they even leave their room?

"You cut your hair."

"Do you like it? She asked.

"I love it."

"It was too long, but you always liked it."

"I missed your voice most of all."

Khalil held her hand, squeezing it, then brought it to his lips for quick pecks. Color rose in her cheeks. He felt like a child. He hesitated to say again, but he couldn't remember much of his childhood. He was able to hide the pain from himself. Music was his sanctuary, where no words were necessary.

From his teenage years he played the baritone saxophone and the bass clarinet. He ran errands and served newspapers. Between the two jobs it was not long before he had earned enough money to take lessons from an uncle who got him started. Khalil played until he was exhausted. His uncle taught him to use his diaphragm. In a year he was able to play any popular tune that he heard on the radio. Reading music came easy to him. He borrowed manuscripts from the library and taught himself pieces by Bach and Gabriel Fauré. He found that he could run away from the issues at home by closing the door to his room and absorb himself in A Well-Tempered Clavier and Sicilienne. What a serious youth he was. With a suicidal mother and an angry, dissatisfied father, where was the place for fun? He wondered what would claim his mother first: the bottle or the bridge. Either way, he was going to lose her. It was because of his mother he decided to follow medicine. Not that he thought he could save her, but it was an ambition that he sought to do good. He revered men like Dr. Carlos Finlay, the Cuban doctor who discovered the mosquito that caused malaria. However, he did not get credit for it, as his supposition was considered erroneous.

The evening had fallen. Khalil walked with Paivi through the narrow streets, where people were singing as they left the movie theater.

"You know, I haven't been to a movie since we were last together," Khalil said.

"We'll do that again soon," said Paivi.

They passed a butcher shop where legs of ham were hanging in the window, and wheels of cheese were on display. A fruit stand full of apricots, green oranges, and plums all looked so inviting that Khalil asked Paivi if she cared for something. She declined and they continued walking. They passed two men standing on the sidewalk, serenading two women on their balcony. Other people approached to take in what was now a little concert. The musicians ended the song to applause. Khalil and Paivi looked at each other with a joy they would remember for a long time.

Khalil and Paivi stopped in a tavern next to the hotel. Khalil had an expresso, and Paivi, a glass of red wine. A woman sang a flamenco. Her voice scraped against the stucco walls. The guitarist gave chase to her. Paivi rubbed Khalil's leg, her fingers brushed against the coarseness of his raw silk pants. Combustion wasn't far off.

The couple asked for their hotel room. The street lights flickered through the diaphanous curtains. The singing continued on the streets below. It was eleven in the evening but the reveling was contagious. Madrid was a city where the night belonged to the young, and Khalil and Paivi embraced it. Who would dare stop the ardent flames that had already seized the unbridled passions that had been patient for years on end?

"Your heart is racing, Paivi!"

"It's trying to keep pace with yours."

Khalil couldn't remember when he had been so exhilarated. Damascus left him with angst. Madrid gave him fervor. Paivi was a big part of that, but he couldn't see himself sharing that same feeling in Damascus. Damascus, as illogical as it was, depressed him just enough to propel him through his courses. He was driven to succeed. Every time he thought of how far he had come, he worked harder to get to the pinnacle. And if that meant climbing Mount Hermon, that is what he would do!

Khalil and Paivi went out for dinner. He walked with his arm around her waist.

"This is something I couldn't have done in Damascus."

He was free to express himself as never before. Paivi felt free as well. As the couple looked for a restaurant, a short black woman approached them.

She looked in need of something. In a moment, Khalil's expression of happiness changed to exasperation. *Even in Spain, black people live in impoverished conditions*, he thought.

He made a gesture with his free hand, but Paivi grabbed it.

"Sorry, we have no money for you!"

"How do you know I want money?"

"Whatever it is, we cannot help."

"Cannot, or will not?" The woman asked.

She might have been a beauty in her day. A Cecily Tyson of her time. Even beauty lasts but so long.

"Either one you choose. The answer is no. *Hasta la vista!*"

Paivi took Khalil's hand and they continued walking.

"You are much too kind. We'll go broke if we start helping every beggar. We are not the reason people are poor or destitute. I work every day just as you do, so that we won't be in such a situation. Seems harsh, right?"

"It does. I thought of how she could have been my own mother."

"Or mine!"

"I don't see how," said Khalil.

"Anyone can ask for money. But we all have to work to earn it. Work has no color. And you remember the definition of work, right."

"Work: a force through a perpendicular distance."

"And don't forget that applies to everybody and everything." She said.

Paivi's words were as clear as they could be. Undeniably clear. *The sooner one started working, the sooner one would have something to eat*, thought Khalil.

And Rocinante, that sway-back jenny, had gotten the last dime she would ever get from Khalil. No more missives of need would he answer. Once a bum, always a bum. No, once a prostitute, always one. She was after all, a professional. Khalil had to laugh at her crooked under-bite as he remembered her. They came upon the restaurant they had chosen. It displayed a glazed round loaf of bread and several bottles of wine by the window.

"I shouldn't have been so harsh on that old lady." Paivi was feeling remorseful. She reached for Khalil's hand across the table.

"I could have given her something, following my first mind. But you are so right. When does it end? It never ends. It's a way of life for some—if not all. I think of all the poor in Damascus and Aleppo. By comparison, there are few beggars in those cities. Here people are free to move about, in relative calm. There, in Syria, your life is always in peril."

Khalil laughed. It was a nervous laugh. He was not someone used to being corrected. He could not remember the last time that had happened. He was so happy to be with Paivi. He didn't want to have anything change that feeling. It didn't have to be perfect. *Life is imperfect, so take it as you find it.* He would be back in Syria soon enough. *Enjoy the bends in the road.*

"So what do you want to do today?" Khalil asked.

"Let's walk. This is such a beautiful city."

They walked until they saw a cinema. They looked at each other, then entered. There was an Almodovar film playing, *Volver.* It starred Penelope Cruz. She was a favorite of Paivi's. Khalil was attracted to her, but had never seen her in anything.

"You haven't seen *Captain Corelli's Mandolin*? You have to!" She said.

"I don't think they will show a war movie in Damascus. If it is about war."

"It is. You'll have to rent it."

They sat in the lobby, with Paivi on Khalil's lap. They were a half-hour early for the show. Paivi lay her head on Khalil's shoulder. She took every advantage to create intimacy. Khalil too, took advantage of what he felt he would never experience in the open in Damascus. It was at these moments that Europe appealed to him. It wasn't America, though. He didn't have a longing for home. Life there was as fetid and brown as the Schuylkill River. It was as Gil Scott Heron described, "It might not be such a bad idea if I never went home again." Khalil was like those Americans who had to learn within the margins. But he wanted to live without the margins. That is why he pursued his education. Who wanted to be marginalized? He didn't want to be American, in the way that blacks were not. He wanted to be like Paivi: a citizen of the world. She was a person who moved freely. Look at how she was, nestled on Khalil's lap, not caring who saw her, or what they thought. That was real freedom. Was it just because she was blond? That fair-headed fact was all too pronounced even in Madrid. Now that she was practically sewn at Khalil's hip, the only reason they couldn't be confused as twins was their difference in pigment. But even that gave little reason for anyone to care. And the initial feelings of uneasiness changed to embolden Khalil. *Is this what being free feels like?*

*

The film ended too soon, thought Khalil. He wanted to see more of Penelope Cruz. Wasn't it enough that she stole every scene? Maybe it was more of Spain that he wanted to see. He wished it had been Barcelona that he had chosen to visit. But he had hardly taken in Madrid. How could he be so sold on Barcelona, if only from one film? Oh, he was overjoyed to be walking along the narrow sidewalks of the Plaza del Angel with Paivi. She got a nod from every man they encountered. She was every bit of a novelty. He, on the other hand, was not an oddity at all. Together they were a pair that did draw some attention.

"Which part of the film did you like most?" asked Paivi.

"Where Penelope sang in the restaurant. She was the glue in that film."

"I agree. I liked the drama between her and the husband. He was a real slime ball."

"He was having relations with whoever was around, to put it nicely." Khalil said.

"There is no nice way to put it!"

"It made me uncomfortable," said Khalil. "No, vulnerable."

"I wonder how much that goes on."

"I really don't want to wonder. More frequently than is reported, I'm sure."

"Did you ever read *Invisible Man* by Ralph Ellison?" she asked.

"Of course."

"I remembered the scene where the main character is in the small town, where he meets a man who is in the company of another man who has come to know his daughter in a way he should not have. Very ugly," said Paivi.

Paivi squeezed Khalil's hand. The signal to change the subject. It started to drizzle. Khalil draped his jacket over Paivi's head. They turned into the nearby subway station. They boarded a train with no destination in mind. They just wanted to explore Madrid.

"What about Cervantes Memorial?" suggested Khalil.

"Let's find it," responded Paivi.

The two set out to locate it. It turned out to be a prominent location.

The couple first returned to Calle de las Huertas. From there they took the metro to Villaverde. When they arrived, it had stopped raining, and while vehicular traffic was brisk, the couple had no trouble getting up close to the monument. Paivi held up a copy of *The Trial* to Sancho Panza, who on his donkey, sat next to *Don Quijote*. She read a paragraph to Sancho while Khalil took a photograph of the three, standing in stoic elegance, immortalized for Paivi's album.

"I wonder what they would have thought of Kafka," asked Khalil.

"I don't know about them, but Cervantes would have had an opinion.

Paivi took pictures of Khalil. An old gentleman went up to them and asked where they were from, and how they found Madrid. Paivi asked if he would mind taking a picture of her and Khalil. He didn't mind, and in return, Paivi took a picture of the man with Khalil. Paivi then took one of Khalil with Don Quijote.

There was much that piqued Khalil's interest. The statuary, swift movement of the traffic and the curiosity of the Spaniards, all were a surprise to him. While the Arabs were people who seldom asked Khalil any questions, the people in Spain were full of them. The Arabs, he had noticed, might have questions, but if they did pose those questions, they would ask each other. Maybe they found it impolite to ask questions to a stranger. It might have been cultural mores that maintained the divide, to include the fact that they only spoke Arabic for the most part. Khalil asked the Syrians questions, but he was inclined only to talk to shopkeepers and always in Arabic.

Khalil and Paivi had been out all day. They decide to go back to Plaza del Angel before dark, since it was the area with which they were most familiar.

Upon arriving at their hotel, they changed and went out, looking for someplace intimate. Again, they found musicians on the street. They had grown used to this atmosphere. At a nearby bar, Cani España, Khalil asked the bartender to suggest a restaurant.

"I think you will be pleased with Algarabia. It's not far."

Khalil and Paivi found the restaurant without trouble. It had started to drizzle again, but Khalil bought an umbrella on the way, so their clothes didn't suffer.

They ordered a paella and an octopus salad and shared a bottle of white wine. For dessert, they had flan, followed by espresso. It was a rainy evening, which ended with Khalil and Paivi lying in bed with the television on. Paivi repeated the words of the editor. The news caught their attention. *ISIS strikes again in Syria. Five years of refugees fleeing into Turkey and countries in Europe. Dead children on the streets and buildings*

riddled with holes. The UN convened, but stood power-
less Dr. Bashir Assad showed no signs of relinquishing his
control. The rebels were not going anywhere as long as
the US backed their efforts for democratic rule. They
were a sovereign nation, so why was the US involved in
their internal fight? As commentary ended, Paivi leaned
on Khalil.

"How can you stand to return there? It's so dangerous."

"You get used to it. I am nearly finished. Then I can
return to the States, or maybe go to Finland."

"Oh, you're just talking. In Finland, you would be
safe. I would protect you. People would appreciate your
contribution."

"It won't be long. You'll see."

"I hope so. I have such faith in you. But you must
know that."

"You are the only one."

When Khalil spoke those words, he saw himself
with Paivi forever. There was no one in the world who
had ever said those words to him, so he took them on
their value, intrinsic and eternal. With her, he saw life
as simple. She presented no hidden agenda. Khalil's
mind flashed to something he had recently read, which
made him reflect. Khalil was not a man like Dostoyevsky described: *a being that goes on two legs and is un-
grateful.* When Khalil told her how much she meant to
him, she was prone to raise a finger to his lips to silence
his thoughts. "I am only as good as the day is long," she
once said, and that was longer than anyone had ever
been good to him. He was, by nature, the grateful type.
So to have Paivi in his life, he would die a grateful soul.

Khalil wanted to ask her if she wanted to see his few friends. But would they appreciate what he saw in her? He doubted that.

"So who are your friends?" he asked. "College chums. Professors."

"Do you go out with them?"

"I do. It can be lonely since you aren't around."

"It's no less lonely in Damascus."

"That's what I was thinking. I should pack up and come live with you."

"Are you serious?"

"I wouldn't have said it otherwise."

"Do you think you could make it there?"

"I could make it anywhere you are!"

"You could make it even if I weren't there!"

Khalil looked into Paivi's eyes, their teal color. When she looked at him now, it was with a serious intensity that only a true friend would feel. She was as he knew her to be: sincere, if not emotional. She could be tender, though. But more than tender, she was sure. She might have been a leopard in her previous life. She had traveled a great distance to find him. She carried whatever she needed to make the journey. Like Euclid, all she needed was a pencil and a straight edge.

"As you are in school, I am too. I enrolled in a PhD program in analytical chemistry. Like you said, it won't be long."

"We may finish together."

"You will have plenty to keep you busy. Dodging bullets and careening cars."

"That will keep us in shape."

"We'll be emotional wrecks!"

"Love wrecks. That could be a movie," he said.

"It would be funny, if it weren't a real possibility. I'll send in my work in real time via satellite."

"Things are so much easier today. It is safer than sitting in a classroom."

"It's got to be nerve-racking." She said. "I need to know you are safe. That's impossible to be sure of, so far away from you."

Paivi wore Khalil's blue cotton shirt, which exposed her legs. Khalil pulled her into his arms, and was again at one with her jasmine aroma. The distance they had experienced for so long melted away. The rain tapping against the tin shutters reassured them, as did the singers outside, impervious to the weather.

Khalil began to think about the impromptu decision of taking Paivi back to Damascus. She was so civilized for the sandy world of Syria. Paivi would have to make her way through the old world. Lying beside Khalil in their holiday bed in Madrid was so different from Damascus. They were free in Madrid. They were an oddity, but nothing like they would be in Syria.

"People will look at us, I mean, really stare," said Khalil.

"Oh, I'm used to that. What about you? Are you used to it, too?"

"I am, but I'll have to get used to it again. It will be a different kind of staring. Arabs aren't used to seeing different races together."

"Do you see how much time we spend on race?" said Paivi.

"You'd have to admit we are an anomaly," he said.

"Let them have their fun. It just shows how empty their lives must be."

Paivi snuggled into Khalil's arms.

"Let them stare all they want. I'll make every man envious."

Paivi sounded like she would enjoy seeing the reactions to her presence there. She would no doubt find work if she wanted. She was not the type to be idle. The fact that she had chosen to return to her studies showed she was up for challenges.

"I wouldn't have guessed you would return to school."

"Before I got married, I was bent on research, which requires a doctorate. Well, I am just picking up where I left off."

"I believe you."

Khalil didn't know if he was happier because she was going to Damascus or because she was returning to her studies. Either way, they would be together. He knew she would be in for surprises. No, devastation! No one was going to Damascus, for love or money. But for studies? Now that was different. If they survived, they could survive anywhere.

It was Ramadan, so there was less fighting. Still, everyone was not observing the cease-fire. It was not a time to expect peace. It was a time to be weary. ISIS had taken to lade children with bombs. There were no limits to their tactics. But putting children in harm's way was nothing new. During the Iraq–Iran war, little green mines that resembled toys were placed about. The unsuspecting children would pick them up, losing a hand immediately. Marvin Gaye and others said it: "War is hell!"

Khalil would leave with his own stories. So would Paivi.

*

"So what do you want to do today?" asked Paivi.

"Coffee for starters."

It was a sunny day. The two walked straight to Café Central. Espresso and croissants were the perfect breakfast meal. Khalil suggested a visit to the telegraph museum. They finished their bite and were on their way.

At the museum, they discovered that Alexander Graham Bell was a physician looking for a device that would help the deaf, and eventually came up with the telephone. The museum held an assortment of gadgets that displayed history. It was where the modern-day telephone got its start. Khalil and Paivi were happy to do anything together. They sat and mouthed words to one another to see if either could discern what the other was saying. It was a silly game, but they were equally amused. They walked around until they came upon a bicycle rental office. They rented two cycles and circumnavigated Madrid. Neither of the two had ridden a bike in ages. Khalil was less sore that Paivi, having done so much walking, and often fleeing, in crowded Damascus.

"You know, I could see myself with a practice here," said Khalil.

"It looks like a fine place to work, but what about Canada? Isn't that where you hope to work?"

"Yes, but this might be great, too."

"We're here on vacation. It may not be so great if we lived here," she added.

As true as her words were, Khalil only knew he did not want to return to Philadelphia. Even she could agree to that. He also knew that Damascus was not what he had hoped it would be. His initial dream had deflated. It was a city with its present in rubble and future in pulverized rock. The country was in the hands of a despot, but with whom could Khalil share that view? The resistance movement was backed by the US. Khalil was not politically involved and only wanted to complete his studies. His fellowship to study offer might have been merely a way to curry favor with the US, or rather, a way for Syria to extend a hand to Americans for future consideration: win the hearts of the American people and they will spread the word of how benevolent the Syrian government is. Khalil was a believer in the vision he had of what Syria could be at first. That was before he had seen the turmoil up close. It was no longer from the vantage point of a story in Newsweek. Color photos or not, he had experienced what a photo could not tell. Upon arrival in Lebanon, he held a victim of violence in his arms. There was no running from the bloodshed. The blood was running to him. He worked to save a life that he never had the chance to know: a man, perhaps his father's age, would never make it home for dinner, or even *Isha* prayer.

But he was beyond those naïve days. His beliefs were shaken. He was in Madrid, a free man in as free a country as he had ever seen. He laughed to himself when he met people eager, no, dying to get to America. He met people in Turkey during his short stay, waiting for a confirmation that their lottery number had been selected. What about all those African American citizens waiting for a chance to work, or, to have their business succeed? Would they ever see their numbers called? They watched foreigners stream in the country (perhaps with superlative education), moving directly to the front of the employment lines, sponsored and happy, their faces beaming with contentment, speaking with only the slightest of accents, responding to queries with new names like Walter not Walid, Freddie not Farid, and Sally not Salma. Yes, his beliefs were not what they once had been, but the notion he had of how Islam was practiced was an academic construct, only based on the reality he imagined. He could no longer confirm what he had once believed.

Paivi had gotten worked up over a problem he could not solve. He was not a politician, and besides that, Syria was not his country anyway! Oh, he harbored some patriotic sentiments for Syrians, but what did that have to do with his foreign student status? Nothing! When he returned to Damascus, staying alive would once again be his priority.

"Of course, I'll have to sublet my apartment. I wanted to find a job in Damascus before leaving the States," Paivi said.

"People are leaving Damascus in droves. If they have someplace that will take them, they are going."

"So finding work shouldn't be hard."

"I can't see why it would be. You might want to cover though. As a precaution."

"I wouldn't want people to think I am a Muslim."

"Women might inquire, anyway. They are always asking foreign women if they are Muslim. It is only natural. And another thing, we wouldn't be able to live together—unless, of course, we were married."

"I thought you would never ask!"

"So you are fine with the prospect?"

"We can do it today!" said Paivi.

Khalil felt an exhilaration that was rare. It was what he had felt when she said she was going to Syria. His emotions then were mixed at first because he was leaving Paivi. Finally, he would be sharing his space with her. He couldn't believe he had asked her, and she said yes. Her not being able to bear children was no longer a concern of his. Maybe there was some way she could have them after all. Science had advanced since she first tried. She was older than Khalil, but still of childbearing age. Maybe they could find an imam in Madrid to marry them. Khalil rubbed her belly, as if she were carrying something there. Paivi blushed with delight. She even looked younger to Khalil.

"I don't think it would be recognized in the States. We may have to wait. We'll live in separate apartments in Syria. I have a friend who worked in Turkey. She really felt the cultural difference there. She was in Konya."

"I don't know that city. She should have gone to Istanbul. It's more western."

"I don't think she had a choice. She stayed six months, and then left for Libya."

"I don't see how that could have been better."

"She liked it, but the civil unrest was overwhelming. She got out of there within an inch of her life."

"Tell me."

"She caught a boat to Tunisia. She didn't know if they would even make it there. The sea was rough. It was night, so it was scary. The men groped her. One of the women embarrassed the guy who felt her breasts. The women who really embarrassed the ignorant pervert gave him a tongue-lashing, quoting the Quran, which seemed to quell his approaches. My friend's Arabic was pretty good, but after the Muslim woman told the man off, she didn't have any more problems with that guy. The odd thing was that the man still wanted to take my friend out once they got to Tunis. Imagine that! My friend just wanted to drive a knife through his eye, and she would have if she had had one. Why are Arab men so aggressive?"

"You can ask one when you get to Damascus. But those were men under stress. It might have happened to any woman on a boat with men of any nationality. Do you remember the movie *Lifeboat*?"

"She lived it! She's a writer, so she can tell her own riveting story, if she hasn't already."

"I am sorry about your friend," said Khalil.

"You know, Arab men are not used to having women in close proximity. That is why the sexes stay apart. Europeans and Americans experience the culture shock, immediately. When I was on the bus traveling across Lebanon, I watched this Arab glance over his shoulder repeatedly at a pretty teenager with long, brown hair. Had he been an American, he would at least have said something to her. But he said nothing. That shows you just how disconnected men and women are in these countries."

"I don't think that would have been the case if it were an older man," said Paivi. "An older man would not have been a threat to the girl."

"The girl probably wouldn't have spoken to him either," said Khalil.

"What happened next to your friend? What was her name, by the way?"

"Frida Al Fil."

"Frida the Elephant. That's an odd name."

"Well, she is quite pretty. Not an elephant at all. She is Tunisian, by the way."

"Her brothers must have been waiting for that guy once they arrived in Tunis."

"Well, you won't believe this. She never mentioned to her brothers what happened to her. In her culture, they blame the women for having gotten in that situation in the first place. No onus is put on the men."

"So the men get a pass in that culture too?"

"It's a fraternity of predators! Not you, Khalil. You are the only exception. I love you so."

"You are the exception, too."

*

Paivi waited to venture along Calle de las Huertas. Not unlike the other streets of Plaza del Angel, it wound down the narrow pathways, as it must have for centuries. A sign, Sol. Imported Mexican Beer, hung in front of Café Jazz Populart. Paivi took Khalil's hand.

"I suddenly have a taste for Mexican," said Paivi.

Khalil did not know if she meant food as well as beer, but she would find beer no doubt.

They walked into a bar with ample seating. They went up to the bar where men were standing, enjoying bottles of beer. Paivi asked for Sol. The bartender brought her a glass of it and said, smiling, *"Buenas tardes. Y usted Señor?"*

"Coca Cola."

The bartender returned with Khalil's beverage with a slice of lemon on his glass.

"I saw the sign saying you have music here," said Paivi.

"Yes, there are the musicians," the bartender said, pointing to the two men standing next to Paivi.

"Are you a musician too?" asked one of the men.

"No, but he is."

"Antonio, mucho gusto."

"Khalil, Paivi. Igualmente."

"What do you play?"

"Bass clarinet."

"I play that as well. Not too often though. I play soprano and tenor the most."

"I have a baritone sax too. I don't play it often either."

"What brings you to Madrid?"

"The culture," said Paivi.

"Where are you from?"

"Finland and the United States," said Paivi. "We are really having a great time."

"That is so nice to hear. Do you have your clarinet with you?" asked Antonio.

"Yes."

"Then maybe you will play with us tomorrow."

"I'd love that."

"What would you like to play?"

"How about *Nardis*?"

"That will sound great. Maybe we can do a blues as well," suggested Antonio.

"A B-flat blues. Okay? Monk wrote so many tunes in that key."

"I love Monk, said Paivi.

"I love *Epistrophy*," said Antonio.

"I haven't learned that one yet. It's on my list though."

"So how does Madrid feel?"

"It's been fun," said Khalil.

"Is it like New York?"

"Much better. It's great for walking."

"And what do you think, Señorita ?"

"I love your food. I love the squid, especially."

"This is the place for that."

The three talked like old friends. They exchanged stories about jazz musicians, movies about music, and compositions they liked.

"Have you seen *Ida*?" asked Paivi.

"No," answered Khalil and Antonio.

"It's a Polish film, which uses the music of John Coltrane. It's set during the Second World War. For me, it shows the versatility of Coltrane's music."

"I have to look it up," said Antonio.

"I hope to see it, too!" said Khalil.

Paivi ordered another glass of *Sol*. Antonio found his friend. The café had gotten crowded. The musicians had assembled on stage. The quartet exchanged signals, and they began playing chords to a tune familiar to Khalil: *Peresina*. It was a McCoy Tyner composition.

Khalil had never played it, but it was definitely one that he wanted to learn. Where would he find the time to learn all of those tunes? He would have to live to be one hundred. Who is to say he wouldn't? Just then Khalil envisioned himself in the auditorium, on stage, at Cheyney He had never played there, but he saw himself there. He had resigned that he would never return to the States, because of the bitter memories of home. But he wanted to play. He had to. No, he was saying that because he was in Madrid, feeling free. Syncopation was his friend there. He didn't have to paraphrase what he felt. Paivi didn't have to explain to anyone what she was doing with him? America was not in the picture. And this group was really swinging, as if playing for McCoy himself. Oh, the pianist played just like McCoy, with his powerful left hand. He played fourths like McCoy. He had total command over the Dorian mode, the way Khalil wanted. The drummer had smooth, almost imperceptible, brush work. The bassist with his steady walking, as if his heartbeat throbbed with every stroke, kept the group in a tight web.

Khalil held Paivi's hand and the night was his. He had arrived in paradise. But he wasn't alone. A group of English-speakers lifted their glasses and toasted to what the evening had become: a night of frivolity. Antonio had set the carousel spinning, and there was nothing to do but enjoy the ride.

*

That night Khalil and Paivi lay awake. The long windows were open. The pedestrians sang popular

songs on the streets below in their own drunken meter.
The cars' tires hissed and splashed, as they lumbered
down the narrow streets. Calle de las Huertas remained
busy night and day. It was a place for lovers, and Khalil
and Paivi were one with them. Khalil listened to the
shower that pattered against the tin shutters, and wondered if he would ever see the city of his birth again.

*

The next morning Paivi went out on her own, ex-
ploring. She did not return until evening. Khalil chose
to practice during that evening. He played his regimen
of scales in all the keys and paid homage to the ancestors of Greece. He danced to the *Gymnopedies* of Satie,
the Dorian, Lydian, and Ionian for several hours. Some
street felines were inspired likewise. They let Khalil
know he was not alone.

*

Khalil put in a new reed. He used a number two
Rico. He began playing the chords to Nardis as he had
played it so many times before. E minor to F major seventh to B seventh then to C minor. He felt an unusual
confidence. He knew he would do well that evening.
The cats outside agreed, meowing in their own peculiar
yet unerring voice. Khalil exchanged call and response
with them while thinking how he carried every American's dreams with him. A voice for the voiceless: those
like his father who stared at the opaque prison walls
that Leeuwenhoek described. Walls, stone and silent.
Khalil was freer than anyone he could point to. Souls

that would never leave the country of their birth. The accident of birth had found them in the US, where they waited for their time to come, when they would no longer occupy one of those cells. After being identified in a lineup for crimes they did not commit, but fit the description: young, tall, and black. The bigger picture was that prison complexes needed workers: people to build computers. Paying under two dollars an hour to build computers. A certain Fortune 500 conglomerate having connections with a South Carolina correctional facility, which, in one year, produced $16 million worth of electronic cables. Khalil played for them, the disenfranchised. He had done well to distance himself from his family: the band of leeches, hook worms, trying their best to poison his system with their nightmares and suicidal daydreams. Physical distance was easier to accomplish than he had thought. He won a fellowship to study in Syria. The only thing he had to do was study, and the next thing he knew, he was on a ship that launched his future. He was away from the environment that had done its best to weigh him down. He had found his way out and there was no turning back. But he had cargo to unload. He played a flurry of notes, trying to free his mind. Could he be as free as those thirty-second notes, the Lydian augmented intervals he borrowed from McCoy Tyner? They conjured the wretched woman on Broad and Dauphin. How do you stoop so low, without having your dreams being squashed in the cradle? That was her catharsis. She was out on the corner by ten every night, even in the rain. This was Khalil's. Oh, he played with such fervor. Would there be anything left to say when he arrived on the stage? *Who can retell the things that befell us?* When had he sung the song that came out of his clarinet? It was from his third-grade class. And a Chanaka song at that! He played it again trying to recapture the old days, but he could only remember two faces: Edwin Dorsey and Joyce Cherkov. He conjured those cherubim and seraphim faces. If he had looked in a mirror back then, he would have seen himself like them. Today he wore a beard and glasses, with only traces of naïveté. He explored the bass range of his clarinet. G, D, A, E, B, F, B-flat, E-flat, A-flat, D-flat, G-flat. The *Fables of Faubus* oozed like hot licorice from his clarinet's silver bell. Then out popped Goffreid Leibniz and the implicit differentiation. Find the slope of a tangent to the curve x squared plus xy plus y squared equals ten. *Two x dx/dx plus (x dy/dx plus y dx/dx) plus $2y$ dy/dx equals zero.*

But how had Leibniz slipped into his practice life? Khalil hadn't thought of him in years, much less freshman calculus. He looked at his watch. He had been playing for over four hours—without a break! He looked in the mirror and saw an Olmec ruler, jowls of putty. Khalil felt energetic when he thought he needed to rest.

*

He picked up a book on urodynamics and reviewed the vocabulary. Nocturia, painful bladder syndrome, and the histology of the bladder. He absorbed the vocabulary and its applications for his patients. He was following his pursuits in a free country. It meant everything to have an open mind where his thoughts were not caged. But Khalil believed what James Baldwin had said, "Freedom is not something that anybody can be given, and people are as free as they want to be."

Just as Khalil had taken himself from the American shore, to the Mediterranean, and on the Atlantic to find freedom, the freedom he was in search of was, and would always be, inside him. He knew he would return to Damascus with a free mind, to continue his studies to the end.

*

Paivi returned at late afternoon. She found Khalil resting

"Are you going to sleep all day?"

"So, you found your way back?"

"I ventured about the city. I may have found the best paella in Madrid. It's across the street!"

Paivi slid in bed with Khalil. She rubbed her nose against his ear and pressed her body to his. A truck rode by, changing its gears and sputtering with a coughing carburetor.

"I picked something up for you."

Khalil sat up and looked around. Paivi got up and walked to the table where she had placed a bag and pulled out a gift. Khalil thanked her as he opened it.

"Beautiful!"

"I hoped you would like it. Mine is tattered. Ooh. It's so soft!

"I couldn't help but noticing that your wallet was falling apart. And this is for you too!"

"It is something to wear, isn't it?"

Khalil opened the box. Inside was a sky-blue silk tie.

"It will go well with your blue suit."

"I'll wear it tonight. Thank you. You know, I practiced all day."

"You must be exhausted."

"I am fine now. This tie is so beautiful."

"I can't wait to see you in it."

"Khalil had not bought any new clothes for the longest time. With Damascus being a war zone, Khalil had no interest in fashion. He spent no money dressing up. He had only worn a tie his first day at the hospital.

Ties were not part of his apparel, so he wondered when he would wear it after tonight. In fact, he had not given any thought of what he would wear tonight.

"What are you wearing?"

"I have a black sleeveless. It's my favorite dress."

By seven o'clock, Khalil and Paivi were walking to Populart. They took a leisurely walk, taking in the window displays and the pedestrians they passed.

The manager greeted the couple and asked what instrument Khalil he played.

Khalil spotted Anotnio and walked up to him.

"Muy buenas noches y bienvenidos!"

Antonio's warm greetings were followed by introductions to members of the musical group.

Antonio, Joan Millet on piano, Carlos Andres on double bass, Pedro Marques on the drums.

Paivi did not escape the eye of any of them. As Khalil assembled his clarinet, Pedro took the opportunity to improve his English.

"So Antonio says you are from America. Where? Hollywood?"

"I have never been there. I live in Philadelphia. It's on the east coast, near New York."

"I don't know America. Perhaps someday."

"Perhaps."

Paivi looked away. She could barely see Khalil in the dark venue. His complexion was lost in the darkness. Khalil walked up to Paivi.

"I am going to warm up. Do you want to come with me?"

"That's all right. I'll have something to drink."

"I'll get it for you. Like what?"

"Sherry, thanks to you."

When Khalil went to the bar, Antonio walked up to Paivi.

"You look fantastic! But I am sure Khalil has told you that."

"Thanks. He likes my taste, and I like his."

"So, are you married?"

"Not yet. What about you?"

"Yes."

"Here you are," said Khalil.

"Antonio, I am going to warm up."

Khalil left and found the equipment room.

Khalil played long tones and harmonics for five minutes. That was sufficient for him. He returned to find Paivi standing with Pedro and a young, dark-haired woman."

"This is Raquel."

"Pleased to meet you. I am enjoying Madrid."

"We like it, too. We are from Salamanca."

"I don't know that city, I am sorry to say."

"You have to go there!"

"Maybe on our next trip to Spain. I am sure it is lovely."

*

The men took the stage. Paivi and Raquel sat near the stage and waited for the introduction of the band.

"And tonight, we have a special guest from America. He is actually studying medicine in Damascus, but plays the bass clarinet. Please welcome, Khalil Baptiste."

The audience applauded. The drummer began his tapping. It was very showy. He had so much dexterity. He was not what Khalil expected. How loud would Khalil have to play to be heard? There were microphones. No reason for concern. Khalil had not used amplification in years. The drummer eased into a softer touch, allaying Khalil's fears that he would have to compete with the percussionist. The bassist and pianist joined in with counterpoint. Ravel's ever melodic line was what he was known for. Khalil recognized a passage from The Concerto for Left Hand. They were runs he would practice. The low register of the bass clarinet, note for note. He knew them well. Oh, he had the urge to join in, but he listened with patience. It was not his turn yet to join in. Why this hesitation? Just jump in! No! Not yet! He was talking and answering to himself. This was not a time for self-doubt. He had played all day. *Now was the time to act. Pick up the bass line. Follow Carlos' lead.*

Khalil found his place without any help. He was playing by ear in E minor Dorian, and it was working! He shouldn't have been surprised. Everything fit in for him, just as he and Paivi fit in. They were where they belonged. They group played through the changes of Nardis, and let Khalil play the head of the tune. When Khalil played the head again, Antonio played a third below him. The harmony fit perfectly. It was better than Khalil had imagined. He had hoped they would play the same notes, but this was more dramatic. Someone in the audience was filming. Khalil looked at Antonio, who nodded that Khalil should take a solo. Khalil ripped right into it, double-tonguing, and finding his lyrical voice. Yes, that was what Paivi had named it years earlier. He believed her then, and since then, gave it his all. How could he ever stop playing? There would always be a place for his horn in his life. The pianist stepped in for his solo: more left-hand octaves and arpeggios. Joan Millet did love Ravel. It was oh-so apparent with the use of whole-tone scales. Khalil stood back, listening to how the musicians gave each other space, creating a wave of harmonies, then dissonance when he thought things would remain calm. The crashing cymbals, the turbulence of a shipwreck, then a lifeboat that announced safety. The double bass bowing of E flat. A tumultuous applause followed.

Antonio embraced Khalil. They took photos to immortalize the moment. Paivi snaked her way onto the stage.

"I took shots! You were marvelous!" Paivi said. "Raquel asked how long we are staying here."

"We all have places to go. I wish we had more time here. We can squeeze in a lunch or dinner," said Khalil.

A patron walked up to Khalil. *"Me gustó lo que tocaba. Le gusta a Eric Dolphy, verdad?*

"*Por supuesto!*" answered Khalil, surprised that the man knew Eric Dolphy. Khalil was enamored by the reference to the multi-instrumentalist.

"*Toca usted alto o flauta?*" asked the gentleman.

"*Solamente este y saxofon baritone.*"

"*Va a tocar mas?*"

"*Me gustaría.*"

Khalil was beaming by now. He felt like a celebrity. In Syria, he was just a face, to be confused with Sudanese merchants and students. There he had not met any vacationers from America. Back in the States, he did not even know anyone with a passport. There were plenty with stories of how they were not living the US. In his father's era, the barber shop was full of stories about how many women guys knew in France and Japan and Korea. Some even married and brought them back with them. He didn't know any of these men. They were a lot older, there were a few guys who had recently returned from military duty in Italy or Honduras. There were engineers who talked of building bridges. That sort of discussion interested him in particular. Much of the other talk bent the truth like a contortionist who had forgotten how to get out of the pretzel he had become. Either those men listening believed in fairytales, or that Saint Nick was still coming to town. Most of the men in the barber shop were not going anywhere further than the blocks they lived in. They were in the land of plenty, even if *plenty* was not theirs to have!

Antonio approached Khalil. "We are hoping you will play another piece. What do you want to play?"

"*Impressions* by Coltrane. When you are ready," said Khalil.

Antonio went back to the bandstand and played two more selections, before reintroducing Khalil to an applause.

Khalil walked up to the stage. This time Paivi sat nearer, her camera in hand. On this number, Antonio played the alto saxophone and the bass player sat out. That meant that Khalil would articulate the bass lines. It afforded him a lot of freedom. He was mindful of the weight his part carried. With freedom came the responsibility of anchoring the group. He maintained his steadiness. It was not something he was used to, but neither was playing with anyone. He enjoyed this rare occasion to play among musicians he had only recently met, but felt that he had met somewhere else in the world.

Khalil was floating on a cloud. He was standing on his own. In Madrid, he and Paivi were living a dream. Who could he point to who was doing what he was doing? He was making friends and sharing happiness with someone he loved. Paivi by his side was all he wanted. Maybe she would stay.

*

They walked back to the hotel. He held her hand and told her he wanted to marry her.

"I can't believe it. Are you sure? I am old."

"No, just older," he said.

"Well, you know what I mean."

"It hasn't stopped us from doing anything. Let's give it a try. If we were in Syria, we'd have to be married."

*

Khalil had an idea, but Paivi would have to agree to it.

"We could go to Córdoba and get married there. It was the seat of Islam before the Inquisition."

"I wonder what it is like now," she said.

"Let's find out!"

Paivi looked up in the indigo sky. That look was his answer. The next day, they boarded a train to Córdoba.

12

It was a Friday. Khalil and Paivi walked down the narrow streets and could hear the call to prayer. *They still practice the faith*, he thought. That meant he would find an imam to do the ceremony of marriage. They walked in the direction of the call, but were unable to find the mosque. Khalil asked a woman to direct him. On their way, Paivi picked out a blue and pink scarf from a street vendor. Now they were ready to enter.

"I have memorized *Al fatiha* since you've been gone."

She recited it.

"I'm impressed. Beautiful."

"If something is important to you, it's important to me," said Paivi.

After the prayer, Khalil and Paivi approached the imam. Khalil introduced themselves.

The imam asked some people to be witnesses, which they were only too glad to do. Without much attention drawn, the two were married. Those who attended, gave money and gifts to the bride and shook hands with the groom. Khalil was not expecting anything. He had not even gotten Paivi a ring yet.

"Let's walk around Córdoba to find a jeweler," Khalil suggested.

"I am so happy," said Paivi.

Khalil did not know what made Paivi happy. He was willing to do whatever it took to make her happy. He already knew he was the happiest man in the world.

*

Paivi looked at the gold band, set with a sapphire, her birthstone, and then looked at Khalil, as they took a tour on the bus. They passed the tall cypress trees, and the medical school, which was there from the time Córdoba was *Qurtubah*. The building was still intact. Córdoba was a city of cultural enlightenment, established by the Moors in 711 as a city of learning. But before the Moors, the Romans had built a magnificent bridge in the first century BC. The bus tour gave Paivi much to absorb and she was able to see what captured Khalil's interest. The bus stopped outside a museum that contained artifacts from ancient times. Boys ran by with boxes, collecting donations from whomever stood still long enough to drop coins into their boxes. The boxes were decorated with crosses, a way to soften the hearts of any vulnerable person. Khalil remembered the little girls in his own town of Philadelphia who paraded from Sunday school with Easter baskets they hoped to fill with "collection money for church" they said. Khalil was taken in by their charitable efforts the first year. After seeing them a year later, leaving a candy store with baskets, he knew he had been fooled.

"You know, this ring means so much to me. I don't need anything else from you. Just finish school. I want that for you."

What could Khalil say to that? *Talk about being in my corner*, he thought. It was something he never doubted, and this was her second go at marriage. All he knew is that her first husband had let her go because he wanted children. Khalil wanted them too, but was it worth giving away a gem of a wife? He kissed her slender fingers, as the bus bounced from curve to curve. The bus rode through the aqueducts and the large courtyard: present-day malls.

"This is the best spot for a honeymoon," she said.

They moved past the Grande Mosque of Córdoba, La Mezquita, as it is called.

"Another architectural wonder," said Khalil.

"Grand scale," added Paivi.

"I hope heights don't frighten you." Said Kahlil. "I have arranged a balloon flight."

"I am so high already!" She said.

"Good, because we are going to take in all of Granada," said Khalil.

*

Paivi held Khalil's hand as the balloon lifted from its moorings. The two were among four couples, venturing nervously in the Andalusian skies. The Sierra Nevada white caps were in the distance. Orange pottery house tiles looked even more dramatic. Sheep herds along with steeples painted the landscape. Mules pulled plows, people carried groceries, as they had for centuries.

School boys played soccer in hopes playing for Barcelona someday. It was very possible, since Messi would eventually retire. And those boys who followed Real Madrid and Arsenal would have their day, too. There were even those who dreamed of being bull fighters. *But why not a sport like jai alai?* Khalil could not imagine getting into a ring with a thousand-pound bull, defying death. When he discovered there were women with the same wish to cheat death, he knew people saw little value in life. The balloon passed over stadia and Khalil squeezed Paivi's hand for reassurance. He felt as alone as he would soon be again. He knew Paivi would go back to Philadelphia, leaving him in Damascus, to fulfill his dream, in a city with its diminishing population, either by death or flight.

Khalil was standing next to all that mattered to him. He floated like a cloud, feeling at once insignificant like a bird, but as majestic as a pelican. So, he was significant after all. They both mattered to each other, so why this feeling of emptiness? It was his inevitable return to that city of death. It was as he had found it when he arrived—how it would be when he returned. Yet, it was the city he had chosen. While it wasn't what he had hoped for, it was as the news media had described. On certain days, it was as the Surah 99 of the Quran read, "When the earth is shaken with its final earthquake." There were those days when car bombs disturbed the equilibrium of life, and one looked for shelter, but getting under cover might no longer be necessary. That day had not yet arrived. And when it did come, Khalil would no longer anticipate the final earthquake. Why was he so preoccupied with death? It would come without his planning. He was no different than those who planned for it with their savings bonds and bank trusts. What was the need for all of that?

"You are so far away," said Paivi, nudging against Khalil's collar. Take me, too!"

"You are always with me." Khalil looked up. Two other couples were pressed against each other. This ballooning was perfect for couples: moving as seamless clouds.

*

"I am going to tie things up on the job. I don't know if they would be sorry to see me leave."

"You know they will be sorry. Who can do what you do?" Said Khalil.

"Certainly a younger me."

"I don't believe that."

"The eternal optimist."

Khalil wanted to forget this conversation. He only wanted to remember the smile Paivi wore on their wedding day. The happiness she felt, looking at her ring. The cheers that rose from those in the mosque in Córdoba.

13

The train crash derailed all that happiness. Photos of the mangled steel were a memory Khalil could not forget. He could not claim the body. Where could he take it? He was a shell of a man: a man whose song had left him. It was July 2013. A year earlier the train engineer had posted that he could only do 124 mph, without being fined. *He must have tested the limit,* thought Khalil. It was the trip Paivi made on her own, because Khalil was going in back to Damascus, in a different direction.

What was the use of making plans, when they dissolved like salt in a glass of water?

Khalil was facing his own issues in Damascus. He returned to the rubble where his apartment building once stood. His belongings were in that rubble. His baritone sax reduced to more memories that meant even less, because Paivi was gone. Another bombing, another pipe bomb. Was there anything new? The journals printed photographs. Just new dead corpses. The opposition forces to Assad were making things impossible. How could one exist in such turmoil, let alone study? But Khalil was determined. Paivi was gone, as were the dreams they had hoped to realize together with her. Life seemed bleak, but where could he go? He would sooner join the Foreign Legion than quit. There was always a desert war to fight! Assad could use another doctor. He could find work right where he was.

Poor Paivi! She could have been happy at the university. She could have taught there and finished her studies for a full professorship. No need to get tangled in the wreck of a relationship. Khalil knew how to be drawn in guilt. He was not much good without a dream.

*

In spite of how he felt about seeing Paivi go into the ground, he knew he had to return to Spain to claim his wife's body. He would bury her there, he would honor her in the only way he knew. She deserved that. He contacted her family—Paivi's mother and younger sister—in Helsinki. Her father had predeceased her. Alcoholism had claimed him at the age of fifty. It wasn't an uncommon experience. Khalil had faced enough tragedy in his immediate family not to press Paivi about her own. Her mother and sister would attend the funeral. Khalil had never met them, but was looking forward to it, albeit the sad occasion. Those plans of going to Finland would never come. Finland would come to him.

*

When Paivi's mother, Mrs. Avo, and Paivi's sister, Pirja, (twenty-three, and as blond as her sister) were quite easy for Khalil to recognize. The three of them wore black. They looked so much alike that Khalil could not get over the similarity. He hugged Pirja longer than the mother. He said the likeness was uncanny. Pirja fought back her tears. Her mother was not as successful. This was a time for grieving, so the airport, with its anonymity, was the place to reveal their emotions. They stood in half-silence. Wet handkerchiefs and sleeves. The three now held each other as if by a lifeline.

From Madrid, Khalil rented a car and drove to Santiago de Compestela, Galicia, a drive estimated to be over five hours. Khalil had not driven in years. The good highways became bad, and Khalil, who had been driving on adrenaline, became exhausted. He told Pirja, who peppered him with specifics about his family that she would have to ease up on all the questions.

"It's just that Paivi talked about you so much, I can't believe that I am talking to you now!"

"But you are, and I to you."

"He has to drive, dear. He may miss his turn," said Mrs. Avo.

"I promise to answer your questions. Just give me a chance to find a place to stop."

Pirja was patient. She looked for a place to stop. She reserved her inquiry for the next roadside restaurant.

"I will need you to find a restaurant. I'm not hard to please," said Khalil.

"Pirja will find one," added Mrs. Avo.

The fact that he was traveling with people he had just met, made Khalil reserved. They were cordial, like Paivi, but still, he did not know them. He would not be with them long enough to get familiar. They were his in-laws, and virtually, the only family he had. *This is not the time to create distance*, he thought.

"So, Paivi mentioned me?" asked Khalil.

"You were all she talked about," said Mrs. Avo.

"We know everything about you," said Pirja.

"That's scary. There are some things that aren't pretty," said Khalil.

"I think we know all the beautiful things."

"You are more handsome than she let on."

"And you are too kind."

Pirja was one for touching. Her mother was, too. Neither was what Khalil had anticipated. *Weren't the Finnish phlegmatic? But was Paivi? No, so what did he expect from her family? Be what you would be if Paivi were there.* Paivi was open, so easy to get to know, and her mother and sister were like her.

"We were both sorry to hear about your family troubles," said Pirja.

"We've had our troubles, too," added Mrs. Avo.

"There is a place we can go," said Pirja, taking the opportunity to touch Khalil's wrist. Khalil was now off the highway, surrounded by farmland. Cornfields and vineyards, and clean, new stucco buildings painted the landscape. The long road led to the town of Linyola, Catalonia. Another very clean town. *No, immaculate,* thought Khalil.

"It's so good to see you laugh," said Pirja.

"Why?" asked Mrs. Avo.

"This is the cleanest town I have ever seen!"

"Madrid was very clean, too," added Khalil.

"And Philadelphia?"

"It wouldn't make the list," said Khalil.

They passed more cornfields before they arrived at a restaurant on Ronda Sant Pau.

They stopped at restaurant Bodega Joan, and ordered paella. Mussels and shrimps on a bed of yellow rice.

"I better take it easy, or you will have to drive."

"My driving isn't the best," said Mrs. Avo.

"I wouldn't think of having you drive," said Khalil. "I'll be fine."

"So, when you are done in Damascus, are you going back to the US? asked Pirja.

"I plan to do a residency somewhere."

"Paivi liked the US. She especially liked New York City," said Mrs. Avo.

"She did, didn't she?" said Khalil.

Khalil went quiet, apparently remembering some moment.

"We miss her, too," said Pirja, stroking Khalil's hand.

"So what kind of work do you do?" asked Khalil.

"I am a mechanical engineer. Paivi mentioned it was an interest of yours."

"I like to build helicopters. I don't have time anymore though."

"That's fascinating. I am pretty busy, too. I am working for a design firm. We are working on wing flexibility. I am especially interested in solar flight," said Pirja.

"I haven't looked into that." Khalil had found a common thread with Pirja. It took his mind off his deceased love. In a strange way, he felt her there with them. Pirja spoke with the same voice as Paivi. It was easy to see how he mistook Paivi for being there. Mrs. Avo was drifting off to sleep. Pirja was ready for another barrage of questions. She was writing notes. She was a busy person.

"What are you writing?" asked Khalil.

"Things about your father. But I don't want to ask if they are too personal."

"Oh, they are, but it doesn't matter. I have grown accustomed to the facts, of our lives."

"I'll save them for later," she said.

"You know, you should do your residency in Finland. Have you thought about that?" asked Mrs. Avo.

"Well Mrs. Avo—"

"Please, call me Sylvi!"

"Okay. That feels better to me, too," he said.

Telling Khalil that opened the door to any conversational point they wished to discuss.

Yes, his father was doing time for counterfeiting. He was doing all right, considering his incarceration: He had gotten his high school diploma, had started memorizing the Quran. He didn't expect Pirja to raise the next point.

"Do you think your father did counterfeiting because of the reparations your people were never given?"

"Slavery is a topic the government never touches. Everyone is an American there, though the differences in class are ever so apparent. They always will be. It is a byproduct of capitalism. We come together for national events: voting, the inauguration of the President, Independence Day, and Thanksgiving, but the playing field has never been level. Work is the only common denominator."

"You will be welcome in Finland. We want good doctors," said Sylvi.

"I wondered about your views on the topic of race," said Pirja.

"Now that I am away from the States, I am not pre-occupied with it. I am in Syria now, and they are preoc-cupied with survival. If anyone thinks about me, it is far from a priority. Explosions go off all the time, so it's 'cover yourself and hope you live to see tomorrow.'"

*

Khalil found a place to stay near the restaurant. It was a suite with two bedrooms.

They settled in. It was time to go to the funeral home to claim the body. Sylvi said she did not have the strength. At several intervals, she pulled out an inhaler, because of her asthma. She was a woman who appeared to like libation. The sacks under her eyes reminded Khalil of Lauren Bacall. Her days as a beauty had left her. She might have been one for some time. She would remain in the suite. That left Pirja and Khalil to go alone.

The hostel owner gave Khalil directions. The location was a half-hour away. When they arrived, there was an attendant, but Khalil was not ready for what he saw. The room was filled with bodies on slabs. This room of death, cold and sanitary, contained bodies, turning grey. Khalil followed the attendant. Pirja slipped her hand into Khalil's. The three weaved their way through the gurneys until they came to Number 45: Paivi Avo.

She lay covered in white. Her face had a broken nose. Black marks ran along right side of it. Khalil touched her left arm. She was stiff and alabaster white. Her wedding ring was not on her finger. Khalil wondered where it was. Her left arm seemed unmarked. Her right arm was not disfigured, either. Her torso and waist were full of contusions and legs fractured with bruises. Pirja held Khalil, and he was aware of her thin frame. She was tall like her sister. They both looked down at Paivi. Pirja broke down and cried without shame. Khalil's body absorbed all of Pirja's wailing and shook as she squeezed Khalil, in every effort not to fall. Some of the gurneys were missing, given the gaps in the large area. *They must have already been claimed*, thought Khalil. Individually, then together, Khalil and Pirja offered prayers. They left the frigid room holding each other for support. They walked to the office window. The attendant returned with reports and a large envelope. It contained Paivi's possessions: her documents, tickets, wrist watch, and the ring. Khalil rolled the ring in his palm. What meant so much to him only a month ago, meant little a month later. The sapphire jewel held no importance now that Paivi no longer wore it. He offered her Elgin watch with its brown leather strap to Pirja.

"Maybe your mother will take the ring," Khalil said.

"No, you should keep that. It is yours," she said.

"I have all the other memories. They are quite enough."

Pirja grasped his hand again. The two of them sat down, while Khalil examined the statement of death.

"The deceased was the victim of a fatal head trauma, resulting from the crash of the train into the steel beams, cables, and debris."

Khalil had no need to read further. It was better to hold onto his memories of the Paivi that no one but he knew. Pirja leaned on his shoulder. Fate had joined them in a way Khalil would not have imagined. She would remain with him for as long as he was in Spain.

*

They stood in the windowless hallway, waiting to confer with the director to make funeral arrangements. The yellowing white walls and lighting threw the elongated umbra and penumbra of their bodies, giving a sense of being that Khalil and Pirja were without hope in a neglected space for the forgotten twosome. Khalil pulled Pirja toward him. Hers had become the sole heartbeat he would feel before returning to Damascus again, and possibly the last time he would be close to the Avo family. The hallway, with its floral displays of chrysanthemums and lilies, all white, was a stark contract from the sterile room where the bodies lay. But even the flowers were cut and dying.

Khalil, Pirja, and Sylvi wished to have Paivi's body laid to rest in Galicia.

14

Khalil had all but finished his studies when Latif approach him with an invitation.

"I know I have never mentioned this before, but I want to invite you to my home. School is over and you may be returning to the States soon."

"Thank you, but that is fine. I appreciate the offer."

Khalil was saying "no thanks," in the easiest way he knew.

"You can't say no when a Syrian invites you to his home. My mother and sisters are preparing a meal just for you! It is a graduation celebration."

"Then it's for you," said Khalil.

"No. It is for us!" Said Latif. "I will get you there by taxi."

"I accept," said Khalil, before he had really taken in the moment. He was still thinking of what had happened to Paivi. Celebrating his graduation with her was the only thing that mattered to him, and she was no more.

"I went away in hopes of starting a new life. It was in Madrid, when it occurred to me that my life could be meaningful. I married my best friend, Paivi Avo. She accepted Islam. But when I left Spain, she was killed in a train wreck. I am only telling you this because you are my best friend here. It's painful even to discuss it now. Yes, I accept your invitation. I am so glad, and I am relieved of the most hurtful emotion of my life."

Latif was moved by his friend's confession. He hardly knew what to say. The words were stuck in his throat. He shook Khalil's hand in sympathy. Latif wanted to tell him about his sister, Zouhoor. She was the real reason he wanted Khalil to come to dinner. Would Khalil even be interested in meeting her? Probably not. Khalil had never seemed interested in any of the Syrian students. No wonder! He was engaged to someone already. Latif's curiosity itched for more information about his now deceased wife. Oh, he wanted to see a picture of her. Was she a Natalie Wood type? She was the most beautiful American for him. No, he would not bring up a reason for Khalil to change his mind about coming to his house for dinner.

"My sympathies, brother. May Allah grant her paradise!"

Khalil nodded in gratitude. The two men departed, but they still had not settled on when they would meet. Latif caught up with Khalil.

"How does next Friday sound? For dinner, I mean."

"Great, just call me on Thursday," said Khalil.

Khalil continued his walk to the room he had found next to the mosque he attended. Khalil had not changed his plans to go to Riyadh. It was all he had in mind to do. He had organized his affairs. It was not as bad as he had anticipated, given the destruction of his apartment. He had to start from scratch. He was numb to the challenges. He had nothing left to lose. But what about the nervousness of going to Saudi Arabia? What nervousness? What was going to stop him? He would not be arriving with the blond Paivi. Nothing for the inquisitive Arabs to gawk at. That was actually a relief.

Khalil came to the frightening realization that he was alone in the world. *Paivi is gone*, Khalil said to himself as he stood where he was used to seeing his neighbors running to the café or the stationery store to make copies of documents. This place, he claimed as a refuge. It was his neighborhood, too. This place marked the cornerstone of the building he knew as home. What was left of it now? Bent lead pipes jutted from the ground. A pile of bricks and tiles made an asymmetrical display of questions without answers, like limbs detached from bodies. He looked up, where his apartment once stood, some ten meters overhead. It was there he lay, where the police exercised their brusque tactics of extracting answers when in a hurry. They didn't want to take up Khalil valuable time with formalities. No, he shouldn't take it personally. It was a war zone, so everyone received the same treatment, save for pregnant girls and older women, or so he hoped. He almost laughed at how insignificant the evening was now. Whose necks were they wringing now? Or maybe they had returned, and were at his door the day the car bomb went off outside, taking with them whoever was in the building at that time. Why was he even looking at the sky? Into space went his helicopter, his manuscripts, and his notebooks. The flights he imagined where the planes would use ten to the minus twelve electronic energy, which they absorbed from neighboring buildings. He thought in theoretical terms, but his ideas were not far-fetched. And even if they were, that would not stop anyone who thought as he did. The single stage Fehskens–Malewicki equations.

*

Paivi was gone. He cared for her. But she was not like anyone else he had cared for in his life, or who had cared for him. He could not remember all the things people had done for him (even the few nice things his father or mother had done for him). His mother had left him, his father too. What was the capacity of a human being? He thought of capacitance as Michael Faraday might have considered it. Some element that contained energy, holding it until called upon. Once the energy contained in a capacitor is exhausted, it dies. Like a capacitor, when your time reaches zero, no person is spared. Death like a sword severs us from all we once knew. Khalil knew all too well the sword was coming for him as well. It was just a matter of time. And he had done his time and accomplished his aim, unless some new capacitance restored energy.

*

Khalil, Pirja, and Sylvi stood on the grass as they dropped flowers onto the casket, watching Paivi being lowered into the ground. They offered their praise and prayers to the deceased, none willing to say goodbye to someone so dear, but all acknowledging the inability to change their destiny.

Khalil felt uneasy with Pirja. He thought that if he showed interest, she would go to Damascus with him.

She made Helsinki so inviting that he would like it there. *How could she be so sure? That she would make it so?* They both felt the void Paivi had left. They leaned on each other, squeezing the depth of her loss out of their sorrow. Khalil felt that he had cast his net already, and whatever he caught would be in Syria.

All Khalil knew was that he couldn't trust anyone. Not Meryam, not Dr.Munir, not even the know-it-all woman down the street. What was her name? He couldn't remember. He would be lucky to leave Damascus in one piece. *No! Don't say that*, he thought. *Alive!* He couldn't remember the last time he had gone outside and returned to his apartment without passing a dead body on the streets. Covering them did not change the fact that they were dead, swollen, putrid; their bloated bodies raising the sheets, their bare feet exposed, with some toes gone, the blood coagulating as fast as it oozed from its source. It was just another day in Damascus, where there were never enough doctors. What good could he do there? He felt useless in a city that ignored him. It was not his destiny to save them. It was never his fight, though he thought it would be. But whose side would he join? He felt he had to choose one. So he chose his own.

Khalil felt nervous for the first time. He wondered if he would make it out alive. He had denied the likelihood of dying on the streets of Damascus for the last time. He was going to test his ability to move freely as someone with an American passport. He was no longer interested in passing himself off as an Arab, or more correctly, allowing his fluency in the language to gain acceptance into that world. He was looking for passage—out of Damascus. But could he trust anyone anymore? How he had survived in that city that juxtaposed death and beauty was an enigma he was no longer willing to ignore. Had he crossed the Atlantic and the Mediterranean to slip into a gutter next to dead dogs? Would he fall like so many he passed by daily? He had come to the end of his road with the wish to do nothing but leave. What happened to the image he had painted of the city he once imagined? The place he wanted to die in was not the same place, and the thought of how he would die there, though so likely, was not the same way he had meant at the time. He was swaying in a hammock in a hotel room with these thoughts crossing his mind. He looked at his diploma on the wall: a proud achievement he would have to hide away. What if they did not let him leave? He had earned his diploma because the host country had given him the chance to earn it.

*

It was not until Khalil met with Zouhoor a second time did sparks ignite. Latif had brought her to Damascus for a musical program at the Bulgarian center. Khalil was performing. He was making his final appearance before leaving the country. A solo number that was no less melancholy than Damascus Blues. He named it *Buildings I once knew*. It was autobiographical, as it was a walk through the different areas of Damascus that Khalil had come to know. It started with the chaos of his arrival, the loneliness of his first days, the melodic pastures of the evening mountains he had seen, to the bounding dance steps of the Bulgarian ballets he had witnessed on his first visit to the cultural center.

*

"I am so glad I came tonight!" said Zouhoor. "Latif told me you were a musician, and you are quite a good one!"

"It really saved me. I mean, it was all I did when I wasn't studying."

Khalil noticed that Zouhoor spoke freely in a way she did not the time he had visited their home. Latif was talking to a Bulgarian woman he seemed to know, or wanted to get to know.

"This is a nice place. Have you been here before?"

"Several times. They always make me feel welcome," said Khalil.

"I hope we made you feel welcome," said Zouhoor.

"Of course you did."

Bulgarians walked up to Khalil, congratulating him on the number he had played. They shook his hands, asking if he would be returning.

"I'll do my best," he said.

"So, you will be staying a while?" asked Zouhoor. "Latif said you are going to Saudi Arabia."

"Latif told you, eh?"

"Of course! It's good news!"

"It is, for sure."

"I am sorry that you are leaving Damascus."

Khalil felt touched by her interest. He wanted to know more about her. Latif had obviously put them together so they could become better acquainted. She was easy to talk to.

"Do you have a personal interest in the Kingdom?"

"I know no one there."

"Then you may need a guide, although your Arabic is fluent already. Better than mine!"

"I don't think so, but thank you."

Khalil found himself admiring Zouhoor's attire. She wore a silk hijab of pastel colors with its paisley and pink form-fitting long dress. Her black sandals with a heel lifted her up so that they were eye to eye. Zouhoor's smile of perfect teeth was every orthodontist's dream.

Khalil had a question for her. "Do you read much?"

"Are you kidding? All the time!"

"Who do you like?" he asked.

"Ulfat Idilbi."

"I have never read her. Should I?"

"I think you should."

"I'll take your advice."

"*Sabriya: Damascus Bittersweet.*"

"It sounds like a movie."

"It would make a good one," she said.

Khalil looked into her eyes and caught a glimmer. He tried not to stare. He was no longer in the doldrums that had held him captive. He had gotten enough of being alone. He was going to ask her father. If he said yes, and she agreed, they would be one.

"I want to ask you if you like me, and then your father."

"I do like you, and my father does, too!"

"And Latif?"

"I think you already know the answer to that."

Khalil found himself falling fast. He could not think of why they would not accept him. He was a man of promise. He thought that any woman would be eager to leave Syria for a chance at anything new and safe. Would his life with her be easy? Easy did not matter. New was what mattered, and new was everything on the horizon.

Zouhoor was beaming. Her freckles danced.

"Will you play again?" asked Zouhoor.

"I'll ask the host if they want me to."

Members of the audience applauded. Khalil, still wearing his bass clarinet around his neck, walked slowly to the stage, as if thinking of what to play. It was easy: *Khalil's Lament*. He announced the composition. It was a blues in F. He was leaving Damascus with all the sad memories living there had engendered. He reached as far back as his dangerous and rickety ride from Beirut. The death and disaster that touched him along the way. But he had also seen kindness in Meryam's eyes, and the pink and purple twilight ribbon of the Damascus sky. Beauty had its place in his memories. He was happy he had chosen to come there, and was equally happy to be leaving. He had reached equilibrium. He knew how to bend the notes. He had had lots of practice. He had learned to dance in Damascus. Now he danced with his instrument like the Syrian women in the clubs. He drew mirth from the Bulgarians at the cultural center. It was a happy time for all there. Oh, he would be sorry to leave, he mused. He switched his meter to the gait of the sheep that controlled the movement of traffic. They could do as they pleased anytime, except during Ramadan.

Then they would huddle in bunches, in no hurry to take their final steps to slaughter. Khalil, just as quickly as he had found himself gyrating, slipped into a motionless state, with only the notes moving through the horn and his body. Now the silver bell sang out to all those listening for what would be the final notes of the evening.

*

"Congratulations, my brother!" said Latif.

"So what will your parents think?" asked Khalil.

"My mother liked you the day she met you."

"But she said nothing that day."

"Nothing to you, but plenty to Zouhoor!"

"Gee, who would have guessed?"

Khalil was feeling confident, but butterflies surfaced when he thought about how quickly he had decided to marry Zouhoor. She was ready to be wed. Maybe more than ready. How could one be more than ready? He was more than ready, if anything. When he had married Paivi, wasn't that on a whim? No, he had known her for years. And their dreams were dashed just as fast. No, he was doing the right thing. True, he could see nothing but good in Zouhoor. But wasn't she the epitome of good? A woman who prayed and read books. She seemed someone who wanted to experience happiness, as did he. She wasn't afraid to leave her native country. No, she was the one for him.

*

"We are happy for you and Zouhoor. No, ecstatic, *al hamdulillah*! said Zouhoor's father. He was so excited.

His eldest daughter was going to be married—to a doctor! And an American as well!

Zouhoor's father wanted nothing to mar the wedding. There had been some ISIS trouble in his city, so he had devised a plan to have a quiet ceremony near Damascus. Also, he would arrange passports for everyone, while he was in Damascus. With all the fighting going on in Syria, he wanted to have everything in order, should the family have to leave. But to where was the bigger concern. He had a cousin in Chile, but that was too far away. Still, he needed to reach out to his cousins, wherever they were. Khalil was a fine man, who would be a great benefit to the family, he believed.

Zouhoor and her sisters were up all night, talking about Khalil. Did he have any brothers in America? He was so handsome. He looked like an actor! Was he an actor? Oh, he could be one! Her sisters passed around a picture of him and Latif in their graduation suits. *Look at the two of them! Brothers they are—and always will be! Huwa Sudani? La. Somali? In nawho Ameriki. Ameriki?* But he is black! He is so black! Her mother wanted Zouhoor to marry a tall, green-eyed doctor. His is tall, at least. But he is like anthracite! And was not Bilal? May Allah be pleased. He is Muslim, and a good man! But isn't his father a criminal? But what about the men who stole those first blacks from Africa. That cannot be considered stealing. There was no law against that at the time! They were not considered men then. And the women either, right? They were all chattel. I did not make the laws. The times are different now. Exactly! Khalil is not a slave. He has a citizenship. His son might be president one day. We will laugh about this talk one day. What about his family? And isn't Obama black? Are we still on that topic? Isn't he American? I guess so! You guess so? Well, he was the President of the United States. He would have to be American then! I guess so. Stop all the guessing! America has everything. Even Syrians. No! Yes! The New York Times reported 12,000 refugees have entered the US since the civil war in Syria began five years ago. America has all kinds of people. Zouhoor is so lucky to be marrying an American. Does he have any brothers? How should I know? Ask him then!

Well, there were loads of questions, even if the answers were not apparent.

*

The wedding drew together the extended family and neighbors alike. There was plenty to eat. Mounds of goat and sheep. Rice, both white and biryani, samosa, fasoolia, lentils, squash, zaatar naan, and eggplant. Milk, tea, and orange juice. There was baklava, too.

Men danced with each other. The women danced with each other, too. That was how it had always been. It was not the West, and no one cared.

Khalil and Zouhoor looked regal in white. They didn't seem to care about anything. The world revolved around them. Still, Khalil wanted the wedding day to move on, given his time in Syria was filled with angst with ISIS always ready to rear its ugly head along with the unstable government. And what about the Russians? Weren't they always ready to destabilize a government? There was never a time when something untoward was not present. Khalil and Zouhoor—he was still not used to hearing those two names in the same sentence—were equally eager to leave Syria.

The cake waited to be cut, and the hour for that had yet to arrive. The women were not tired of dancing. Their beautiful dresses of every color in the rainbow (and many not) gave the men thoughts of who would be next to announce their wedding.

*

The time for Khalil and Zouhoor to leave Syria came one morning right after *fajr*. Everyone embraced and Zouhoor's parents were most reluctant to let her go. Her mother wept openly, as did her sisters. They all wanted to know when the couple would reach Beirut, as they were leaving by taxi. From there, they would catch a flight to Riyadh. Zouhoor's parents were frightened for the couple to leave from the Damascus airport. They felt it safer to leave from Beirut. Khalil agreed, though he never shared his experience of his arrival in Beirut with his new family: the bus ride and the ambush he had encountered. As he thought about it, he remembered that there was never a time during his stay when he was not in a violence-prone environment. Still, mixed with all the tragedy were the resplendent nights of shooting stars, the moon that kissed the mountains, iridescent rains, and sands, where lizards peeked out over the dunes and moved when they felt safe. Khalil took all that in as he said goodbye to his chosen homeland.

"So, what will you miss the most?" asked Zouhoor.

"The sunsets. The sun hanging there, a huge orange sphere. Magnificent."

"I will miss my family," she said, hiding her face in Khalil's sleeve, now moist from Zouhoor's tears.

Khalil thought of how his mother would cry at times when she thought of how far away her mother was from her mother in New Orleans. Khalil's parents had ventured to Philadelphia is search of a life far away from the segregated South. He knew that the distance weighed heavily on her. She never realized her dream of becoming a teacher. *A teacher of what?* asked Khalil. Children, he guessed. He never asked. He had his own questions to answer: how many moons did Neptune have? How long was the short intestine? Those were the questions that were within the realm of reality. But reality extended to the present: traveling through Syria to Beirut. The taxi chauffer was used to traveling on rugged terrains. Zouhoor chose this time to squeeze questions out of her husband. Saying the word "husband" was still so new to her that she loved saying it. And all the questions about his family burned inside her.

"What was your mother like?"

"She liked to write."

"So, we have something in common. I would have liked to have met her."

"That's something that might have made her happy. She had so little happiness in her life. You would have brought her joy."

"Why was she unhappy?"

"She felt unfulfilled. She settled for a life of low expectations."

"America has so much to choose from. Isn't that right?"

"Yes. You have to be willing to take chances."

"And she wasn't?"

"She married a man who didn't reach very high, and she didn't have the courage to leave him."

"If she had, you might not have been born."

"I would have had a different father."

"Speculation."

"Still, the situation would have been different. Maybe better," said Khalil.

"But not better. How could things be better for us?"

"I can't see how," said Khalil, rolling Zouhoor's ring around on her finger.

Zouhoor was peeling away the layers of Khalil's life. But for once he did not feel that his privacy was being invaded. He realized that Zouhoor was not afraid to know about how marginalized life was for him in America.

"You will see, if we go to America," he said.

"Of course we will go. And I don't expect to find a Disney movie."

Hearing those words made Khalil realize that she must have been preparing herself for what she would find; the country that shaped Khalil and what made him so different from others that looked like him but were not. What did it mean to be marginalized anyway?

"It is not so easy to see, unless you go beyond the center of the city. You experience economic segregation, initially. Next, there is the more discernable racial distinctions. When blacks engage in conversations with strangers, it is invariably about money. Take Rocinante, for example. She is never without a ruse in her conversation, if you can call it that. 'Mister, can you loan me a dollar?' She doesn't know the person, so why pretend she would ever pay him back? But she is not finished. 'Just a quarter, then.' That's the way she starts and finishes her day: begging. She is shameless, but she represents her social class. They sit on the 30th Station and the 15th Street Station, slowing down people on their way to work. This is how these indigenes *earn* their daily bread."

"But the Quran says we must help the poor," stressed Zouhoor.

"But these people will never help themselves. They are poor, but they are more crafty than poor. If one day I see one of them with a broom in his hand, I will give him a quarter, but I know I never will."

Zouhoor looked at Khalil as if he were a sage. He knew his countrymen in a way she did not. She lifted his hand, which was in hers, and kissed it.

"Rocinante?" asked Zouhoor.

"Oh! She is the neighborhood leech. Every community has its parasites," he answered.

"Don't waste your fertile mind on sewer rats. Toxins will destroy themselves. But I realize there is so much I have to learn," she added.

"Fortunately, you won't have to face the embarrassment I have."

"Let's catch the sunrise," she said.

Khalil marveled at its singular beauty as it moved in autumnal copper over the Jibal Lubnan ash Sharqiyah, the mountain range that divides Lebanon and Syria. Crabapples grew along the range. The plant life took

Khalil's mind off the less attractive thoughts about his own homeland. His thoughts now revolved around what was in store for him and his wife in the Kingdom, as he had gotten used to saying.

"I will have to keep myself busy in the Kingdom," said Zouhoor. "I am going to enroll in a university."

"You will make many new friends," said Khalil, not at all sure of what either of them would encounter. Living in a kingdom would present a new set of challenges: segregation was not new. The States had prepared him for that. But segregation of the sexes would have its own set of particulars. Oh, and mathematics was the requisite that prepared one for parallel universes the way no other discipline could. Khalil called on his work with partial derivatives and complex conjugants, equations of Euler and Maxwell, in anticipation of the anomalies he was, no doubt, going to negotiate.

*

Khalil and Zouhoor arrived at the Beirut Airport with plenty of time in hand. There were many families on their way to Saudi Arabia. Khalil could not help but notice how large and out of shape many of the Saudi men were. Three hundred pounds was heavy for even a weightlifter. He chose not to say anything about the women shrouded in black. Zouhoor looked about for someone she might know. She recognized no one. Armed men and women in uniform walked around. Their stoic demeanor gave nothing away. Khalil and Zouhoor sat together. Their faces brought stares from all the Islamic people around. The fact that they switched from Arabic to English gave the children and mothers reason to look at what, to them, was an oddity. The circus had never come to their town, so this was like having celebrities in their space. The space was devoid of song or merriment of any kind. No mothers sang lullabies to their babies; no birthday celebrations, no after-parties. Some men were reciting the Quran to themselves. Khalil and Zouhoor took out their books and started reading. Khalil read *Damascus Bitter Sweet*. Zouhoor was finishing *A Man* by Oriana Fallaci, written in English. She looked for it in Italian, but had no success at finding it in Damascus. The couple did not appear like the newlyweds they were. They were without anxiety, like the family of six a row of seats away. All boys, all looking very animated. Khalil was sure the boys would be looking for a football field to expend that energy, if there was one available. Khalil wondered when the day would come that he would become a father. There was time enough for that. It was too early to check in their bags. Thanks to the bomb that had destroyed his apartment, Khalil had little to take with him. His baritone sax had been lost in that building. His books and papers as well. He was going to the Kingdom with new diplomas, the suit he was wearing, and the garments that he and Zouhoor carried. Khalil's in-laws had given him a set of silver fountain pens and a medal with Surah Maryam enclosed, and the silver chain that he wore. They knew it was his favorite surah, which Khalil often recited at *namaz*.

The time had come for the couple to check in. Khalil presented their papers to the clerk, who examined their passports and marriage certifications. Another person arrived to reexamine their documents.

"Why are you going to the Kingdom of Saudi Arabia?"

"For work and further study," answered Khalil.

"What is your work?"

"Medicine."

The second examiner looked at Khalil quizzically.

"And the two of you are married?"

"Yes."

Khalil wondered why the man asked questions that the documents clarified. They were in clear Arabic, which anyone there could read. The man wanted to clear things up in his own mind. He was witnessing something he had never seen before: an African American married to a beautiful Syrian woman. *How could this man have what he did not?* Khalil could not answer that question. The clerk was finally allowed to do his job. Khalil only knew that he and his wife had tickets to board the Saudi Airlines' flight to Riyadh. Their seats were A4 and B4. One reaches a point where gravity or logic prevail. When people realize that three into two go! Khalil remembered a line from the Bible 1 Corinthians 13 "when that which is perfect is come, then that which is in part shall be done away."

The plane was in the air.

*

Khalil and Zouhoor arrived in Riyadh at night. The queues formed and Khalil was surprised to find stacks of forms both on the counters behind the clerks, and the piles on the floor. How could anyone justify the disarray? Who was in charge? Did that person even care? The crowd of men pushed in vain to get to the front of an imaginary line.

The clerk shouted in Arabic for the men to be quiet and step back. But to where, if they were all gridlocked? The smell of underarms was a stench Khalil would not forget. These men were a long way from home. Perhaps this was their home. Khalil looked ahead and there was more confusion where more men waved their paper-work and passports. The clerk stopped shouting when he looked at Zouhoor, then at Khalil. Khalil was already familiar with the stares. Some things one learns quickly. The clerk spoke in English, but after "hello," he reverted to Arabic. The men who waved their Bangladeshi pass-ports had gotten the best of him. The men stared at Zouhoor like she was the first woman they had ever seen. What would they do if they saw a movie star? Khalil looked at Zouhoor. She leaned into him, hiding her face. The clerk's arrogance started to show. He threw one of the passports back at an Indian. Khalil saw how that behavior would have gotten him fired in the States. But he wasn't in the States. What was the proto-col? Khalil paused, looking for an opportunity to talk, and then decided to merely tender his passport with Zouhoor's.

*

They were put up at the Mövenpick Hotel. It was the finest hotel Khalil had ever seen. Zouhoor beamed with delight. She called her family as soon as they got to the suite.

Her mother was full of *hamdulillahs* and *allah hu akbars*. Her father spoke to Khalil.

"I am proud of you, my son. Take care of Zouhoor."

He could not remember a time when his own father had said that he was proud of him. Some things were a given. Still, it meant a lot to hear someone say it. Khalil was walking on air. He was away from everything familiar. He immediately noticed that Saudis spoke a different class of Arabic than Syrians, and were very different from the Algerians, like Meryam, with whom he had spoken more than others. He was able to make himself understood, but he noticed that the Arabic spoken in Riyadh was full of slang. *Where is the pride in speaking well?* He asked himself. *Get with the program,* he chided himself. This was going to be home. *See how quickly you can learn something new.*

*

After three days in the hotel, they moved into a condominium, which was a fifteen-minute ride from the Sulieman Hospital. There he would work making rounds and studying urology. He was supposed to examine surgical and medical disorders of the male urinary tract. Females were assigned to females, as far as he knew. He saw patients with bladder and kidney bladder and prostate injuries, much like he had seen in Damascus. Those experiences served as good exposure to what he now saw in more detail in Riyadh, because now he encountered problems with male genital disorders and adrenal gland injuries. Khalil enjoyed his experience in Riyadh. He worked in a safe environment. Strict, but safe. Given a choice, he could stand strict. He was married to a woman who did everything she could to make them both happy. Zouhoor kept the living space immaculate. She was also able to work toward completing her studies in journalism. She picked up her interest in Italian, finding some women from Italy and some women living in Riyadh who wanted to practice their language. She started a cooking class with some of the doctors who cooked.

Things went well in paradise for a few years, but even in the land of sweet dates, one has some bitter pomegranates. They had attempted to have children, but what were the reasons for no positive results?

"We'll get out of here as soon as I get an answer from one of these hospitals."

Khalil waited, but no hospital in a city of his choosing had responded. He did hear from hospitals in Kentucky, Mississippi, New Mexico, Montana, North Dakota, and Idaho, but none of those places appealed to him. Then he heard from Montreal.

15

Montreal

Khalil carried his lunch meal to a table where an attractive young doctor was sitting alone.

"May I?"

"Of course," she said, barely looking up.

"Khalil Baptiste, urology."

"Fadime Baran, anesthesiology."

"Pleased to meet you. I am new here."

"Two years for me. Welcome to Montreal."

Khalil attempted to twist off the bottle top of his pomegranate juice.

"Here, let me," said Fadime, taking the bottle, and using the opener on her keychain.

"Resourceful."

"I am sure you are, too."

"So are you from Canada?" she asked.

"Philadelphia, originally. I have spent the last seven years away from my homeland.

"Where?"

"Four years in Damascus and three in Riyadh."

"I can hear the Arabic in your speech."

"It's that noticeable?"

"Maybe just to me. I was born in Damascus, but spent most of my life in Turkey. I am Kurdish-Turk."

"So, I speak a few languages, like you, but I have just started using the French that I learned in college. At least it isn't hard."

"A matter of survival for me. We moved around when I was very young. We left Syria when I was eleven and moved to what was then Kurdistan, then we moved back to Istanbul. While Kurdistan is still where its surrounding countries claim it to be part of their own. I can say that Turkey has provided me with the opportunity to study."

"I can't say I understand much of it," said Khalil. "Kurdistan must be very rich."

"That is only one of the reasons we want it back. It belongs to us!"

The more he listened to her, the more he liked Fadime. He immediately understood what she meant—something his own being taken from him. His forefathers had been taken away from a land he never saw. Africa still remained, but owned by few indigenous to it.

Fadime possessed a smooth dark-olive complexion that drew Khalil's interest. Were they sister and brother separated at birth? No, that was too much of a stretch of his desire. But Khalil liked that they might be distant cousins: another fantasy he entertained, as he had no relatives even. He had to acknowledge that she was the most beautiful woman he had seen in Montreal. He was not looking for comparisons. It was just an undeniable fact.

*

"'I find myself talking about politics, only to be left with questions. It's such a frustrating issue."

"Politics or Kurdistan?"

"Kurdistan."

They both fell silent. The sound of chairs sliding across the polished floor and the laughter of the nurses who passed by them sprinkled the air. It was no longer busy, as the late afternoon shift started. Khalil was happy to have met someone so engaging.

*

"Golshifteh Farahani! Her name just came to me. That's who you remind me of! I hate to appear intrusive, but I would like to know about your background. I will start reading more journals. That way I won't appear so dull," said Khalil.

"Oh, I am sure you are not dull. You surely have your own interests. How do you know Golshifteh Farahani?"

"I like Iranian films."

"I would never have guessed you know her! That is one of the benefits of the exposure we have here. On films. But I can't say I'm an expert on films, watching them is something I like."

"Any other interests?"

"I have an interest in flying. I might have been an aeronautical engineer. I also spent a lot of time practicing music. I play the bass clarinet and baritone saxophone. I don't sleep much. I have always had an enormous amount of time to myself."

171

"You have used it wisely."

"I am fortunate to have discovered the joy of reading early on."

"Are you married?"

"Yes."

"And children?"

"A son."

"Oh. That changes things."

"And you?"

"No, I am not married."

"I find that surprising. You are so vibrant! Forgive me, again."

"Oh, compliments are nice. Do you know what I find surprising? We have the same nose! Now that is incredible! But why do you find it surprising?"

"I was certain that you were married."

"I fell in love with a foreigner. He was Christian, and it didn't last."

"Only because he was Christian?"

"No. Our cultures were different in other ways. He tried to convert me, and I told him I didn't need to be converted."

"So, have you made any films? With your looks, you could have been offered roles. But I have not seen you on Netflix."

"And you won't. I can't see how you find time to do all these fascinating things?"

"All those things were before I was married. I am fortunate to be working in this country."

"I feel the same way."

"Speaking of work, we may soon find ourselves in the operating room together," suggested Khalil.

"I think you're right."

The two stood up, and exchanged cards and hand-shakes.

Khalil wanted the conversation to continue. Partly because he was in no hurry to go to the apartment, partly because he was drawn to everything about Fadime. *Wake up! You are so easily smitten!*

"Any pictures of your family?"

Khalil pulled out his wallet, and showed her a photo of his wife, holding their son.

"She is quite beautiful. Is she American too? Your son looks like you!"

"Thanks. She is Syrian. You will meet them."

"Does your wife share your interests in flying?"

"Just the flight from Saudi. No, she likes to travel. She studied journalism."

"Fascinating! I have never been to Saudi Arabia."

Khalil wanted to turn the conversation around: to find more things in common.

"You must have to be running," she said. "I am sure your family is waiting to see you."

"We'll have to see each other soon. In the mean-time, I will read about Kurdistan."

"Oh, you will learn a lot."

Khalil walked away. His reluctance was evident from his gait. But he knew he would see her soon, so his spirits brightened.

"I still can't get over how you know Golshifteh Farahani."

"She is hard to forget."

Khalil wondered if it were Golshifteh or Fadime he was fascinated by. He could get neither out of his head. A bird in the hand . . .

"You know, I will give you a list of great films," Fadime offered, interrupting his thoughts.

"Thanks a lot."

"I hope your wife likes them, too."

Well, even if she doesn't, I'll like them, he thought.

Khalil was looking forward to seeing what new things his young son had learned. He was so clever. Which of Khalil's interests would he pursue? Maybe he would become an engineer or maybe a skillful writer like Zouhoor. What had his wife prepared for dinner? He was not hungry for anything that did not concern Kurdistan. He wanted to eat out at a Turkish restaurant. There he could be close to his new geographic interest. He was captivated by Fadime's black hair, cut just above her shoulders. He had to force himself to not compliment her large, dark-green eyes. Oh, he was certain he would find a way to say something about Kurdistan their next encounter. Why did his adopted country have some of the most intriguing women? He was better off in the cloistered world of Syria. Or, the fact was that he did not pursue anything apart from his studies. Speaking of studies, he remembered he needed to pick up some reeds for his clarinet. He had a rehearsal with Daniel Noisy, a pianist colleague, also a physician, who lived in the same neighborhood on Rue Sainte Catherine. He was born in Montreal, of Haitian parents. He had never been to Haiti though. so, his knowledge was what his parents shared: the years under Papa Doc

Duvalier, the earthquakes and reparations to France in spite of it all, the survival.

*

Just as Khalil was trying to find ways to dim the glow in his heart, he received a call on his mobile from Zouhoor.

"Hello."

"Habibi. How is my sweetheart?"

"Fine, thanks. What a surprise!"

"I know. It's an hour early! You are out of surgery. I'm glad."

"So I am! I think you have a telepathic sense."

"I feel I know your every move."

"If so, what do I want to eat tonight?"

"When you ask me that, it must be Middle Eastern. More than that, I can't say."

"That's good enough. I am coming straight home."

"See you soon."

Zouhoor was so joyful. How could Khalil think of anyone else but her? Still Fadime had him doing the unthinkable. He hoped he would get over Fadime. First meetings were always exciting. He would have to immerse himself in one of his projects. That would do it.

The drive home gave Khalil some space to sort out the fantasy he had conjured about Fadime. Hadn't he already embroiled himself in enough entanglements when he was in Syria? Hadn't he vowed not to look for labyrinths, no matter how alluring the face, attractive the scent? Yes, of course, he had. Wasn't Fadime nothing more than a trap for him to step into? Or had he already fallen?

*

Khalil stopped at the music shop he frequented to get some reeds.

"I'll take Rico, size 3, please."

"So, how is your piece coming along?" asked the merchant.

"Fine. I'll have to record it for you."

Khalil was eager to share his new composition with Daniel. Baritone saxophone and piano sounded so good together. Khalil drew on Fadime's dark features for inspiration. The midnight color of her hair, the clearness of her green eyes, and the clarity of her thoughts. He just liked being around her. The time out of the operating room, he looked forward to spending with her. He knew, however, he would ultimately leave her, or she him. No matter how many compositions he dedicated to her, she would remain nothing more than a source of inspiration. But what a source! He wondered how Fadime would feel about it. There he was, thinking about her again! Better to switch gears and find inspiration in his wife. She should have been his sole inspiration. She was gifted as well. But how could he reconcile her, and the fact that his wife was with him? She was there with him during the lonely, empty years in Saudi Arabia. She cooked his favorite meals: baked eggplant, stuffed artichokes, lemon meringue pie. She lay out the prayer rugs where they prayed side by side. He loved Zouhoor who was perfect in every way. But for Fadime, he held a lust. And there was no cure for that. It was completely irrational. She was the square root of negative one. So, why was he trying to fit her into the realm of real numbers? He had two real numbers, his wife and his son, who depended on him making the right decisions. *Wake up!* He had to keep telling himself that as he approached his apartment. Then he did something unusual: he turned the car from the driveway and drove to the florist shop. He saw some white roses and decided to buy them. Then he returned to the apartment.

*

"Oh, lovely!" said Zouhoor. She beamed with delight. Their son, Riaziat, crawled toward him. He had recently taken his first independent steps, but still relied on crawling. At seventeen months of age, his father saw him as average. "Each one learns when he is ready," Zouhoor would say. She had no doubt Riaziat would be brilliant like his father. "He watches you, so how could he be otherwise?"

Khalil did not argue with her logic. "In a free society like Canada, *how could he fail?*" asked Khalil. He would experience none of the degradation he had known in Philadelphia. The City of Brotherly Love was the one where he had been most required to produce identification.

*

"What's the hurry?"
"It's cold!"
"Mind showing me your ID?"
"It's in my pocket."

177

"Take it out."

"A student, eh?"

"Yes, sir."

"You fit the description, you see."

"Of course."

The policeman had wound up his window, then checked his clipboard. He quipped with the other patrolman in the car. Something the driver said made them chuckle. Their humor was not something Khalil shared. He massaged his numb hands. February was no time to be outside without gloves on. Khalil would not be going back out once he got home. He was freezing, but his wit was sharp, and he meant the sarcasm in his words *of course.*

"You're okay," said the officer, returning Khalil's student ID.

Khalil moved away quickly, generating the heat he had lost in the inane interrogation.

Have they nothing better to do? Bastards!

*

He opened the door. The house was quiet. *Just as well,* thought Khalil. He was not in the mood to talk anyway. He kicked off his shoes, and threw the blanket over his frozen body. He was still dressed, though that didn't matter. When he was upset, he would often go to bed fully clothed. He missed Paivi's company. She was the only one with whom he shared his dreams. He slipped off to sleep.

"How soon before we arrive in Helsinki?"

"Four hours, sir."

Paivi held Khalil's hand. He lifted it up to his lips, and then lay it back into her lap. The scent of pomegranate cream lingered on his lips.

"You will love Helsinki."

"As much as I love you?"

"No, as much as I love you!"

Buzz—buzz—buzz.

Khalil's alarm clock rang. He had to study for a microbiology exam. It came easily to him. He loved it. Flagellar motility was his particular interest because of his interest in aerodynamics. He was working on drones that would send messages to friends, with six-digit coordinates. But that would not be on the test. Bacterial cell motility would for sure, so he changed his focus. Flagellar motility was where the e.coli moves itself forward by rotating its flagella, thus, moving forward. When the bacterium changes its rotation clockwise, it somersaults.

Khalil drew a few capsules that rotated, putting himself in them alternately, imaging himself in flight. He drew the capsules rotating alternately counterclockwise, then clockwise. The colored pencils were both instructive and entertaining.

That was back in undergraduate school. Paivi was with him then. He had dreamed his earlier school days. He had another dream as well but it was wed with reality: Khalil had successfully completed a prostatectomy in Riyadh, but his mind was already back in Damascus where he studied years earlier. There he sat in contemplation on a mound of Jabal Qasiyun, where he found himself every Friday afternoon. He conjured a vision of Paivi Amo, dressed in aquamarine. Her silver eyes, smiled at him, her fingers snapped some rhythm she hummed. Maybe it was Finnish. He did not recognize it. It did not matter, because he missed her all the more. They were more than 9,000 kilometers apart. After two years his vision of her was growing dim, and depression was gaining space in his heart. Then a citrine wagtail fluttered by and landed in front of him.

It was a sign of hope.

16

Khalil arrived at Daniel's apartment at 9pm. Daniel opened the door to an ebullient Khalil.

"You wouldn't believe how creative I am feeling! I think I could write a symphony!"

"Good! I am eager to hear what you have come up with. That is, if we are still working on your new piece."

"Oh, I am most interested in your thoughts," said Khalil.

Khalil warmed up. Long tones from a Lydian scale, followed by intervals in fourths, then triplets. He played half-notes and quarter notes, and played the lowest octave C sharp minor seventh, F sharp seventh, B major seventh, A sharp minor ninth, D sharp seventh, G sharp major. Daniel played the 1-3-7 chords with his left hand. He played with familiarity. He left lots of space for Khalil to explore colors of the chords. Khalil liked Ravel, so there were moments of silence and moments of whole tone passages.

"I like what you did with your right-hand 3 runs in A sharp minor. I thought you would do more with it, like 3-7-9-1, 3-7-3-9-1, 3-9-1-3-7."

"Well, that's what you did, so I did something else," said Khalil.

"We can always try it out, and see where it goes."

"Right, that's the beauty of exploration."

"What's the piece called?"

"*Baran.*"

"Nice. What does it mean?"

"Rain."

"A quiet rain."

"A female? Of course."

"You have a daughter on the way?"

"She is at the hospital."

"Better explain."

"She is in my system. I am trying to shake her."

"By composing a tune?"

"It's the safest way."

"And what will Zouhoor say. No, I already know."

"She knows I'm not going anywhere."

"I would leave it alone. You're only setting yourself up for disappointment. Ask me, I know. Then too, music is a safe bet."

"That's how I feel."

"Just don't write a symphony."

"I am trying not to, though she gives me enough material."

"I wrote a long piece before I was married: *Damascus Blues.* It got me through the lonely times there."

"So, you write when you are lonely? I go out."

"I don't, but you know that already."

Daniel played riffs from *Baran.*

"It sticks with you, eh?"

"It does."

"I think you'd like her. Maybe you'd make a good pair. It would make life easier for me."

"I think I should stay out of it."

"Look, for me she'll be musical inspiration. A safe distance."

"If she's free, I would rather see her with you that with me, screwing up our lives. Of course, that is assuming the two of you make it."

"I think you have an advantage. She was with a Christian before."

"I can't see how that matters."

"I will ask her if she wants to meet a friend of mine."

Daniel embellished on the riff he had played earlier.

"I think you are already showing interest."

This time they both returned to *Baran* from the beginning. Daniel played arpeggiated chords from the Lydian blues scale.

"In your hands, it turned into a bright song. It turns the way I was feeling about her around."

"Well, she may have a bright side you haven't explored."

"And I don't plan to."

"You have enough on your plate!"

Baran became more and more Daniel's piece. Khalil played the melody with rich, long tones in the low register, leaving plenty of space for Lydian scale runs. Daniel took full advantage of the space, like a harpist might: hand over hand.

17

When Khalil arrived home, Riaziat was asleep. Zouhoor greeted Khalil warmly, having looked forward to having him all to herself. He breathed in the aroma of tahini and freshly baked bread, mint and red lentils, and rice.

"Are you hungry?"

"You bet," he answered.

After all that playing, he was ready to eat what she had prepared.

"Oh, I missed you," she said. She nestled her head onto his shoulder. The smell of lilacs whispered into his collar. It was her trademark fragrance.

The candles on the dining room table were already lit. Ravel's string quartet with well-rosined bows made the evening perfect.

"I picked up *Corriere della sera* for you. You must miss reading that."

"I do!" Zouhoor got wistful. That was her life before marriage. She was still interested in keeping up her Italian. She was going to call the Italian consulate there. They were sure to have an activity calendar. She and Khalil would find a sitter so they could go out one evening.

*

"You may not know it, but since the day we first met, I have been thinking about you."

The awkwardness of Khalil's words gave way to a comfort he did not anticipate.

"I have thought about you, too. I wondered why you sat across me that time. I thought that you might have just wanted to talk to someone. Anyone. Then a more honest thought came to me. I think you know where I am headed."

Khalil became nervous. He knew exactly what she meant.

"I never thought you would say that, or even think that. I prepared myself for a let-down—that you would have no interest."

"Having an interest and acting on it are two different things."

Fadime examined Khalil's face with interest. Was she ready to act on her feelings?

"Before we go any further, let me tell you what I have in mind. I have someone for you to meet. He is a young, handsome Canadian doctor. I think you will like him."

"Before you go any further, let me tell you that I am already interested in someone. I think you know that. The problem is, he is married. Do you see my predicament?"

"I wouldn't have guessed that you'd be interested in pursuing me."

"Oh, I don't plan to pursue you. I just wanted to let you know how I felt. I don't want to complicate your life, or mine either."

Fadime and Khalil had already gone too far. They sat alone in a hotel lobby in Montreal. They had planned to have only lunch that Saturday afternoon. They did. Now a dessert would be nice. They ordered a crème brûlée, which they shared. Cappuccinos followed. He walked her back to her car. She wanted to take advantage of the afternoon together. She held his hand to her cheek, let it fall, then entered her car.

He wanted to ask her if she still wanted to meet his friend. *Not now,* he told himself.

Khalil watched her drive away. He felt he had done something wrong. He knew it, but he couldn't have predicted she would say what she did. He had resigned to free himself from the inevitable outcome: the hotel bedroom. He had escaped, but not without a scratch. Fadime had touched him, and getting her out of his mind was going to take some effort. He needed to put her and Daniel in the same space, to see if she would allow herself to be with Daniel the way she was with him.

"Where are we going?"
"Only where you want to be."
"But it's not right!"
"Because you feel guilty?"
"Because it's wrong! You know it and I know it."
"You can still say no. But I don't think you will. In fact, you and I are already there."

186

*

"Khalil."

"Yes."

"Who is Baran?"

"It's the title of a film by Majid Majidi. Great film! Why do you ask?"

"I've got to watch it. You mentioned it in your sleep."

"It's is also a composition Daniel and I are working on."

"I'd like to hear it, too, when it's done."

"Of course."

Just what had Khalil said in his sleep? Too much, to be sure. It was going to be hard to keep all of it inside. He had to get Daniel and Fadime together.

"So when am I going to meet Fadime?"

"When I get back from the conference in Toronto. We can even play *Baran* for her."

"I hope she likes it," said Daniel.

"How could she not? A composition carrying her name? Wow, you'll score big points!"

*

In Toronto, Khalil was alone, except for his several colleagues from McGill University Medical Hospital. They did not sit together during their two-day conference. In fact, they did not seek him out, as they were senior doctors. And as for the seminars on kidney failure, Khalil did not find them so informative. They rehashed what he already knew. There was one case study of complications with fecal deposits that interested him. There was little else, however.

Khalil later asked himself why he was so eager to attend lectures on kidney failure. That reason got him out the door. Did he know Fadime would be going, too? Not until he met her on his way to the dining car.

"So, are you on your way to Toronto?"

"I have a cousin there. You're going there, too? You never mentioned it."

"Lectures on kidney failure. Any excuse to gain more knowledge."

"So glad to see you!" she said. "Still, I can't believe you never mentioned it."

"I was going to be away for only two days." If it had been for more time, I would have told you, I'm sure."

Khalil knew very well why he hadn't mentioned to Fadime that he was going to Toronto, as did she. He didn't want to increase the opportunity where he would fall for her, or rather, with her. They had to avoid the inevitable plunge from which there would be no life raft to save them. What made their working relationship harder was that Fadime now pursued him. She had shown little interest in Daniel, after mentioning that he was "cute." She chose to limit her views about him to his piano playing.

*

One Saturday afternoon, Khalil had arranged to take Fadime to Daniel's to introduce them, and to let her hear the composition that carried her surname.

"It's a pleasure to meet you, too!" said Fadime.

188

"When Khalil told me he wanted me to meet a colleague of his, I was curious."

Fadime showed her characteristic charm. "You have a beautiful apartment. What a view!"

"Thanks."

"You have a baby grand. I thought I was going to hear you play an electronic piano. This is going to be a concert."

"We hope you'll like it," said Khalil.

Daniel had walked Fadime into the adjoining space that displayed his bookshelves and wall of certifications.

"So, how long have you been playing piano?"

"I can't remember a time I didn't play."

"Were you a prodigy?"

"No, nothing like that. I just loved the instrument. My parents encouraged me."

"Are they musicians?"

"No, but we share similar interests."

"You and Khalil share music. It's great that you have more than medicine in common. And you write music, too?"

"Not as much as Khalil. He's the real composer."

"Hey, I heard my name mentioned," said Khalil, walking into the room where Daniel and Fadime were.

"Well, I waited as long as I could!"

Daniel handed Fadime a glass of sparkling pear water. She sat facing the piano. Khalil assembled his saxophone. He played several long tones in different registers. The oak panels absorbed the sound from the horn and the piano. The tune was lush with its intervals, and there was give and take between the two men. Daniel was completely at home with his flurry of notes, following strong statements from Khalil. The musician had mastered the piece, bringing it to a triumphant close. Fadime stood up and applauded.

"Excellent! I didn't know what to expect! You are both so good!"

"I am so happy you like it," thanked Khalil.

"Like it? I love it!"

"Daniel really gave it body," said Khalil.

"You were quite amazing, too, Khalil. It felt so special hearing what you have done. You will have to play it for my family."

"We'll record it," suggested Daniel.

Fadime shook hands with both men, then embraced them.

Daniel's mobile rang. Five minutes later a delivery arrived at his door.

"I arranged for lunch. I hope you like Turkish cooking, Fadime."

"Of course I do!" said Daniel.

"Well, this is your day," said Khalil.

Daniel placed out everything on the table for them: rice pilaf, artichoke hearts, bread, baked chicken.

"Where did you find ayran?" she asked.

"Just a block from here," said Daniel.

"I haven't had that in years."

*

Khalil saw that Daniel and Fadime were getting along well.

"I am surprised I have never met you before," he said.

"The hospital is so big. It's understandable."

The three of them exchanged stories of how they came to work at the same hospital; how Montreal was the magnet: they could not imagine meeting in any other city.

"It is a special place. Like Tokyo, maybe! Really, I have no idea what Tokyo is like!" said Fadime.

"Well, music brought us together. You were the perfect audience," said Khalil. A minute later Khalil saw that it was time for him to go. "If you two don't mind, I'll be leaving," said Khalil. "I am going to see what my son is up to."

Daniel smiled at his friend, as Khalil wiped down his saxophone.

"That thing looks so heavy," said Fadime.

"You get used to it," said Khalil, closing the case. He put on his overcoat.

"We'll talk tomorrow," said Daniel.

"Au revoir, mes amis," Khalil bid farewell.

Khalil caught the elevator down to the garage. He gave out a sigh of relief, as he walked to his car. He was sure the fresh reed he had put in his instrument was a wise choice. He had played with such clarity. Even if Fadime had not found *Baran* beautiful, he thought it was. But that was not the case. She loved it! He had poured his heart into it. He played a flurry of sixteenth notes, which caught her by surprise. Her eyes had brightened. The pale-blue color of her dress, the gold Hand of Fatima she wore around her neck, her hands clasped around her glass were the composite of a portrait as lovely as a composer could imagine. Daniel followed his lead, taking off, playing thirds in both hands

from the lowest octave, racing up the keyboard at a diz-
zying pace. More importantly, he felt he had done a
good thing: the right thing. His conscience was clear, no
matter the outcome. He did not need this entangle-
ment, the one outside his marriage. He wondered how
other people did it.

18

It was Saturday. Afternoon was the time to go shopping. Zouhoor bundled Riaziat in his winter one-piece snowsuit with mittens, and tied a woolen cap to his head. She was in the habit of taking Riaziat out for walks, and Saturday was no exception. She hoisted him on her back, while Khalil carried an empty canvas bag for the groceries. Two blocks were as far as they would walk to find what they were after: fruits and vegetables, a bottle of cherry juice, and some Turkish cookies Zouhoor liked. It was more important for them to make this jaunt together than buy anything at all. It was thirty degrees and the three of them wore wool on their heads and scarves round their necks. Despite the temperature, people were out in the crisp air, taking full advantage of the season.

*

"You know what I did today made me proud. I introduced Daniel to a fellow doctor, Fadime Baran."

"So you found a name for that movie."

"Well, that's a coincidence. We had lunch together at Daniel's.

"Great! I like Daniel. I hope they make it," said Zouhoor.

"They are off to a good start. We played for her, then had lunch."

"I haven't heard you two play in a long time, since before Riaziat came along."

Khalil realized they hadn't even been together for several months. When she did hear them together, she would no doubt recognize the theme, *Baran*. Khalil hummed it frequently. He had yet to compose Zouhoor a tune. He thought he had better get cracking, if for no other reason, to placate his wife. Why must it be that way? Never mind trying to weasel his way out of this. *Write a little ditty, and embellish it!* He could give the melody to Daniel, and he'd turn it into a movie score. Walking in the winter air made Khalil remember his days back in Philadelphia, but that city had little diversity. The harshness of winter was coupled with the phlegmatic air of the Philadelphians. It was nothing hard to try to convey. It came naturally to them. And the winter brought it out in their faces of steel. Khalil could not forget them. No matter how grey the sky in Montreal was, it would never be as morbid as Philadelphia.

"Khalil! Where are we going?"

"To the market, near the mosque."

Khalil had not said a word, being lost in his reverie, momentarily. He held Zouhoor's hand, looking at Riaziat, nestled in his mother's coat. They entered the market. The overhead lamps replicated the rays of the sun. Zouhoor loosened her cap. She kept her coat buttoned. She filled the cart with the items she wanted: eggs, fig jam, yogurt, pine nuts, and pita bread. That was all.

Khalil had wandered away from his wife, but caught up to her at the cashier. He paid for the items and placed the plastic bag into his canvas one.

He held Zouhoor's hand, as they walked back into the winter air.

*

"We'll have to have Daniel and Fadime over," said Zouhoor. "What kind of a doctor is she?"

"She's an anesthesiologist."

Khalil thoughts went to the flurry of notes he had exchanged with Daniel, when they were playing *Baran* earlier that day. Now he could speak her name out loud her without the guilt of lust that had accompanied the melody before.

"Oh, I forgot to tell you. You got some mail today from Philadelphia."

"I wonder who that could be. My father maybe. I haven't written him in a while."

"You should. It must be lonely where he is."

"Yes. He'll be out soon."

"It wasn't from him. The letter is on your desk."

Khalil's circle of associates was no longer so wide. He had long since distanced himself from his family as well. Being out of the country for so long, he had little contact. His father was the only person with whom he had a link to his neighborhood. Neighborhood? Even the thought made him chuckle. It was a place he had run away from. No, it had chased him away! It repelled him and he was glad to breathe the crisp air of his new home. No. He had lived in so many other places, and the neighborhood was as Gil Scott-Heron sang, *it wouldn't be a bad idea if he never went home again.*

*

Paivi! He thought about her, but she was in Galilcia. She was his lifeline, during the lonely years in Damascus. How they had shared enough joy for a lifetime! He was no longer the naïve, needy undergraduate student. His life was full now. He wondered what hers might have become: a middle-aged divorcee who still reached out to him, but was now in another dimension.

> *Dear Khalil,*
>
> *I know you must be surprised to hear from me. I am writing because I still remember all that we shared. The hopes of one day reconnecting are not something I believe in anymore. You are a man with responsibilities, as you have been for a long time. So why am I writing? I have contracted ovarian cancer. Yes! A woman in great shape otherwise, but like so many women who never had children, I have fallen victim to this dreadful disease. The good news is that after a hysterectomy, I may still survive. I say "may" because like poker, no outcome is certain until you play your cards. You know, my only solace these days is the memory of us listening to Sebelius on the floor in my apartment, that autumn, when the fall colors*

*were so vivid, and our dreams were the
threads to the future.*

*I am out of the hospital and undergoing
therapy. The future still looks bright, because
my condition was diagnosed in time. I would
love to hear your voice again, my dear.*
                              Pirja

Immediately, Khalil wished he could run catch a
plane. But why had Paivi's sister written him? They
were never intimate. She obviously felt she could share
with him a detail she would have with her sister. He
would not have caught a plane for his father, but he
would have for Pirja. That was crazy! He had a family
now. That seemed so wrong, but that was what he felt.
She was part of his patch-quilt that was unraveling: his
security blanket that he no longer had the need for.
Maybe she reached out to him because she felt the same
way about him! He had not known her to have any
friends. He knew little about her family. He looked out
the window. Snow had started to fall. It was the season
of death. Could the quiet only add to the absence he felt
for his first love, Paivi? He watched the snowflakes col-
lect against the window of his third-floor apartment. He
was safe where no sickness lurked, and still, he felt the
absence of freedom he had experienced during his undergraduate days. *The sanctuary of your arms.* That was
a phrase Paivi used to describe how she felt with him.
But people say things without realizing how or when
the words will surface in the silence-—in the distance
when you are no longer able to touch the one who had
said them. As silently as the flakes collected, they

formed a mound that reminded Khalil of back when he was a child, staring out the window, looking away from his book of riddles. Life was full of questions, but no one was there to answer them.

"Do you want some tea?"

Zouhoor appeared, breaking the silence of his thoughts with a tray of tea and a bowl of mixed nuts.

"You're so thoughtful."

He looked up at her. She wore a white silk dress with a pattern of pierced petals throughout. She set the tray on the table next to his desk and left without asking about the letter on his desk. Khalil watched her leave, catching the full length of her figure. She was so graceful. If she wanted to know something, she would do her own research. Khalil saw no reason for bringing up Pirja's letter. And Zouhoor deserved more than a ditty. She was an inspiration of the highest order. By the simple act of bringing him tea, she had elevated herself to the sonata status. Khalil had never written a sonata, but now he knew he could. *Baran* would take its place to the rear of *Zouhoor,* and he had yet to play the first note.

19

"I was hesitant to come here today," said Fadime. "I anticipated some music, but not you. That you would be smart, I had no doubt. But you are quite handsome as well. That must be a distraction for most."

"I haven't heard that in a long time. I mean, apart from hearing it from my mother's friends. Thank you."

Daniel sat at the piano and played a series of chord progressions. A ballad that he was developing before he met her, now took more shape.

"You are so talented," she said, crossing her legs, as she sat facing him.

"You are so kind. I am glad we met. I would ask you to stay for dinner, but like you, my time is limited."

"But my time is not limited," she said. She sipped her pear juice.

"In any case, I will invite you to dinner, but you'll have to say when you are free, of course."

"Is next week too soon?"

"No, I will play for you again."

"I would like that. This is completely new for me."

Fadime giggled, as she had never felt so playful before; certainly not as an adult. She was a serious woman. She engaged in political discussions, not artistic ones.

Daniel was filling the void she hardly knew existed. For her, it was work and the problems of nationhood. She wanted to put her past behind her and slip into the Canadian citizenship. It was a more comfortable suit to wear. It was the only passport she carried.

Daniel ended the piece he had started.

"Could I take your picture?" she asked.

"At the piano?"

"Yes," she smiled.

After the photo, Daniel had the intention to ask her for a photo, but he decided to save something for the next visit. Fadime put on her overcoat and scarf, and picked up her gloves.

"It was a pleasure to meet you," she said smilingly.

"And a great one for me as well."

Daniel extended his hand, and they shared a handshake.

As Fadime waited for the elevator, she could hear what she was sure was *Baran* at the piano. Those flurry of notes cascading down the keyboard made her certain. She smiled and felt flutters in her heart. She jumped up with joy, and had to find her composure when the elevator door opened. She was still smiling when the elevator arrived at the ground floor. It had been three years since she had been that happy: when she began working at the hospital.

20

"Comment ça va, mama?"

"Ça va bien, merci," answered Daniel.

It was Sunday, and Daniel always visited his parents on Sunday, unless he had to work.

"Your father just went out for some bread. You know his ritual of buying bread for his coffee. Nothing has changed since our days at Port-au-Prince."

"Habits are hard to break."

"So why try?" said Daniel's mother.

"I am always glad to see you. So what brings you by so early?"

"I just made a new friend, and wanted to share the news."

"Is it a female friend?"

"Yes."

"Someone from the hospital?"

"Yes."

"I can see on your face she makes you happy."

"Is it so obvious?"

"Anyone can see," said his mother.

"She is a simple woman, very intelligent."

"Oh, you make the best of choices, *mon fils.*"

Daniel's father walked into the apartment. The two men greeted each other in the usual manner: a kiss on each cheek.

"And are you getting your rest, Daniel?"

"I get enough, *Papa.*"

"So, are you chief urologist now?"

"There are many ahead of me, *Papa.*"

"Who is brighter than you?"

"Well, your view isn't unanimous."

"It needs to be!"

"Well, let's just say that they are pleased with my contribution."

"Are you wearing the tie your mother got you?"

"Oh, yes! I received several compliments."

"Then keep wearing it."

The repartee continued, and nothing was ever different. Gerard Noisy was very proud of his son, but wanted him to excel further. They had had two miscarriages in Haiti, before going to Montreal. With Daniel's birth, came none of the complications Gerard and Nicole had experienced in Haiti. Nicole carried Daniel to term, and when she gave birth, he weighed six pounds four ounces. Daniel had his mother's complexion, *café au lait*. He was tall like his father, just over six feet. He had an athlete's build, though his only physical activities were swimming, and cycling on the bike in his apartment. For either activity, he did not have to leave the apartment building.

"So, will you have some coffee with us?"

"Of course. You and I like the same things," Daniel said.

Nicole served the coffee and placed the bread out with fig preserves and *Port Salut* cheese.

"Daniel has a new friend," said Nicole. "They work at the hospital."

"Is she a fine nurse? They have beautiful nurses there!"

"She is beautiful, but she isn't a nurse."

"Oh, well, is she nice? That really counts."

"I agree one hundred percent!"

"So how did you meet?"

"Khalil introduced us."

"Khalil Baptiste! *J'aime bien cet homme là!*"

"Do you have a photograph of her?" asked Nicole.

"Give me a minute to pull her up on the computer."

"Is she a movie star or something?" Gerard joked.

"Not that she told me. We have only met for dinner, so I am just getting acquainted. *Peu à peu.*

"Here she is," said Daniel. *"Elle est douée."*

"Et tres jolie, d'ailleurs."

"So, is she a star?" asked Nicole.

"She is a star to me!" said Daniel.

"I see that she is an anesthesiologist," said Gerard.

"She is so much more than that."

"When will we meet her?"

"Soon, I am sure. We don't have a lot of time, with our work schedules. We have never worked together, but that may change."

*

Daniel sat with his father at the chess board. It was already set for a game. It was another thing they did when he visited. Like Daniel, his father was a urologist, too. He had a private practice, but had slowed down taking on fewer and fewer patients. He shared an office with two other Haitian-born doctors. One was a pediatrician and the other practiced family medicine.

*

Daniel's father moved first.
"So how did you meet the lovely one?"
"Khalil brought her by to meet me."
"And where is she from?"
"I don't know, really. I know she speaks several languages, including French. When we speak again, I will have many questions."
"Is she a Muslim?"
"I am sure she is. She wears the Hand of Fatima. Then again, I can't be absolutely sure."
"Her name makes me think she is," said Gerard. "Do her parents know?"
"Papa, we just met! We are barely colleagues! Give us a chance!"
"It's so unusual, but this is a land of possibilities."
"Exactly. I have no idea. We are not dating, so there is no telling where we will end up."
"Just be careful, son," said Gerard.
"Yes. Check!" added Nicole.
"You know, I hope she turns out to be the one," said Gerard.
"If she doesn't, I won't throw in the towel, as the Americans say. Check."

The two took out each other's pawns, and then the knights. Gerard put Daniel in check with a queen. Gerard trapped one of Daniel's rook. The exchange went back and forth until a rook held Gerard immobile, and he resigned.

"You're not easy to beat," said Daniel.

"Toi non plus!"

"On s'amuse."

The two men shook hands, and it was time for Daniel to leave.

"Deja?"

"Mama, I cannot stay forever."

"Promise me, next time you will stay for dinner," said Nicole.

"I promise."

Daniel looked at his father's hands: gnarled like doughnuts. Nicole brought in two demitasses of coffee.

"You still have this china?"

"It will be yours when you get married."

"Vraiment?"

"It's a day every mother prays for."

"Maman, I pray for it, too."

Daniel finished his coffee. His mother extended him his scarf. "You forgot this last week."

Nicole was one for details. She draped it around Daniel's neck.

Daniel left as quietly as he had arrived. His parents lived in Vieux Montreal. They stayed close enough to make a weekly visit. On the way back to his apartment, he remembered that he could have played *Baran* for his mother. She might have liked how he had spent some of his free time. No sense in overwhelming her with this new woman.

*

Daniel opened his door and heard his telephone ring. It stopped before he could take the call. He played the answering machine. There were three messages: Khalil, Giselle, and Fadime.

Khalil: *So, what do you think? Are you the happiest man on the planet?*

Giselle: *I haven't heard from you in a while. Maybe we can take in a movie. Call me.*

Fadime: *You are such a gentleman. I would love to see you next week. Call if you are not busy. That was such a special afternoon!*

Daniel smiled. He was indeed happy. If not the happiest man in the world, but he didn't care that he wasn't. Happiness was relative and he was glad to be in the company of Khalil and Fadime. They enlightened him. They awakened what was important to him. He was just glad to see the smiles on their faces. He could not ask for more than that. And Giselle? Five months it must have been since he had last heard from her. She was on her way to Barcelona. They had gone for a movie just before that trip. He liked her enough, but she really didn't want to be more than friends. He was beyond the casual, and for intellectual stimulation, he had books. But he said yes to the movie. It was an old film, *Arrowsmith (1931)*. Sinclair Lewis' classic was published in 1925. And Giselle Brune wanted company. Daniel was willing to have popcorn with her. They were friends after all. Just friends, so what was the harm? She had told him she wasn't interested in more than that. She had put her cards on the table. He was left with his in his hand, so there was no point in showing his ace of spades. Was she back from Barcelona? Did it even matter? He would call her back when he had something to tell.

*

"Hello. Fadime?"

"Daniel."

He could hardly believe he was talking to her. A week had passed before he could muster up enough courage to call, but he had done it! She was just a human being when it came down to it. Not a carnivorous monster out to devour him.

"I did not think you would call. You must be so busy. I just wanted to see you. Do you have time for a cup of coffee?"

"Sure, I do. How is tomorrow?"

"That sounds good. Will you be at the hospital tomorrow?"

"I am there until five in the afternoon," he said.

"Can you meet me at six?"

"In the cafeteria, then."

"Cafeteria it is."

He had done it! All that angst had been overcome. Why was she so much easier to face than sheet music on the piano? He didn't know but he had done what he had been running from.

21

"Have you been here long?" asked Daniel.

"I had something to read, so the time went by fast."

"On my way over, I had two thoughts: One, to have something to drink, coffee I mean.

"And the second?"

"Go directly to the cinema and then have something to eat."

"I like the first, though we could have a cup of coffee at the cinema."

"Let's go to the Cinema Banque Scotia. It's close by." Daniel suggested. "How do you feel about James Bond?"

"*Tiens*, I'm with you!"

Daniel and Fadime took off. Daniel's black 2012 BMW 535i series was recently washed, which Fadime noted.

"It must be hard to keep this clean in the winter."

"I don't mind. Car washers are plentiful."

"It's a beauty. Is it brand new?"

"Two years old. It runs well. It is the first car I have ever owned."

"You know something: I drive, but have never had a car."

"The transportation is good here."

"Clean and punctual."

"Exactly," Daniel agreed with her.

"Is that a CD playing?"

"Yes."

"I don't know much music, but I like it. Who is it?"

"Sol Gabetta, from Argentina, although she speaks a lot of German in her interviews. Maybe, she is of German heritage."

"Very likely."

"She is very smooth. And you are so cultured."

"Thanks. You too."

"Here, there is so much to engage the mind."

"Oh, I just love this city!"

"Were you born here?" he asked her.

"I was born in Damascus, but grew up in both Syria and Turkey."

"So, you and Khalil have something in common."

"We have a few things."

"What languages do you speak?" he asked.

"Kurdish, Arabic, Turkish, French, and English."

"That's impressive!"

"What about you?"

"Just French and English."

"Don't say just!"

"I get by with those two," he said. "And when do you speak Kurdish?"

"When I talk to my family and friends."

"Do you live with your family?" asked Daniel.

"They are spread around. My parents are in Turkey. My sister and brothers are in Bulgaria. And I am here!"

"I guess you have to go where you find work." Said Daniel.

"Or school. My sister and brothers are studying mechanical engineering."

"So, all of you embraced the sciences. Or all of *us*!" said Daniel.

"Ha! Ha! You're right!"

*

Daniel and Fadime arrived at the cinema with enough time to have their coffee and biscotti. Then they found their seats.

Fadime sat back and laughed with Daniel, exchanging glances and quiet moments of tension. She allowed herself to grab his arm. Perhaps, it was an inadvertent gesture, or an advantageous one. Either way, Daniel liked it, as it only drew them closer. The tender moments found their heads touching, then moving away, as if to mean it was an awkward experience. It was too soon. Or was it?

*

Fadime was not a child, but she had never gone out with a man who was not in her family. She had finished medical school at the age of twenty-six and spent her time pursuing her career in Montreal. Apart from working, she had the concerns of her family. Her parents were in Turkey, true, but that was only part of it. They were not together because her father was in prison. He was struggling to reestablish Kurdistan as an independent country. He was snatched out of bed and carted away in an unmarked vehicle. He might have been able to answer the questions and be released, but he could not justify the seditionist literature and the Kalashnikov, whose serial numbers had been burnished. That wasn't all. He had been identified as an organizer by an "informant", (someone that no one knew since spies were everywhere). Who could you really trust? Some Kurds were encouraged by financial incentives. And with an abysmal economy and high unemployment, people risked their lives in hopes of a better day. At thirty-one, she was at a disadvantage. Women from the Western countries had the first choice of eligible bachelors. She was not married and had had little experience, but she was so eager to fill the void in her heart. She had carried the weight of her father on her shoulders for far too long. With whom could she share that embarrassing secret? Nobody. She could not talk about her family, other than to mention those in Bulgaria. Yes, Yusuf had graduated with honors. He built helicopters that flew. Bursa had memorized twenty-six places of Pi; Ridvan could build a carburetor with the ease of a mechanic. That was easy to talk about. These were the safe topics that any family would be proud of. Her prior contacts with men had been in the hospital, so going to the cinema was a real stretch.

She felt so overdue for a date, she gave herself latitude. The laughter. The seating, the infrequent, though all the more meaningful, touching of his wristwatch, the request for the program from Daniel, although she could have easily picked one up on her way out of the theatre.

"I don't know about yours, but my heart is racing!"

"Absolutely! Like a race horse."

They walked through the heated mall, pausing to look at the dressed mannequins in the windows, and the expensive timepieces. In one of the photographs suspended in the hallway of the mall there was a man playing a saxophone.

"What type of saxophone does Khalil play?"

"A baritone."

"And that one?"

"An alto."

Daniel enjoyed the space he and Fadime shared. It was something he had missed. He hadn't been to the cinema in a long time. He hadn't even watched a movie since the time he and Giselle were together. What a staid rendezvous that was! She left him feeling lonely, so why was she calling him again? He needed the company of someone like Fadime. No, he needed Fadime! But did she feel the same way? *Don't push it,* he warned himself. He at least had a chance with her, so there was no need to be desperate. In fact, he couldn't remember the last he had felt so comfortable.

"So, have you ever been married?" asked Fadime.

"No. And you?"

"No. In my culture, women tend to marry very early. But I pursued my studies. We all did."

"I'm glad you did."

"In just a short time we have grown close. I am comfortable talking to you. This is quite unusual."

Fadime spoke with candor, but just how open could she be with Daniel? Was she willing to share facts about her family so soon? Was she willing to lose her friend? Wasn't he becoming more than a friend?

"You must be feeling hungry by now," said Daniel.

"I don't care about food. I want to know about you."

"Like what?" He asked.

"Well, tell me about your childhood."

"I have lived here all my life. When my classmates were playing sports, I was playing the piano. I was never good at sports. My mother encouraged me to continue, and wanting to please her, I did. Like anything you work at, you get better. It was the same way with science. It wasn't as easy, but that's not to say I found it hard. I can't say it was hard, because I liked it. My life may seem dull."

"No! I want to know."

"I went to McGill and I have never been anywhere else. I would love to travel like you have. You have seen the world."

"Some things I wish I hadn't seen."

"I would like to see Damascus."

"That is a place I miss. Just to walk through the market place: to smell the bread and see the shawarma. I can taste the falafel again."

"You paint a picture."

"The landscape is hard to forget. But now that is all changing. With all the fighting, it is not safe anymore,"

"Is that why you left for Turkey?"

"My parents missed their parents. They were getting older and needed care. My father taught biology, and took a post there. Have you heard of Dersim?"

"No, never."

"It is documented in history. It was the scene of a bloody rebellion that the Turkish government put an end to 1937. Needless to say, many people died. I don't

213

like to talk about it, but it is another ugly page in the chapter of human suffering. In 2011, Recip Tayyip Erdogan apologized for the tragedy committed against the Kurds who died during that time."

"There is so much in the world I don't know," Daniel contemplated, after hearing of a history unfamiliar to him.

"Much of it is not discussed because of the wounds it left."

"We all have them," said Daniel.

"Yours do show, too."

"I am glad. But they come out in my playing."

"Maybe even when you aren't at the piano."

"They would have to. No one is completely in control of his feelings, though he may try to be."

"You know, you are easy to talk to," she said.

"Maybe we should be getting back."

"Let's walk just a bit more," she suggested. They wandered into a music store. Daniel took the lead, pointing to the classical section.

"I want you to have something."

Daniel found a CD by Sol Gabetta.

"I think you will like this. It is Sol Gabetta. I hope you like it."

"Well, I like you."

Fadime had spoken without reservation. She was through hiding her emotions. The winter, if nothing else, put people's guard down. The cold broke their heart's chains. It melted the chamber of ice, drop by drop. Fadime had held back for so long. She was now ready for whatever came next. But that *whatever* was a calculated step. She had done her homework. She had made her choice. Yes. But she still had her parents to confront. Cultural mores could not be circumvented. The heart did not need a precedent, but her ancestors might. Was she like the Kurdish poet, Nali, described in *Birds*:

> *Yes, Kurds are birds! And even when*
> *there's nowhere left, no refuge for their pain,*
> *they turn to the illusion of travelling*
> *between the warm and the cold climes*
> *of their homeland. So naturally,*
> *I don't think it strange that Kurds can fly.*
> *They go from country to country*
> *and still never realize their dreams of settling,*
> *of forming a colony. They build no nests*
> *and not even on their final landing*
> *do they visit Mevlana to enquire of his health,*
> *or bow down to the dust in the gentle wind,*
>   *like Nali.*

But Fadime was through with flying. She wanted no more of that. Back and forth from Damascus to Istanbul, from Istanbul to Montreal, to who knew where next? She wanted to build a nest where she was. Flying in the winter was most challenging, if not the most dangerous! She had opened up to Daniel. She had carried the weight of her journey for so long. Only now was she exposing her life to someone she was befriending.

"I am talking to you in confidence. Where I come from, they imprison you for 'thoughtcrimes.' People sometimes express themselves artistically to circumvent exposure, and prison."

"I think art is the truest way to express oneself," suggested Daniel.

"If not the truest, it is not even always the safest! Consider films from certain countries. I won't say which but a director may portray women in the films often as ill. This is a way to show the society as suffering. Or, a director might show the father unable to work because of some infirmity, while those with wealth move uninterrupted by flaws in the economy. In these situations the director makes an attack, but cannot be accused directly as exercising a thoughtcrime." Fadime said.

She did not want to talk. She wanted to listen. If they were in Daniel's apartment, she would ask him to play for her. He might do that anyway. That way the piano could do the talking.

Fadime began folding paper on the table. "You know, I haven't even the talent to fold paper."

"Your talents lie elsewhere, I am sure. You are kind with people and you make friends readily. That's how we met.

Fadime unfolded the paper and wrote the following lines: *My fingers knit with yours a fabric full of doubt. What will tomorrow bring? Dream come true, rain or drought?*

"Is that for me to read?" asked Daniel.

"It is," she replied.

Daniel looked at the paper, quizzically.

"Why the doubt?"

"I have been on the run all my life, and never by choice. Stability came with studies, but even that was broken up with turmoil. In Istanbul, I distanced myself from the troubles that dictated my moves. It was either do that or remain in limbo."

Fadime paused, collecting her thoughts. "I don't want to complicate your life," she said.

"You're a breath of fresh air," said Daniel, touching her left hand, which held the Waterman pen.

"So, do you write poetry?"

"If that is what it is, this is my first one."

The color rose on Fadime's cheeks. Daniel was encouraged by this show of emotion. He touched her free hand first. Then, held both hands. Fadime felt the thrill of being with a man like never before. Is this what people mean when they call it *the free world*? Things moved very quickly. But she had waited so long. She started to tremble. She had every reason to be nervous.

"You seem so calm, and I am shaking like a willow!" she said.

"It is winter, you know."

"You know what I mean."

"Well, don't think that I'm not nervous," he said.

Now they walked to where the car was parked. Halfway to the car, Daniel held Fadime's hand. She was no longer trembling. She had resigned herself to her heart: to her emotions. She had neglected her emotions for a lifetime. All those springs and all those summers where even butterflies found mates—where even crows found a reason to caw, Fadime had only her studies to console her. She was saving herself for someone her father would choose. She was not like her Canadian peers. That special someone would be her life partner: she would die in his arms. But the man her father had in mind had already spent four years in prison, and unless he obtained a reprieve from the government, he was going to do his twenty years in Diyarbakir Prison. And what had he done to find himself there? He was having a conversation with her father in Kurdish. That was a sufficient circumstance to be arrested and carted off to prison. His whole life put on hold, not to mention his career as an attorney. None of the latter meant anything to those who held the power in their hands. It would take an international tribunal to see that justice was served. But what could Fadime do in the meantime? She had kept herself busy with work, sixteen hours daily. But her lonely heart had been touched when she had heard Daniel play *Baran*. Here was a man she barely knew, but had fallen for. She would not last sixteen years. Life just was not fair. Daniel was a man unlike any men she had ever known. He was a professional from a good family. What would her father say? Daniel was not a Kurd. He was a Canadian, of Haitian parents. He was a copper-skinned black whom one might mistake for Kurdish, but that was not the issue. She had made her choice without her father's consent. True, she made decisions for herself every day. She was confident in doing so. But, wasn't she getting ahead of herself? Daniel had not proposed to her. They were still getting acquainted, albeit at lightning speed.

Sol Gabetta was bowing sixteenth notes in sharp contrast to Daniel who explored the floral pattern of Fadime's bracelet.

The car windows were steamed, so Fadime and Daniel were visually cut off from the outside world.

22

Khalil was on duty the next time he ran into Daniel.

"Hey, it's been a while!" he said.

"I've been spending my free time with Fadime. Didn't mean to neglect you."

"Good! I was giving you some space anyway."

"It's amazing how your life changes when you are with a person you love."

"Glad to know you have someone to spend it with."

"Look, we'll be in touch!" said Khalil.

"My best to Zouhoor."

Khalil walked away thinking about his friend's happiness in his newfound relationship. He could see that Daniel's life had changed for the better. Khalil had his cup full with Zouhoor and Riaziat. Riaziat had been rejecting Zouhoor's breastfeeding, preferring the bottle. Zouhoor had not been the same lately, feeling rejected herself.

Later at home Khalil stood with Zouhoor. "He's growing up," said Khalil.

"But he's still an infant."

"Yes, but he's giving you a break."

"Maybe I don't want a break!"

Khalil drew Zouhoor close to him, holding her like he used to: long before Riaziat was even a thought.

"You are still my everything!"

Zouhoor smiled, revealing her perfect teeth. She had a winsome smile. *She is so uncomplicated,* Khalil thought. She walked around with the expression of Mondigliani's Girl with Braids. She was not a girl, but a woman. Even when she did not speak her silence held wordless grace. She was the beauty of a Coriolis force: She was an inertial force that acted on you as you rotated about a sphere. She was magical. Khalil could write the equation for her movement. But marveled at her ability to grace his world. He loved the way she reduced everything to its lowest terms. She was the essence of humility.

Zouhoor took Khalil's hand and placed it to her lips.

"If I ever say something that you don't like, let me know," she said.

"Where did that come from?" he asked.

"You talk in your sleep when you are tired. You were talking to Fadime: how you like listening to her. That was all you said. Still, I wondered what she had said to you that made you mention her."

"I don't know. It was Daniel who mentioned her. They are seeing each other. Why I should mention her is beyond me."

Zouhoor said nothing else, but Khalil was put on notice that his thoughts were being recorded.

"So, are they serious?" asked Zouhoor.

"They must be. Daniel was beaming from ear to ear when I saw him at the hospital."

Zouhoor went back to preparing the salad and lentil soup they were having for dinner. Riaziat played with blocks in his playpen.

Outside, the snow fell and accumulated on the streets.

"You haven't played your saxophone lately," said Zouhoor. "I miss that."

Those words reminded Khalil that he had yet to work on a composition for his wife. Guilt was a terrific motivator.

He looked out the window. He could see the cars moving cautiously down the boulevard in the twilight. The trees, nude to the night, exposed their thoughts, as the wind howled. The emptiness of winter with its mysterious indigo shadows danced on the snow. Khalil had all the inspiration he needed to capture *Zouhoor at Twilight*. Now that he had a title, all he needed were the notes. He assembled his instrument and played some scales. E flat minor nine caught his attention. He played runs in A flat minor seventh, moving to D flat major seventh. Then he moved on to D flat minor, G flat seventh, and on to C major seventh. He added elevenths to each of the chords he had already played, looking for melodies to unify everything he had found. As snowflakes fell, Khalil peered out his window and thought of how he had first met Zouhoor; how he sat with her in her father's house; her engaging conversation; his wondering if he would see her again. He liked her, but was not overwhelmed. He did not want to appear too eager. But now he was with her, so far from Damascus, with their son. He could not think of living without her. She was the melody that captured his heart and he was glad to play it. He continued to embellish the tune he had discovered. The notes gave way to a form he had learned to live with. She liked the music he played. It was a fabric, like the clothes on his body. They were one with every stitch: a mosaic of blue wool and tan silk that warmed him. He felt he could do no wrong. Any pattern of notes modulated into a beautiful phrase. He thought that he would have a problem writing her a sonata, that the form was too ambitious. But it was what she deserved, he felt, so why not?

"What is that you just played?"

"I don't know."

"Please play it again."

Khalil play the motif again.

"Was that it?"

"Yes."

"No. It was this."

"Yes, that was it!

"I will record it, so I can go back to it later."

"Then you and Daniel can play it."

"He has a real gift," said Khalil.

"He is no more gifted than you."

Khalil played the entire piece as the cassette recorded everything.

"That was gorgeous!"

Khalil embraced Zouhoor.

"Which finger played the last note?"

"Gee, all of them. They work together," said Khalil. He had never been asked that question. With Zouhoor so enthused, he was equally eager to pen them down on a manuscript paper. He had an idea for an introduction in 6/8 time, as he listened to the flat tire slow to a halt in the snow.

"This one, on A flat."

Zouhoor smiled appreciatively. Khalil's answer to her question made her feel connected to him and the huge instrument he wielded.

"See," said Khalil, pointing to the note that he had written on his manuscript paper.

"From now on, I will look for it when your music is out."

Zouhoor felt part of the world of black ink on the music stand. Music was not of interest to her, save for listening to it. It soothed her most when she was rocking Riaziat to sleep and when Khalil occasionally picked up his sax. He was so tired. But then he remembered his days of practicing in Damascus:

"And it is such a beautiful instrument. Even the case is lovely."

"You're right." He passed his right hand along the lush burgundy interior.

Zouhoor placed her hand on his. She glided her right hand onto the soft interior as well. The two walked over to the window, peering at the empty, and now quiet, boulevard below. The wind blew fiercely through the oak trees that stood in defiance.

Zouhoor walked away to check in on Riaziat. He was sleeping. She returned to Khalil, who was writing notes on the manuscript paper. He wanted to preserve what he had just composed. Riaziat might play one day.

23

When Khalil put down his pencil, it was three in the morning. He had completed eight pages of the manuscript paper. Zouhoor would be pleased to see her name at the top of page one.

Khalil crawled into bed dressed in his robe. He was too exhausted to put on his pajamas. He had to get up in four hours. The habit of rising early was well-engrained. He did not have to be at work until noon. His eyes closed as soon as his head hit the pillow. He was so tired he slept and dreamed of his times in Damascus.

Khalil walked the length on a date-palm-strewn street. It was humid and empty. It was a Saturday, and Khalil lowered his cap over his eyes.

"Khalil. Who are you hiding from?"

"No one."

"Well, I haven't seen you in school. The brothers have been asking for you."

"What for? Besides, I am busy."

"Too busy for friends?"

"Yes. I'll talk to you another time."

Khalil had already distanced himself from the broth-

ers, and Meryam as well. She was part of that group. And Khalil was in no need for the distraction they imposed. He was sure that they wanted to get him involved in their Arab Spring endeavors. He was not Arab, and did not want to cut short his fellowship. He risked a greater danger of losing all he had worked for than they did. He was a guest in their country. Something he was quick to remind himself. He did not pretend to be something he was not.

He went to pick up some lead for his mechanical pencils. He left the store and walked to his favorite cafe.

No sooner had he sat down, he was joined by Meryam.

Khalil looked at Meryam, exasperated.

"Oh, I am not following."

"Good," he said.

Khalil buried himself into his book. He pulled out his pencil and began to draw the urinary system. He began with the abdominal aorta, followed by the renal artery, left kidney, cortex, medulla, renal papilla, calyx, and renal pelvis.

"Isn't it fascinating?"

Khalil had all but forgotten Meryam was there. He looked up. "You'll have to excuse me, but I have no time to talk. I don't mean to sound rude."

"Oh, I understand," she said.

The waiter came over with tea for both Khalil and Meryam. Khalil had decided not to say another word to Meryam. He continued to draw from memory the renal vein, the inferior mesenteric artery, and the internal iliaric artery.

Khalil was pleased with the rendering. He was comfortable with his knowledge of the system and how it functioned. He had started to draw the urethra when he was interrupted.

"Brother! So here you are! This is so disappointing. We look all over for you. You are not ever at home. We know because we even send Meryam for you, but without success. You do not find her to your liking?"

"Actually, she is quite beautiful. But I have a mission, and you keep getting in the way."

Khalil was surprised at his boldness. There were the three students who had appeared at his door and interrupted his music practice.

"We are so disappointed. We want you in our association. We want to forge an international group, and we see you as a brother, and want you to be a part of our growing membership. You will be our link to the West. We have followed your background and you are just the kind of brother we need."

"I am flattered, but I have to decline."

Khalil gathered his notes, and packed everything away.

"Brother, it's not that simple. When we decide on a brother, that's it. They are in."

"Sorry, I have gotten used to democracy and free will. I don't want to be a part of your group, no matter how much you want me."

"Oh well, we'll just have to convince you anyway."

One of the three grabbed Khalil by the shirt, and Khalil did the same to him.

"Khalil! Wake up!"

Zouhoor held her husband, as he struggled to free himself from his imaginary demons. Khalil was out of breath with his fists clenched.

As Khalil's heart raced, he shook away the last of the student organizers he wanted no part of. It had been a long time since he had first met those young part-time gangsters. They were the enforcers who were out to derail the easily-convinced ones who wanted change so badly, they could taste it. They would soon taste the blood from the bullets lodged into their bodies, or knives across their throats. The Arab Spring had awakened in Syria, as it had in Tunisia and Algeria. In Syria, forces were out to depose Assad, but were up against a formidable opponent with Russian and Iranian backing the Syrian leader. Khalil stood on the side of the family who had taken him in. Why would a Syrian family invest in an American doctor without wanting something tangible in return? And now with a Syrian wife at his side, had he sealed his fate?

Before leaving Syria, members of a family he had not met earlier threw a party for this brother from another country they now embraced. Oh, they were all so cordial to someone they knew only on paper.

"Brother Khalil, we are all so proud of your accomplishments. You did it! It must have been difficult being away from your family. But you did it! Now you are Doctor Khalil Baptiste, and on your way to the Kingdom of Saudi Arabia. How do you feel?"

"Exhausted!"

Those near Khalil, laughed. The laughter reverberated throughout the crowd, as people translated what he had said. A line formed as was the custom in Syria, to shake his hand, as he stood next to his wife, Zouhoor, fashionably dressed in white and green, from head to toe. Next to him, she measured almost six-feet tall. Her face was aglow with pride, and you might have thought the celebration was for her. Her family felt it was. Her mother, grandmother, and sisters stood side by side making that clicking sound so familiar to gatherings. The men in the family shouted "Mabrook!" in succession. That was the happy culmination. No one but Khalil carried the anguish it took to reach that day.

*

"You see, brother, Meryam has fallen for you. That wasn't what we had in mind. She was only there to get you in our organization. She went further than we intended. In addition, she did not accomplish what she was supposed to do. She has been reassigned. She is on her way to Aleppo."

Aleppo did not sound like where she would be studying medicine. Rather, she would be assigned to a medical unit. She would be attending to the wounded. Skirmishes were happening daily. Rockets pierced the stucco rooves so frequently that the mosques were the safest refuge.

"I will always miss you, and what was never meant to be."

Those were the last words Khalil would hear from Meryam.

*

"There is so much you haven't told me about those years in school," said Zouhoor , still holding Khalil.

He needed her warmth now, more than ever. He was such a solitary person. No, lonely was what he was. He was solitary in Damascus, but now that he was in Montreal, he was lonely. He had always been lonely. At home in Philadelphia, he watched his mother drift off while clutching a four-ounce heavy-paneled Dewar's Scotch glass, only later to be fished out of the Schuylkill River. He watched his father waste his skill counterfeiting money, which ultimately landed him in prison.

At home, he was surrounded by losers. When he had met Paivi, his luck began to change. He never looked back. His parents had chosen their fate, and he had chosen his. If he could save *himself*, it was the best he could hope for.

*

Khalil got ready for work. Zouhoor prepared the usual breakfast: olives, cheese, and tea.

"That was some dream," she said.

"Sure was."

Khalil didn't elaborate. He did not know where to begin. Should he talk about his family? He never did. They were such an embarrassment. But he would have to. That would address all the anger he held inside. He had nothing to lose. He would have so little to explain. Plates in the basement told their own story. His father was no Gutenberg, although his engravings were superb. It was a wasted talent, where he now stood. What else was in the basement? The plaque for some basketball team Khalil had never heard of. The dust had shaded the lettering.

*

Khalil went to the hospital where he had one patient waiting for him. His problem was incontinence. He scheduled a battery of tests: the bladder stress test, the urinary analysis, and the urine culture test.

The second patient wanted to undergo a vasectomy. He was forty-five and had two children. His wife agreed, as she did not want any more children.

Dr. Baptiste asked the patient that if he and his wife divorced, might having children not be considered in a subsequent relationship.

"I am through with that! I'll sign the papers that I am of sound mind."

Dr. Baptiste looked into the cold platinum eyes of the man and saw no glimmer of doubt. He was willing to discuss the joys of fatherhood, but sensed that this patient was completely convinced.

"I have daughters and both are hellcats!"

"They may both surprise you."

"And I may hit the lottery. Let me pick a date for the surgery."

Khalil tendered the papers to the patient. There was nothing left to say. The patient was on auto-pilot.

"You see, I married young. My wife and I were the same age. Love was young, like us. Should I be telling you this? Probably not."

"Sir, I don't do counseling. I don't think I can help you with that."

"No, you're most likely right. But I am going to tell you something. Don't marry for love."

It's too late for me. I'm married."

"Happily, hopefully."

"Hopefully."

"Hope you make out better than I did."

"Tomorrow will tell."

The two men ended their short conversation, smiling, but Khalil felt uncomfortable sharing a personal feeling with a stranger. A moment later, he was sitting with another man, who seemed relaxed.

"So, how can I help?"

"I need something for this burning down here."

Dr. Khalil examined the man. It looked like chlamydia. He would need the results of a biopsy to be sure. He prescribed some antibiotics to attack the infection.

"Get this prescription filled and follow the pharmacist's directions." The man looked relieved by the prescription.

"Be safe in your sexual choices."

"I will."

The man left the office almost sprinting. Dr. Khalil took no further interest in his patient. He was concerned that the young man would make wiser choices, but that was something he had no control over. His life was complicated enough. What about the dream he had to unravel? He hadn't even given Meryam a thought in the longest time. After she was whisked off to Aleppo, he was relieved. He had felt they were being followed whenever they were together. He was right. And the stares the two of them would engender, gave him an uneasy feeling until his stomach churned. An afternoon with her had him taking Pepto-Bismal when he arrived home. He expected to hear a crashing in of his door, shortly after he arrived. That never happened, although his guilt kept him close company. On one occasion, right after Meryam had just left, there was a knock on his door.

"Hey Latif."

"Hi Khalil. I haven't seen you for a few days. Are you okay?"

"Sure. Why do you ask?"

"You haven't been in the library. Your usual place."

"Oh, yeah. I move around."

"Okay. Just don't forget who your friends are."

Latif had left without another word. Khalil considered him a friend, and perhaps his only one. Those other Syrians were only trying to use him: to gain favor with him. He had an American passport, and what he at first viewed as genuine interest, he later came to see as a façade. He was a vehicle to either promote a personal interest or a political one. Either way, he was being used: a USA-approved prophylactic. They had an agenda of which he wanted no part. With the exception of Meryam, they were not really students. Khalil never saw them in the library—nor with any books. They were political activists. Those were the telltale signs. He never sought them out, as he shared none of their interests. When he did run into one of them, it was to remind him of a meeting, or a party with the brothers. He hated the latter most of all. Sitting around, smoking shisha was not what he cared to do. He did not wish to be anywhere they were. They might have called him a snob, or perhaps worse, when he was not around. He didn't care. How were they in any position to call him names? Their country was bursting at the seams in anarchy and disillusionment and spiritual decay. He had become a callous pragmatist. Meryam once said something to him: "If you don't expect anything, you will never be disappointed." It was so true, and *that* was how he viewed life. When he first arrived he enjoyed the meal *freekah* a delicious meal made from durum wheat, served with cinnamon, cumin and lamb tail fat. Khalil had tasted nothing better. Now however, he had lost had even his taste for something so unique. He certainly had enough experiences in his life to have drawn that conclusion on his own. His mother had checked out on him early. His father was of no use to him, or to himself. Meryam was only there on the margins, but distancing herself by way of her political allegiance to *the cause*, as she called it. No, Syria was not what he had hoped it would be. His medical education was not really free. It was exacting a price he did not anticipate. He needed to pray, again. That is what he lacked. Apart from his music, he had all but lost his connection to the higher ground. Oh, he continued to go through the ritual motions, but the words did not penetrate through him, as they once had. And with all the bombs exploding, his spiritual nucleus had been shaken. He remembered the scenes in Sarajevo, when just to buy milk and bread, one risked life. He found himself avoiding going too far. Life was reduced to going to school, and picking up what he needed while he was out. Crepuscule was very beautiful, but not when it came with *the rockets' red glare*. Night trips were out.

Things changed once he got to Saudi Arabia. There were no protests. He arrived on the evening of a national holiday. Youths were driving their cars. Those that were not driving, sat on doors, the upper halves of their torsos exposed. They waved flags. If one looked hard, one could even spot some women in the myriad. There could not have been a greater celebration if they had won the World Cup, a feat no Gulf State had ever come close to accomplishing. The noise was deafening, but no police presence impeded it. Khalil came to understand that the populace spent its time going out on the desert in their trucks, racing up and down the dunes, watching movies about cars, and going to the mosque.

There was always the pastime of eating. Goat over a bed of rice garnished with long, hot peppers was popular. That was every day, so the men were quite corpulent and short of breath. Smoking was another pastime. The yellow-stained smiles they displayed gave an idea what the blotches on their lungs must look like. If only they knew there was nothing to smile about! Khalil remembered the cadavers. Carcinoids stared back at him. And those were the dead ones! He remembered a woman sitting in a clinic in Damascus one sunny day. She barked, her voice barely audible, her sallow look, her eyes grey, like daggers of the night that foretold of pallbearers. She barked again. Her chest heaved. She was out of breath. She craved a cigarette, but craved oxygen even more.

"There is nothing we can do. You are too far gone. Please stop smoking."

Khalil was only talking to himself. The woman forced a smile. Those were the days he was doing his rounds. He learned to accept that those patients were going to die soon: either from smoking or a piercing bullet. Death was on its way. It was amazing that Khalil had become so resigned to the realities of Damascus. Death was inevitable for everyone, but in Damascus, it was as close as your best friend. When would the next explosion occur? In the market place? Outside the wudu station? In a restaurant? The streets were never without pieces of red-clay pottery, or shards of colored glass. Potters would not lose the opportunity to stir them into their own mosaics. Nothing was wasted. Life continued. There was no waiting for what misfortune would over-take them. Damascus was a vibrant city. Had it never been without turmoil? Since the time of the Greeks and the Romans, harmony had come and gone. Now, the Sunni majority inhabited the same land as the Alawites and a fair number of Christians. One walked from Antiquity to the twenty-first century in a span of five minutes. But who backed the group of patriots that pre-sented itself at Khalil's apartment? They were not from the standing government. They were trying to bring that government down. The sooner they did that, the sooner Khalil would find himself outside with no foot-ing in Syria. Oh, the country was in turmoil and no one Khalil knew was above suspicion. Meryam, whom he had learned to trust, was no longer around. Was she even still alive? He hoped she was. Aleppo was under attack, so he did not dare try to reach her. But he need-ed information. He needed to find a way to reach her. He hated that he had treated her with indifference. One needs friends, or at least one. Meryam was someone who had befriended him. She was unlike the others.

While people looked at him as though he had some nefarious purpose to be with her, he had none. Khalil noticed no other couples who garnered any such scrutiny. He hated that about Syria. If he could change anything about that beautiful country, what would it be? The landscape was breathtaking. The night sky was ablaze, a frequent light show: bombs bursting in air. Maybe he could elicit some help from his fellow classmates that knew her. There was Frida! Why hadn't he thought of her before? She and Meryam were inseparable! That was until Meryam started spending all of her time with Khalil. That is when he was certain Meryam was trying to recruit him. Oh, she wanted him in their group, but did she want even more than that? Khalil felt himself growing weak. Loneliness was getting to him. He saw himself as a clump of graphite in the sand, and people sought him out, to put in their pocket, to display at their own discretion. That is when he reassessed his worth. Unlike some students, he could return to the country of his birth. He had the passport everyone wanted. While he did not consider it of such value, it was worth more than he initially thought it to be.

Were that not the case, why would students make such a big deal when they found out that he was *Ameriki*? One Pakistani student thought all Americans were white. Khalil's reply "They haven't killed us all!" was delivered with a smile, which conveyed no meaning to the student, who apparently knew nothing of America's political history. Khalil knew little of his, save having seen Benazir Bhutto on a weekly news interview. Her looks were as riveting as her oratory skills.

Frida was who Khalil had to talk to. She must know Meryam's whereabouts.

"Well, there isn't much I can tell you."

"That's hard to believe," said Khalil.

Frida sat with her pudgy hands folded. She looked at them. She wore a bracelet of jade and topaz. When she looked up at Khalil, it was really the first time he noticed her eyes were topaz as well. *So different from Meryam's*, he thought. Meryam might have been African American, were her accent different. She had the look, but that was where it ended. She did not possess the ugly language of the women living in Khalil's neighborhood. They had all the answers until it came to "Who was the baby's daddy?" If they knew, and they did most of the time, they would not say. And the government didn't care. But that was not the point. Meryam was as beautiful outside as inside. If Khalil felt that way, why didn't he tell her? Well, there were two reasons: he did not trust her, and he didn't trust himself. He was right on both accounts. He was not looking for love in Damascus. This was a dangerous land, and he was being watched all the time. He was not approached for anything other than academic questions. When he noticed students holding hands, he turned his head away, he thought of Paivi, and what he shared with her. He was not going to see her again, or meet anyone like her in that dry land. Still, he found himself looking back at the days he used to sit with Meryam, discussing histology and dashing any other interests of theirs. What a predicament!

*

"But Meryam isn't Syrian. She's Algerian."

The news came as a shock to Khalil. How could he have known? She did have something African about her.

"I had no idea!"

"No, she is a foreigner, like you! Well, maybe not like you. You know what I mean."

Khalil nodded in agreement, but his head was now spinning with questions. If she weren't Syrian, then why did she agree to go to Aleppo? Would she learn more medicine there? Did she have someone in her life there? Was she a part of a political movement there?

"So, is she still studying medicine?"

"Oh, of course. She asked about you."

"She did?"

"Sure. You spent a lot of time together."

Khalil would not have guessed that she had given him a thought. He was glad to be thought of. Gee, he had considered himself insignificant in Damascus.

"Why would you think that? You're an American after all!"

True, he was. That alone made his every move important, whether he thought so or not. Here, it was not the color of your skin that mattered, it was the color of your passport.

For as much as Khalil hid his American accent when he spoke Arabic (actually, he was losing it, as he spoke almost no English any more), he absorbed the Syrian culture, totally.

"You have become Syrian! Just ask anyone!"

Khalil took Meryam's address from Frida. He felt happy to have a link with her again. He had not been so delighted since he played his bass clarinet. For him, there was little joy in that desert land. His time with Meryam was what he missed. Had he fallen in love with her? No. He was lonesome, and she was a human being. That was all he cared about. He would have been just as happy with Frida, if he knew her! He might end up spending time with her. She was friendly enough, and they shared the same classes.

"Thanks Frida."

She smiled. She had perfect teeth. Her eyes brightened with delight. She adjusted her paisley headscarf, and walked to the bus stop. Khalil walked to the library. It was going to be a waste of time to try to study there, because protesters had formed a chain around the entrance. Who was studying anyway? Only the med students were serious during such times. They wanted to leave the country the most, and knew their only way out was to graduate. But they were likely to encounter resistance. The government was holding back any national eager to leave the country with a medical degree. Some wanted to stay to see what the outcome of the revolution would bring, but they might not live to see it.

Rat-tat-tat. The automatic gun's fire perforated the air. Khalil hid behind a date palm, not sure of the shots origin. He had one more year to complete. If he survived it, he could leave—in one piece. While he had the government to thank for his education, he was not required to remain once he was done. The government wanted him to go back to the States with news of how wonderful his education had been, and how hospitable his host country had been. An ambulance siren sang its tune. Khalil thought of his arrival in Beirut and the wounded and the dead on the streets. His heart sank on that day of bloodletting. What a reception, he had thought. He was sure his American colleagues were facing nothing like that.

The policemen went right to work. Their batons rapped against heads and bodies alike. Men and women covered themselves with little success. There was no warning to stop what the protesters were doing. Just a lot of running. But where could they go? They ran from the batons and into others. The police seemed to enjoy the chaos they created. A man went to the ground. His face became quickly disfigured. A baton in a skillful hand could rearrange a face like putty. Oh, he and others like him would need surgery. *Thud*, and there went another young man to the ground who might never walk again. Thud! And there, a woman was down. *Was she pregnant?* Then that was really two down! There, more automatic fire, and Khalil ducked under a crate of melons. Would his brains be splattered with the fruit if they were in the crosshairs? The writhing of the woman, the scurrying, and stumbling of the disoriented. The children who looked up at the faces of their parents without answers were the portrait of a nation in transition that might very well be the last one Khalil would see. How many times had he taken the prone position since he stepped off the ship in Beirut? How many people had he watched fall, who would not get up?

"Khalil! Come with me!"

Who was calling him? Khalil did not move from behind the crate, petrified he was taking his last breath.

Yes, he was sure Death was calling him. He surrendered himself to the voice.

"Come!"

The shooting stopped and Khalil stood on wobbly legs.

"Let's go over there."

It was Latif, and Khalil was never more relieved to see his colleague. Latif knew his way around better than Khalil did. He knew the cul-de-sacs. They were seeking the same refuge: survival.

The two men ran together, though only one knew where he was going. Down one narrow alley after another, they bustled, tripping as they went. Khalil took no time to take in the stares his sweaty face engendered. Latif knew the way past the vegetable carts, and the blind beggar. The café sanctuary Latif came upon was not open. They were off and running toward another one. Feeling the safety of being away from the turmoil, they began to walk. Still panting, Khalil took furtive glances behind. Through another street they walked, briskly. This street showed none of the frenzy of the tension that was twenty minutes away. A tranquility resided where none existed elsewhere.

"*Ithnatain chai, shukran,*" said Latif.

The waiter brought two steaming glasses of tea. The two men looked at one another. Khalil smiled, but without confidence Latif had grown accustomed to reading the face of this self-assured American.

"Things have gotten worse," said Khalil.

"If you were from here, you would not say that. Things are getting better. The people are waking up."

Khalil thought before he spoke. He was not at liberty to even venture an opinion in a fight that did not include him. Still, he felt he should say something.

"I see what you are saying. People will remain silent for only so long in the wake of what they feel is injustice," Khalil said.

"Even as a foreigner, you are touched by it," said Latif. "You feel the anxiety we all feel. But that is part of what makes people act with passion."

"I just don't know what to say about it. I am a guest, do not forget, and on a government scholarship."

"You are free to study without impunity."

"I would say that too, except that everyone doesn't feel like you do."

"What do you mean?"

"When I first arrived in Damascus, a group approached me. Came right up to my apartment while I was practicing music. They introduced themselves as students, wanting to welcome me to the country."

"What did you do?"

"Well, I didn't know your customs. I had tea with them. I found out soon afterwards that they had political motives. They wanted to unseat Assad. I told them that it had nothing to do with me, since I was a foreigner."

"So, they were trying to recruit you into their ranks."

"Right. I told them no thanks."

"Those guys don't give up so easily."

"You said it. I mean night and day they're at it."

"Then what did they do?"

"Well, one of the students was a female. She would appear at a café I frequented."

"Meryam?"

"You know her?"

"Only because she approached me. She wanted to know about you. She had seen us together."

"Why didn't you say anything to me?"

"She only asked me once. I didn't think anything of it. I haven't seen her in a while anyway. I figured she had dropped out of school. She wasn't my concern anyway."

"True. I have my studies to worry about, like you. She was involved in politics, though we studied together too."

"You were right to leave her alone."

"That's true, but I had grown accustomed to her company. As a foreigner, we don't have the contacts you do."

"So, did you fall for her?"

"I miss her, if you know what I mean."

"What do you mean?"

"She kind of grew on me. I fought with myself. I told myself I could make it without any companionship. She was there whenever I looked up. We studied together. Histology, pathology, radiology, like that."

"And then she got under your skin?"

"It's crazy. She's gone, and I now I miss her."

"Well, you might be better off without her. She's being sought by the police. She appeared in the paper. I don't know the extent of her involvement in the Arab Spring, but her name is among those mentioned. The fact that she's foreigner doesn't help. I mean, it's always easier to blame a foreigner. You know, as instigators. The newspaper linked her to an Algerian group that came into the country to bring about change here; not the kind the government wants."

"I just found out she was Algerian," said Khalil."

"Yeah, she told me she was, but we have loads of foreign students here, so it didn't alarm me. Of course, politics is a dangerous business."

"A dirty business," added Khalil, not feeling at all like discussing politics.

"But it's all around us," said Latif, after sipping his tea.

"It's a shame I couldn't find someone who isn't an anarchist. I am just so used to conversations with females."

"Conversation. Is that all?" asked Latif. "Conversation, and what goes with it!" he added. "I know what you Westerners are used to. I have watched enough of your movies."

"Movies aren't reality. But I could stand for some repartee."

"Excuse me?"

"Conversation. That is what I had with Meryam. She made great conversations. I didn't take advantage of it like I should have."

"Maybe you did. She wasn't going to be here too long, as it turns out. And now, the police want her. Better to distance yourself.

"Well, today I talked to a friend of hers. Do you know Frida Azmeh?"

"No."

"She gave me an address."

"With the police after her, she is no doubt on the run. They will be looking for you, too. I would stay low, if I were you. The less you know, the better."

"I have nothing to hide."

"The police here may not see it that way. They like to rough people up. Break joints until they get the answers they want. At least that's the way the movies portray them."

"Let's hope the movies here are like the ones in America: exaggerations, as you say."

Khalil was hoping so, too. He didn't fathom the notion of broken joints. How could he hold a scalpel, or even tie his shoe laces?

He was not interested in finding Meryam now. Funny how new knowledge had him running from his past, not that he had many fond memories. He certainly thought he would not revisit the States. That past he had all but forgotten. No, that wasn't true. He remembered selectively: Paivi, a few guys from college, and that was it! But Meryam had pursued him. He was not interested in her romantically. He was in Syria to study. Sure, he expected to make some friends. He had done that. But those with political agendas were not what he had in mind. He was reluctant to engage with the first Syrians who had sought him out, under the guise of a cultural embrace. He could be as friendly as the situation required. He did not want to offend the country that had extended itself to him in a way his own never had. That fact had him in a quandary. Was it true that people only do what serves their own purposes? He was sure that most did. Recent history had convinced him. As for Meryam, he was glad he knew so little about her.

He did not like being wrong about people. And there was Latif. He had been a real friend to share what he did about Meryam. That was vital information, albeit disappointing. How did she get involved with that band? How did she know them? What was her interest?

Those were the questions she would have to answer, and not to him, but to the police.

"More tea?" asked Latif.

"Please," replied Khalil, still pondering what he would do with all this knowledge.

"You might be questioned, given your relationship with Meryam."

"Relationship! Wait a minute! We are friends, nothing more!"

"Look, I believe you. But I may be the only one."

"I didn't even know she was Algerian. I didn't even care that she was."

"You don't have to convince me. I am your friend."

"You may be questioned, too."

"Let them. I have nothing to hide.

"Nor have I."

The tea arrived. The waiter looked at them and placed the glasses on the table along with a tray of biscuits. The men smiled at one another.

"You know Khalil, I want to invite you to my home. It's something I should have done before."

"It's all right. I am almost ready to go home, except that I don't really have a home to go to."

"What do you mean?"

"I came here with the intention of not returning. Now that I am feeling the heat, I am suddenly thinking of leaving: studying someplace else.

"But your scholarship? Besides, if you try to leave, it will create more questions. I don't think you will be allowed to leave."

"You are right. Better to stay the course, and not to appear a fugitive," said Khalil.

"When the semester is over, I will invite you."

"Thanks."

Khalil sipped his tea with a newfound pleasure.

The men finished their conversation and left the café. As they walked through the alley out to a familiar street, they parted ways.

The afternoon was quiet. Khalil walked back to his apartment. He had regained his composure, no longer thinking of leaving Damascus. He would finish his term here, though he did not have the same desire to stay that he had before. Meryam's situation had opened his eyes to the danger his association with her brought. He was relieved to get to his apartment that late afternoon. He was not tired, despite the long day. He looked forward to hitting the books. Never before had completing his stay in Damascus been more meaningful. He opened the door.

*

"Okay, drop your bag!" a plainclothesman ordered.

"What's going on?"

"We will ask the questions," said the second one.

The second man displayed a badge.

"Put your hands in the air!" he said.

The first plainclothesman put handcuffs on Khalil. He then frisked him for weapons but found none.

"Where are you from?"

"The United States."

"Why are you in Syria?" the second policeman asked.

"I am here as a student. I am in my third year at the medical school."

"Don't they have medical schools in the US?"

"This one is less expensive."

"Of course."

"And what is your name?"

"Khalil Baptiste, sir."

"Sit down."

The men were obviously in the habit of ordering people around. Khalil was used to what policemen were like in the States, and did as they ordered. The first plainclothesman remained standing, his back facing the door. Khalil sat facing the second man. He was the one in charge, asking the questions.

"We are here because of your association with Meryam Bashir. How do you know her?"

"I know her as a student."

"How else do you know her?"

"I know her only as a student."

Khalil's heart raced. He tried to catch his breath. The handcuffs were tight. "Sir, these cuffs are tight. I will not escape. Please loosen them."

The first plainclothesman, who already had his automatic handgun trained on Khalil, relented, then loosened the cuffs.

"May I lower my arms?"

"Why yes. Just stay in the chair."

The momentary relief ended once the questions resumed.

"So, you are not romantically involved with Sister Bashir?"

"I only know her as a student."

"Why do you study with her, when there are so many male students?"

"Is it a crime to study with a woman?"

"We will ask the questions," answered plain-clothesman number two. "But no, it is not a crime. It has come to our attention that Sister Bashir is linked to the people in the news. We are questioning anyone who knows her. Do you know where she is now?"

"I cannot say for certain. She left school some months ago. We have not been in touch since."

"I want to believe you," said inspector number two.

"I am telling you only what I know. I spend my days studying."

"So, what do think of Damascus?"

"It is a city of singular beauty."

"Yes. We like it, too."

"Do you plan to return to America when you are done with your studies?"

"I don't know, sir."

"And what about Sister Bashir?"

"I don't know what her plans are."

The first plainclothesman unlocked the handcuffs.

"We do not want you to leave the city while the investigation continues. Sister Bashir is at large, and anyone in her circle is subject to questioning. That includes you, Brother Khalil. Do you understand?"

"I do."

Until the men left, Khalil had not thought to question how they had gained entry into his apartment. Of course, the landlord. It was an unsettling thought. He looked at his bass clarinet case, and his baritone sax case under the clarinet case, and walked over to them. His instruments were still inside. *Of course, they would be.* The police had not even bothered to ask him about them. They may have already looked in. They knew everything about him. The landlord or other tenants might have informed them. The women in the apartment, who were there all day, must have told all they knew about him to the officers. Those were reasonable assumptions, he figured. What he did know was that he would not be contacting Meryam. He did not like the way the Syrian police extracted information—like teeth without Novocain. They weren't so different from American detectives: come in pairs: one to rough you up, while the other pretended to be rational, but either way you ended up sore and in need of a hot shower. While their English reminded him of Sherlock Holmes and Dr. Watson, that was where the comparisons ended. Since the time he had gotten off the ship, he went from dodging bullets to protecting himself from explosions, carting the injured, to having his arms twisted. That was the hospitality he had experienced to round out his education. It was almost laughable, but Meryam was in danger, and now, so was he. No, there was no humor unless he took the matter lightly. Someone could wind up dead. Someone named Khalil. No, that was not funny. He was ready to pack his bags. But didn't they say not to leave? That didn't mean he couldn't pack. He had better forward those instruments—somewhere!

Rat-tat-tat-tat-tat! A car sped away. Oh, Damascus was no longer safe. Who was he kidding? Damascus had never been safe. Only livable within the thin margins: the alleys and streets, the walls that stood with crumbling stucco, chronicling the centuries of stories in a plethora of languages. Khalil hoped to add his to the others.

Oh, he had stories to tell. All he had to do now was to live through it. He hoped he had answered the detectives adequately. He did not want to make trouble for Meryam, but did she feel the same way about him? She was a fugitive of justice. He said the same, as he rubbed his wrists. They were still aching. No, Meryam was going to have to get herself out of this jam. She and her associates were in the newspaper, so they had to know they were on the government's radar screen. And now he was as well! Suddenly, his studies did not seem difficult anymore. Wasn't staying alive difficult enough? And now, he was being watched by the police. The consolation was that apart from Latif, he had no friends. No one he could trust, anyway! He was truly alone, so he trusted no one. He looked at his calendar. Two more months and his exams would begin. There was nothing more eventful to him. He would hold himself up in his room, and bury his head in his books. He would arrange the café down the street to bring his dinners to him, not to risk being watched. He had seen enough of "this country of singular beauty."

In the final analysis, everything is stone and sand. That is what Khalil had to admit. He looked out his window. Didn't the Damascus landscape say the same?

Yes, but his decision to stay inside his apartment did not last one day before the walls seemed to squeeze the life out of him. What about Jabal Qasiun? He would venture there when he was most lonesome. Was it not a treasure of a mountain no one could deny? How could he stay downcast when that mountain range was just a taxi ride away? He grabbed his Family Medicine text and his notebook, and went outside to find a taxi. The driver wound through a few streets, then took to the serpentine hills that leaned forward, until Khalil arrived at Jabal Qasiun. He would remember the cumulonimbus that announced a rainstorm that never came. The following day was a sunny day, which transformed Damascus into a land of peace. It was no longer the war-torn land that depressed Khalil so much. He wanted to leave it, but he would always remember that mountain. The location where he sat, Damascus resembled areas of parked cars, all of them granite-colored. And the rectangular forms stood in defiance of the rifle-wielding citizens. The buildings were not going anywhere. That is, until a mortar round pierced a wall. But that evening, for that was when he arrived there, the breeze had its way and conducted itself through the mountains. The sounds of birds filled the air, as they passed by. Then there was stillness again. Khalil opened his book. When was he not preparing for board examinations? His memory was his best friend, an equal match for his ability to untangle complicated concepts. He was equally able to disengage himself from all personalities. Meryam had put herself out in the cold, more distant than where he sat and farther than the farthest residence he could see.

24

The next morning Khalil left for the university by bus. It was the usual ride on the rickety, crowded transport. There were no fireworks going on; not even the backfire of a car. Such would have been enough to rattle anyone's nerves.

Khalil was happy to see Latif at Family Medicine. It was not unusual. It was just after his harrowing experience with the Syrian police. Khalil surprised himself: he didn't as much as mention that afternoon to Latif. Khalil did not want to appear needy, but that is exactly what he was. He now anticipated visits from the police. But he had nothing else to say. No new information. But they did not know that. He just as quickly resigned himself to his studies. *Worry about those who worry about you!* But there was no one. *There, wasn't that easy?* He thought. He was alone, nothing was new. "Get your lessons done," as his mother would say. He even found a way to smile. There, life wasn't so bad.

"Khalil, want to review today?"

"What about tomorrow?"

"Good. Right after class?"

"You bet."

The two friends sat down for their lecture. The professor asked a general question: if any of the students had any experience with head injuries related to sports. One of the men did: someone he knew had been hit in the face with a soccer ball. He was wearing glasses at the time. His glasses did not break, but he was rendered dizzy by the blow to the head.

The professor said that now footballers were seen wearing head protection, to avoid concussions: that the students should conduct research to find at least one study regarding head injuries resulting from sports; it would be very likely that some of them already knew of such a case.

The professor must have been close to the topic because he spent the entire lecture discussing case after case about Real Madrid and Manchester United.

"I was hoping he would say something about Barcelona! Who cares about Real Madrid anyway?" asked Latif.

"Well, we certainly know your favorite team," remarked Khalil.

"I just like the best, that's all."

"If he wanted to talk about head injuries, he could have asked me. I have seen my share since I have been here—and none of them on the pitch!"

Khalil felt like he had spoken out of turn, but the reality of quotidian Damascus needed no embellishing or diminishing. Body injuries were something everyone faced. The professor knew he was keeping the examples safe, because to talk about what was happening on the streets, might mean that he would have to talk about who was being killed in these senseless gun battles: the mothers whose entrails were left apart on the gurney or the grandfather whose teeth were separated from his jaw. Those were some of the things Khalil had witnessed. He wanted to talk about those injuries, the ones that pierced him like the bullets that had lodged inside the innocent victims. Those were the people he thought of, but from whom he remained detached. If he thought of them too much, he would never get through with his studies. He would not have enough to delve into the whys and wherefores of war, and probe the reasons why men just could not live in peace. It must have been prescribed for a man to fight, as his friend, Latif, had once remarked, "Didn't a baby have to struggle to emerge from the womb?" So, it must be that the struggle continues until death. Did the battlefield even matter?

"While heading the ball can cause an injury, the greater likelihood is that an injury will be the result of colliding with another player, or a goalpost," the esteemed doctor ended his topic. He gathered his notes, closed his book, and found his way to the door. One female student followed him outside the lecture hall.

"Are you okay?" Latif asked Khalil.

"Odd, I am still confused about why the police came, looking for me."

"They are probably making their rounds. Anyone who knew Meryam, and you happen to be one."

"Yeah, you must be right."

"You are doing rounds today, right?"

"Sure. Talking to the patients will take my mind off those cops."

"They were pretty rough, eh?"

"I still feel their grimy paws," said Khalil, rubbing his neck.

"At least you're smiling," said Latif.

"That was not the reception I ever anticipated from Damascus."

"Another year, and it will be history."

"You know, I'll never forget it."

The two men walked out in different directions. Khalil took a taxi to The Italian Hospital, Jamal Abdel Naser Street. It was there that he felt he was doing something worthwhile. He knew he was a good student; many said great, but if there was anything he knew, it was that he was great with patients. He reported to the desk for his first assignment.

Dawud, 21, had lost tissue from his right eye in a car accident. He had no seat-belt on. Most people did not wear them in that city. Who enforced a law so few observed? Dawud's spirits were high. He smiled broadly and shook Khalil's hand. They exchanged pleasantries.

"And how is Arsenal coming along?" asked Khalil.

"They beat Liverpool! That's all I care about!"

"I hope they go all the way!"

"I didn't know you followed the Primer League."

"I do now."

Khalil had gotten quite an education in European football, since arriving in Syria. He certainly knew as much about soccer as he once knew about baseball. No one knew, and cared even less about the American pastime. Khalil was one of the four third-year students examining Dawud. One of the three other students had examined Dawud's eye, which was now uncovered, exposing the blue-redness, now healing. The swelling had reduced. The doctor advised the nurse to wash and bandage it. He said nothing else. They all left him with the attending nurse.

Emeraa Amina, 65, whose lung cancer in her right lung had progressed beyond help. She would live the rest of her life with one lung. If she gave up smoking, she might live another year. Amina coughed, and the pain on her face made Khalil wince. It was a sound very familiar to him. His uncle Roy had the same one. Those Chesterfields induced the exact results. He died at the age of thirty-five. Amira had out lived him, but she had also abused her body. Her jaundice complexion and emaciated body bore the signs of poor diet.

"Do you think I will live, doctor?"

"Yes," said Khalil.

They were all living then. Who knew what the next hour would bring? Where medical aid had come too late, Khalil gave her a smile and hoped her remaining days would be less painful. He could not stop the time bomb that had started ticking long before he met her. He thought of his own mother, a woman he hardly knew, who had given up on life, before she had a chance to taste it, save for the Dewar's scotch. Here was yet another woman who would soon join his mother.

Death claims every soul. Still, he wished he could do something. Say something that could comfort her. He thought of the words of Richard Wright, from *Black Boy*, "I would hurl words into this darkness and wait for an echo, and if an echo sounded, no matter how faintly, I would send other words to tell, to march, to fight, to create a sense of the hunger for life that gnaws in us all."

*

Wright's words were so profound. They addressed every thought that Khalil wanted to express, but at the time, he could not. He was an empty vessel in a place where breathing was a challenge. He had no voice of late, so if he threw words like projectiles, who would hear them, when they fell on deaf ears? Would it matter at all? But it had to matter! He had to find someone who would listen. He had to climb out of that valley of gloom that contained him. Maybe he had made a bad choice with Meryam, but he did not know that at the time. Bad was such a relative term, anyway. She certainly didn't think it as a bad choice. When Khalil set his sights on Syria, he could not have anticipated being questioned by its authorities, much less being hurled about in his room. Those were memories he would not forget, or at least, not soon enough. He chuckled to himself as he said *memories*. There were those that rushed back to him. There was Rose, or Rocinante as Khalil called her. She was a top toothless septuagenarian, with a decisive under-bite, and square jaw. She perhaps ate soup, since what else could she eat? The only words she seemed to utter were, "Any spare change?" which she uttered in the most pitiful atonement: her piercing dark eyes, with raccoon circles, made people give her something so she would not ask again. She stood outside the gas station for hours on end. Once, Khalil asked her why she didn't get social security. "I does," she answered. "Dis just ma liquor money." Rocinante loved her Calvert's Gin. Gin with its 96% azeotrope of water and ethanol contains juniper berries, nutmeg, and sage. Even the Quran states that alcohol has its benefits, though they are never extolled. It chides one for its detriments far outweigh its benefits. Khalil imagined that she couldn't have weighed more than ninety pounds. *Old Rocinante might have already slipped into the next realm*, thought Khalil. He had his own concerns. She was a willow he was not going to weep for.

*

Khalil and Latif stood at a pharmacy, waiting to buy hair products and toiletries.

"Khalil, I have been meaning to invite you to dine with my family. I imagine you might be lonely for the company of your own family."

"That is very kind of you."

"Do you miss your family? Yes, you must."

"I don't think much about them." He said those words and felt their emptiness. He wished he had a family to think about. He wished to take back his words. "I think about how far away they are."

"All the more reason for you to come by. After exams end, you will come for a feast."

"Well—could we meet before graduation? I see myself hanging around much longer."

"I hoped that you would make Syria your home."

"That is a generous offer. I have heard from a hospital in Saudi Arabia. I am going to take their offer. It is in urology."

"Great news! When were you going to tell me?"

"I was hoping to hear that you had received good news as well about residency."

"Actually, I have. I will be doing orthopedic surgery here, in Damascus."

"*Mabrook!* Wonderful, my friend!"

The two men shook hands and cheered. Their enthusiasm brought cheers to their surprise from the students standing nearby.

25

Khalil wrote his final examinations in the crowded auditoriums of Damascus. He had studied enough. He felt no reservation about the time he had given to each exam. He walked into each room with a clinical detachment. He had already left Damascus. His heart was elsewhere. He was leaving Damascus, but not like those Syrians who took only the clothes they were wearing. Leaving was not the same as fleeing. He knew where he was going. No, he had never been to Riyadh, but people were waiting to greet him.

*

Six month after graduation, Khalil married Latif's sister, Zouhoor. She was even more eager than he to leave Syria, and its doubtful future. She was not ready for having to shroud herself in black, but that was a small price to pay for the new freedom. The different freedoms. No, she could not vote, but she could shop. She could travel, as long as she had her husband's permission. Khalil and she would make the pilgrimage to Mecca. But what Zouhoor loved most of all was that she was now married to an American. That, for her, was the gold standard. Khalil had promised her that she would someday see the Statue of Liberty. She believed him when he told her that, though she did not know when that day would come. She knew he did not share her excitement. She only began to understand when he countered her question, "Do you think we will see Mickey Mouse?"

"If he comes to Philadelphia, we'll see him."

For the time that seemed sufficient. Zouhoor came to know that her husband harbored serious questions. Dark questions. What would the climate be for an African American and his Syrian wife? She was a woman who did not know what racism was, except through films like *Bullet* and *A Patch of Blue*. What would it be like for her? She would have to see for herself.

"There is no getting around it. It's woven in the fabric—like the legacy of slavery."

"I have so much to learn," she said with childlike eagerness.

"I will give you some books to read, if you can stomach them."

"If you can, I can!"

Khalil needed to share some American history with her: things he was sure she had not heard of in her native Syria. How could he articulate the level of degradation the blacks experienced in the States? How do you express the sadness of being told to go around the back to be served out of the backdoor of a restaurant? No, you can't drink from that fountain! Those were the kind of experiences she would not understand. Khalil had traveled to countries like Turkey and Syria, where people did not have much, but no one he met treated him with the distain he had only known in the States. It had this notion of a high standard of living everyone could aspire to, but few experienced. That was why he could embark on a voyage to complete his medical education with the courage that his compatriots could not muster. He had the faith to seek his future.

Khalil gazed at the date palms looking like florets, as far as he could see. The green was all that broke the monochrome of ochre. Camels and Toyota pickups. Highways that led to nowhere, rickety buses and school girls dressed in black were what dotted the sandscape. A call to prayer was the closest thing to a song. If you played a car radio, the windows would be rolled up. Life existed, but joy was experienced behind the high wall, and left to your imagination. There was lots of football. Every other child wore a Messi shirt, even if they didn't know where he came from or even where in the world Barcelona was. Those questions had answers, but what was more important was getting the ball in the back of the net. What were the boys back in his hometown up to? Were they still looking for trouble to get into? That was on every corner. The summer was the season for the deaths of minors. Summer fun was joining a basketball program; seeing if you could learn to do ceramics; or seeing if you could cross the Schuylkill. The last one was a death-defying feat. Some would not return to school in September.

Khalil returned to his apartment and looked at himself in the bathroom mirror. A mirror he had salvaged from the rubble of Damascus. Broken, but so valuable to the traveler, this trapezoid of memories was more than it appeared to be. It was frameless. It had survived thousands of miles of travel. How old was it? *A century at least*, he thought. It was like so many other relics, tossed when a car bomb went off. Who knew its origin? When Khalil picked it up, there was no one to ask. Death was like that: it left you with your suppositions, or conjectures. What you came away with mattered only to you. He had gone halfway around the world, lived through precarious situations, and finally asked himself, "Why?" He questioned why he had chosen to go places where no one looked like him. Was he running away from himself? That was not possible. He was himself, wherever he landed.

26

Montreal, Quebec Airport, 2015

Khalil stood with Zouhoor and Riaziat. They were among the crowd waiting for the flight to arrive from Damascus. Latif had arranged an interview at McGill University Medical Hospital. It provided the opportunity for the family to have a reunion. Latif was now married, and Zouhoor was eager to see her family, and catch up on the news with her brother. He had married a distant cousin, Jadida, also a physician.

The crowd assembled, as if they were going to miss something if they were not vigilant. The waft of tabouli was in the air. Someone had just opened a bag of pistachios, too. He was passing some around to his newfound friends.

Khalil had invited Daniel on this occasion. Daniel and Fadime were now engaged. This was something her father was against at first. Fadime's mother was easier to convince that their daughter had made the best choice in their absence. Her parents were still in Turkey: her father still in prison; her mother not leaving her husband without hopes of getting out of his predicament. Things were bleak, based on the charges levied against her father. He would no doubt spend the rest of his life in prison. He had taken to reading Rumi and quoting him, "There is a loneliness more precious than life. There is a freedom more precious than the world. Infinitely more precious than life and the world is that moment when one is alone with God."

There was no more trying to alter what was his destiny, nor that of his family.

*

Fadime had spent more winters than she wished to remember watching the snow accumulate on her windowsill, letting the tea steam in front of her, turning from piping hot to tepid. She had a comfortable apartment without the comfort of a companion. Her life needed more than a successful career and a safe, progressive country. Daniel's family accepted Fadime with open arms. Daniel's father enjoyed when Daniel would bring her with him on his Sundays of chess and demitasses of coffee. His mother had acquired a taste for Fadime's homemade mujaddara with fresh lentils and bulgur, which Fadime prepared for everyone.

There was also the view that Daniel's mother shared about her son's choice: *You have found someone with kindness in her soul. That is not easy to find.*

Like Daniel's mother, Fadime believed to her core that kindness is pivotal, and more than that, it is monumental! In increments are how glaciers move. Kurdistan doesn't exist now, but it is only a matter of time. Who was it that had said, "Hope springs eternal?" And Fadime's energy affected Daniel, who prior to becoming involved with her, had shown little interest in Haitian politics. He was always ready to serve for emergency health care in the poorest island country in the Caribbean.

*

Khalil looked at himself in his mirror. He wondered how his life would have been different had he not gone to Damascus. He would have had a tremendous debt, to be sure. The physical bruises he endured would have been exchanged for verbal and mental ones in America. He had avoided them, and he was even happy to have skirted them. His wife would not have to endure them either, except, vicariously, through the literature of Wright, Baldwin, and most recently Amira Baraka. Zouhoor did not understand the anger in *Dutchman*: "I do not even want to discuss it. If that is America, I don't like it. I am very angry, but I don't know what to do."

"Be glad you didn't have to endure what Baraka did."

Zouhoor fell silent. *It must be her way to digest her emotions*, thought Khalil. To him, it appeared more like she had indigestion. A swelling in her throat seemed to have blocked whatever words she wanted to say. She had lost her ability to breathe. She collapsed into Khalil's arms. He walked her to an open window. The air helped her come around, though she remained pallid.

Khalil lay Zouhoor on the top of his briefcase and began giving her mouth-to-mouth resuscitation.

Zouhoor came to, though she spoke incoherently in Arabic.

"*Tamam, Habiba,*" said Khalil.

Zouhoor smiled weakly. She said nothing.

"I am going to get you to the hospital."

"Na'am. Il al mustashfa."

*

Was Zouhoor now carrying their second child?

"Your wife is pregnant," said the doctor.

"Thank you, sir. I am relieved to hear that."

"I wonder if this one will be a writer," she said.

"If it is a girl, she will have the best example in you," added Khalil.

Khalil and his wife left the hospital. They would need to find a nurse, and enlist her care.

This time they were expecting a daughter. Whatever they had, they were most happy to be in Montreal where health care was the best, and they were living in a tolerant atmosphere.

Khalil still had his own challenges to face. But he was in a place he could exercise his thoughts and deliberations. He had a partner who encouraged him in his every endeavor.

27

Philadelphia, Thirtieth Street Station

Khalil finally relented. He took his family to the city of his birth. It was just as he remembered it with a few improvements. The streets had fewer potholes.

When he spoke Khalil couldn't believe it was the same man Khalil once feared. He was only a cicada shell of who he once was, but he was the same one whose voice bellowed like a tempest through the halls of Sayre Junior High. He was full of himself then. He had a degree in something and was a teacher of health and physical education. He was in a word intimidation, and perhaps a father figure to some. It was a time when teachers were full-time disciplinarians, even if they could not teach. In retrospect, coming from a strict family and a good elementary school, Khalil didn't need the heavy-handed approach this man of action doled out. But this was an uncivilized lot of youngsters. (He might have seen himself in the scrubbed black faces. He was after all from an all-black neighborhood in North Philly. Maybe he was operating from a mandate of those who were really running the show. He was just a dutiful straw boss. Khalil would never know, since anyone in those positions were deceased.) They were the sons of men and women with dreams, too. The sons reached for stars that they would not have to reach for much longer: the war in Bosnia (like the one before it in Vietnam) was looming, and Camp Lejeune would need new recruits. The trajectory of those tough guys was soon enough to display itself when they would show off their new uniforms as they strolled through their neighborhood as young peacocks with a plumage of colored ribbons on their dress uniforms.

The body bags were not in short supply. This teacher cum basketball player full of wizardry might have known that, too. He taught by analogy of what a player would exhibit on the court. If he read any books on the basketball he kept that knowledge to himself. Oh, if his knowledge of physiology matched what he knew about dribbling, he might have been up for teacher of the year. (Years later when he made a name for himself as a college coach, he was also known for threatening other coaches with language that he should have kept to himself, or gotten out of his system when he was in junior high as a teacher. For all that intimidating talk, many of those boys still ended up in Vietnam, no better off for the sermons, but in body bags, still.

Those—from William Cullen Bryant—banned together as much as they could, but in this new environment they were separated by race and gender. Khalil's Jewish playmates formed new alliances, and were on their way to Central, the top academic school. Now when they sang Shalom Aleichem he was no longer in the chorus. They didn't sing that at Sayre. They were also separated by intelligence, or merely by skin color, for all he could see. Antigone Floret was in our group from Bryant, but she managed her way without being noticed. With two names like that, and being very gifted at the bassoon of all things, who were her friends going to be anyway? She said nothing to anyone except her white friends. She was passing perhaps, though Khalil didn't know the meaning of the term at that time. The term light-bright was circulating, and *passant blanc* to which she might easily have been ascribed, however. None of that mattered to him. She stayed to herself as far as Khalil could tell. As girls went, he had not developed an interest in them. The Jewish girls who would chase him around the school yard at Bryant had moved on to boys their parents thought as prospects for the future. His interest was in mechanical drawing. He excelled in layouts of objects: top, front and right or left side. There was nothing more satisfying.

As for learning, everything was hard to gauge. Maybe he was too concerned about hygiene to be thinking about anything else. Khalil could say though, eight grade was a total waste. The boys in his class were a banal bunch with little home training. The only thing they did well was to get suspended. Fights broke out everyday, so little teaching was done. Some of the same ones who loved to fight were able to show what they were made of when they arrived at Fort Bennington, Georgia. Some returned to the neighborhood wearing their dress greens decorated with infantry ribbons, and badges they might not have earned, but sure looked good, as a magnet for those who wanted to be like them. At the time Khalil did not understand why females were attracted to uniforms, but later he realized that someone in uniform represented a paycheck and health benefits, ergo, the closer you were to that soldier, the better your chances were to PX privileges and survivor's benefits.

"You talk like a white boy," he remembered one guy telling him. Khalil had not learned any comeback expressions. They would have been lost on the urchin anyway. We are all a product of our environment, thought Khalil. Khalil might have shared a story by his favorite author of those years, Robert Louis Stevenson, but the strange guy showed no signs of ability to discern anything past *Fun with Dick and Jane,* so why bother? That strange kid, call him Duff, found his way from a school that had no white boys as far as Khalil knew. Boone was the school everyone dreaded attending, where Duff might be have been destined. The only requirement was that you had to know how to fight. Khalil was never good at boxing, although he could defend himself. Sayre was not even a school with a debating team. Boxing was where it had potential. And when some of those did eventually find their way to some foreign land defending their country, they would have the chance to test their strengths, but a better chance to show shortcomings. Many of those tough guys Khalil remembered were draped in stars and stripes, with their names etched in one of the memorial walls in Washington, D.C.

It was not until ninth grade that they were introduced to Shakespeare in the form of *Julius Caesar.* Khalil was always good at memorizing. He knew all of the TV commercials, so Shakespeare came easily to him. Also by then, some of the roughnecks had found their way to the Youth Study Center or the graveyard.

But Khalil had digressed. This man, now less than six feet tall, could have been a scarecrow if he had had a straw hat. Khalil was inclined to buy him one, just to see what he looked like. The boxer's knuckles were now gnarly. Arthritis had set in. Sure, he could have been the character in the Wizard of Oz! But that film had no black actors. Besides, Khalil didn't know if this shadow of a man had any acting talent. Back then he had a strong voice, though, and Khalil was sure he could have been taught to act. But that was not the path he followed, or was available to a black man in the Jim Crow Era. Had Jim Crow ever ended?

"Got a quarter?"

"You need more than quarter!" Khalil said, surprised at his own honesty and feeling sorrow for this one-time stronger than Samson, but now ever so vulnerable street-person. How had he ended up that way?

"I do, don't I?"

Khalil was shocked by his own baritone voice as he was Mr. Basketball's shrill reply. This man tilted his head and now resembled Picasso's painting of the old man playing a guitar.

"You know me, or something?"

"I know who you *were*. A teacher at Sayre. That was so long ago. You were a real tough guy then. I was only thirteen. Sayre was a beautiful facility, but a den for thugs."

"It was a beauty!" The old man said, looking melancholy.

"We never got to us the handball courts, except for air raids. That was an architectural waste. Can you tell me why? No, I think I know: The administrators were waiting for another population to come, and until that time they would remain the immaculate athletic facilities they were."

Khalil's query was lost to this prune-skin of a man. What had happened to all the raging fire? That panther was at a loss for words. He had been declawed. Where were all the sounds that made us tremble? Had Alzheimer's set in? Ah, he would have made a good drill sergeant. The black man's prowess was never lost on the battlefield, or when it came to drill and ceremony, thought Khalil.

"We had a lot of characters," the old man mused.

"I had come from a good school. Maybe a great school: William Cullen Bryant, named for the attorney-poet whose poems a teacher had often recited to us. By contract, Sayre was a school for hoodlums. It was a feeder school for Boone and Catto, and the penitentiary."

"Well, you made it through." The sage said.

He fell silent after that, as if looking for words that might make his audience stay. He was not too articulate back when he had all of his faculties. Now even less. He was quick with his hands or his paddle. He had grown up in North Philly, so he represented the hard life and schools he attended.

"Got a quarter?"

"I heard you the first time. This is Philly, just as I remember it. How did I expect it to change?"

"Just because you've been away, doesn't mean you would find it different now. I know you got it!"

"You are just as arrogant as I remember you being. But not the intimidator, as we called you. I have been away for seven years and am just passing through."

"You been to prison?"

"Try med school."

"Wow!"

"I would say the same thing to you, but *will* give you a dollar and be on my way."

"No, I can't get nothing for a dollar."

"But it's seventy-five more cents than you asked for. It's all you'll get from me! I am so sick of this city. A city of bums."

Khalil was again surprised at how curt he was. He had become indifferent to paupers. He knew he could not save the world. It was just too vast. Indifference was not an admirable characteristic in anyone. Who was it that said "Charity begins at home, and spreads abroad"? But Mr. Basketball engendered no sympathy in him, given the reputation he had and all the times he had paddled the impressionable Khalil. Years later when he told his mother, she asked "Why did you tell me?" Khalil responded that he didn't think it would change anything. "It was a prison setting," he told her. Still he knew that he would have given a Syrian money, had he been there. But if someone was in need there, he would go to the mosque to find alms. In the City of Brotherly Love people made a livelihood of having their hands out, to the extent that one mayor asked the citizens to stop the charity for street peddlers.

"Doctor!"

This man had caught up with Khalil, even after he had put some distance between them.

"Who are you? Were you a student of mine?"

"You can say that, but I can't say I learned anything. Call me Ishmael."

He heard him mumble the name, as if ruminating something tough to chew. Khalil crossed the street and descended into the subway station on 30th Street.

*

Khalil had to meet Zouhoor at a small café on 5th Street near South Street. She was not familiar with the city, so Khalil did not want her to be alone. She was anxious about Philly anyway: the stories Khalil had shared about his growing up there were sure to play on her mind. But she wasn't alone, Khalil thought. She had caught up with Leila, the wife of Bilal a doctor friend Khalil had reconnected with. The two women stayed in touch via emails for years. Like Khalil, Bilal had married a foreign woman, someone he met in med school. Leila was Palestinian. She had grown up on the West Bank, but had moved with her family to Chicago where she finished high school then moved to Philadelphia where she studied and met her husband, Bilal at a Muslim meet-and-greet while at Jefferson Medical School. Bilal was smitten immediately by Leila. Her large dark brown eyes was all Bilal could think of as he spoke to her over tea in the student center. Her voice was so pleasant. She wore silk hijabs, and simple blouses. She had a penchant for brown and beige. Bilal was unable to see any flaw in her personality, and she was quiet which made her all the more attractive. It was summer and Leila's olive skin was dark from the strong sun. After the initial meeting they met everyday. It was not long afterwards that they met for Isha prayer, as they were free of classes at that hour. Fortunately, Bilal had stayed in touch with Khalil while Khalil was in Damascus. Both Khalil and Bilal had stories to share when they got together. They could not have guessed they would have married foreign women, although, they never discussed their wives. Since Zouhoor had wanted to see Philadelphia forever, and Montreal was just an eight hour train ride to Philadelphia, Khalil relented and took Zouhoor there. A week was what Khalil agreed to. Riaziat stayed at a preschool center for that day while Khalil and Zouhoor had the day to themselves. The women had agreed to meet, and Khalil would catch up with them later. Leila offered to show Zouhoor some of the city. Khalil was to see them that evening.

Khalil was eager to hear how Zouhoor had found Philadelphia. Her insights might help to change Khalil view of that city.

*

When Khalil arrived the women were sitting at a Turkish café on 5th Street.

"It is so good to finally meet you, brother," said Leila.

"And you, too, Sister Leila. It was so kind of you to show Zouhoor around."

"It was a pleasure."

"So how did you find this city?" Khalil asked his wife.

"So many colorful people! So animated!"

"We walked around Independence Hall," said Leila.

"That's a great place to start."

"It's too big a city to see in one week," said Leila. "You will have to return."

"We will arrange another visit," added Khalil, suddenly finding interest in his birthplace. There were places that even he would like to visit. Why should he dismiss the opportunity to share the adventure with his family? He was no longer the marginalized citizen he once was. Now when he walked the streets he felt he was no longer someone the police would stop and question under any pretext. No. But he was not so naïve to believe he could not be stopped under so new disguise called profiling. There was always a ruse, because nothing of the fabric had read really changed, only the outward appearance. As quickly as Khalil had entertained his initial thought, his memory grabbed another one he could not ignore: the reality of growing up in Philadelphia, walking the mean streets. No. He and his family would be returning to Montreal, his new home. That was the city his son would know. He would learn several languages and grow up to be an international man.

Khalil and Zouhoor returned to the daycare center in West Philadelphia where Riaziat had spent the day. He ran straight to his mother who hoisted him up. He then reached out to his father who held him as they left the center. That evening they would with meet Bilal and Leila. The three stood at 42nd and Spruce where they boarded a bus that took them back to center city where Bilal and Leila lived in a condominium on JFK Boulevard.

To amuse Riaziat, Khalil and Leila played a counting game. Khalil began with *un*, next Leila *deux*, Riaziat *trois*, and so on until they reached the number *cinquante*.

Riaziat fell silent by when several raucous boys and girls boarded the bus at the University of Pennsylvania Hospital. Riaziat clung to his father, apparently frightened by the noise. When the rowdy ones got off at 22nd and Chestnut the bus became quiet again. Khalil and family descended the bus at 17th Street, and walked to JFK Boulevard. Khalil carried Riaziat as the stretch of several block would have been challenging for the infant.

*

Both Zouhoor and Leila were three months pregnant, so they shared spirited conversation about the joys to come.

"We have been waiting for this moment, hoping for this miracle," said Bilal.

"There is nothing so joyous," said Khalil.

Leila showed Zouhoor around the condominium. There was a breathtaking view of the city, the lightshow that of the buildings that seemed to be competing for attention, their reflections bounced off the glass and steel.

"This is the Philly I never knew," said Khalil.

"We have come a long way, eh?" said Bilal.

"It's easy to forget the old times way up here," said Khalil, standing with Bilal at window, viewing the cityscape.

"Things have changed for us, but the masses have seen few changes," said Bilal.

"It's painful to go through some neighborhoods. Some I never even went through, and won't be going through now," said Khalil

"We are some of the lucky ones. Some of the guys have grown old on the corners, stretched out on sidewalks," said Bilal. "Do you see that in Montreal?"

"Montreal is a place where the poor aren't left out of the health equation. We see where our taxes go. It's so refreshing."

"I don't think we will ever catch up with you," said Bilal.

"I toughest thing for us is the winter weather. Thank Allah for four seasons," said Khalil. "And I wouldn't trade it for the world."

"We'll visit you one summer," said Bilal. "But Leila, is used to the cold," he said watching her return into the room with Zouhoor.

"We spent a lot of winter evenings doing puzzles," said Leila.

"Since we are all together I wanted us to share this story I have written. We can read it aloud then comment afterwards," suggested Khalil.

"Bilal told me you wrote, but I thought it was just music," said Leila.

"Why stop the muse," said Khalil. I really need to hear what you think of this piece."

"I want to read it, since it will be my first time," said Zouhoor.

"Brother, you are full of surprises!" said Bilal.

Khalil pulled out the copy of his story, and Leila made copies of everyone.

Two Down And One to Go

By Khalil Baptiste

Mary Magdeline Jones buried her boy last week. He was a "good boy" she still says. And good he might have been back in the third grade, sitting in Miss Nathaniel's art class. Oh, he was fond of seizing four crayons, letting them hit the large sheet of white construction paper, simultaneously. He found they created motion. Even a still life gave the impression the oranges and lemons were rolling off the table.

But at seventeen he was not a boy anymore. Now doing things that most of his friends did left no time for art, except maybe reciting the words to a rap CD. A day spent selling bags of different colors was as close as he would ever be again to the spectrum of light and dark shades of blue that delighted him so, nine years ago. School years were too long a time frame, with no connection to a Mercedes-Benz and chains around the neck. How ironic! The police found him in a red Mercedes, gold chain tangled in the steering. A .45 caliber slug was found to have entered the rear of his head. Portrait of a Still Death. But then again, all death is still. Warren would make no more colors come to life. Springtime and youth had rushed right through to winter, and the raw cold of reality that accompanies it.

"When we take life for granted, it doesn't grant us much. Can I get an Amen?" asked Pastor McKinney. "And where do our young think they are going in such a hurry? Why the great rush to the grave? Isn't life short

enough? Killing each other in these undeclared wars . . .
And we are nowhere near Bosnia or Iraq!"

The little funeral parlor was a sea of tears. This was
not a lone tragedy. Only sixteen months prior, death
had knocked on Mary Magdeline's door. Warren's older brother, Ted, was a victim. That was what a newspaper described as a senseless act of violence. Senseless
because he was standing next to the intended victim,
when the Uzi let fly its volley of heat. Oh, Forty Dugan,
the one whose name was on the bullets, fell dead, too.
He keeled over like a domino as his shoulder touched
Ted's. The punctuated pattern etched diagonally across
Forty's chest strangely resembled musical notation, the
final notes of a requiem. Ted's eyes were open, but his
ears were closed, so he never heard the elegy. The par-
amedics remarked that cars drove by, paused, and then
moved on as songs from CDs vibrated windows and
pounded eardrums, droning their hip hop anthems of
the dead. Later, Ted and Forty away, in death as in life:
black, side by side, but in identical body bags.

The suspect, Tone Ross, was picked up at his mother's
house residence hours later, the Uzi still warm, stowed
the mattress and box spring of his sister's bed. Tone,
escorted in handcuffs down the dank, narrow staircase
of the public housing project. No stranger to cuffs behind his back, he walked with a defiant gait. Once outside he displayed his steely-eyed, granite face any and
all onlookers. He dipped his right-shoulder, his shaved
head glistening and sweating black rain. He vanished
into the police wagon, but not before he was given a
shot in the ribs with the officer's night stick. The policeman took relish in doing this almost imperceptible

gesture of the public servant. Tone winced when he felt the sharpness of the blow to his ribcage. The office registered the anger in Tone's eyes, brown agates. Didn't cattle going to slaughter need prodding?

*

Mary Magdeline held her head erect, he eyes shaded by black sunglasses, her cheeks stained with crystals, and droplets fell into the salt-lake folds of her black dress. Attendants viewed the casket, and tendered a hand when they came up to the mother, and young Joseph. Yes, there was a third son. He was nine, and sat holding his mother's left hand. He registered the faces as they passed, and the words Pastor McKinney had said earlier that morning: that he was now the pillar of the family. *How could one pillar standing alone support a building?* He thought. He would need help. He worked after school at Mr. Kim's grocery store. Joseph's mother had asked Mr. Kim to give her son a chance. "You bring him by. I see," said Mr. Kim. That was how Joseph got his break. But some of the neighborhood toughs had a plan of revenge. They believed in an eye for an eye. They believed in "get back." Tone had brothers—and sisters!

"We gone wipe out all them bastards!" said Billy Powell. "We gon catch 'em in they sleep!"

"No!" said Joseph. Nothing you do will bring back my brother. Besides, they already caught Tone. We don't need any more killing. *Vengence is mine, I will repay saith the Lord.*"

*

"What? You a preacher, now?"

"No, I'm a pillar!"

"I don't know what a pillar is, but you got some *heart*, talkin' back to me."

"We don't want any get back. Let the law take care of that. We will be all right."

For the moment Billy was without words. Oh, he wanted revenge, even if it wouldn't bring Ted and Forty back. It was his only understanding of fairness. He was at war with the world, so somebody had to die. And if he succeeded in wiping out Tone's family, what about Tone's mother? She hadn't done anything to him. His sisters hadn't either! And if he took revenge on Tone's family, what would happen to his own mother? When would the killing cease? No, the young boy made sense. Still, killing seemed the only way Billy could express his pain. He was not in the habit of listening to reason.

*

"That's a lot to take in," said Leila.

"When do you have time to write like that?" asked Bilal.

"It's not a long piece," said Khalil.

"You've never left Philly, have you?" said Bilal.

"Oh, I have left it. It is only when I write I return to some of these shadows."

"They are dark to be sure." Said Zouhoor. "I prefer your music. There is more hope in those tunes."

"I would like to hear some of them," said Leila.

"I brought a CD of a composition I wrote for Zouhoor. You can keep it."

"Thank you so much," said Bilal.

"And thank you for everything," said Khalil.

"I will have to read it again, and send you my thoughts," said Bilal.

Leila prepared the guest room for Khalil, Zouhoor and Riaziat (who had already fallen asleep). They would spend a few more days before returning to Montreal. It had been a great stay.

About the Author

Nadel Harvey was born in Philadelphia, Pennsylvania. He studied civil engineering and mathematics. He has worked most of his life as a civil engineer. He enjoys reading and playing piano when he is not writing. He is inspired by listening to music of Thelonious Monk and Elis Regina. He speaks six languages and lives in Pennsylvania, USA.